Time as Power

Evan D Thomas

ISBN: 0-6480899-1-6
ISBN-13: 978-0-6480899-1-9

CHAPTER 1 - JEAN

Jean Pierre's heart was racing, a fact the onlookers would never discern, his pale face hidden behind the metal visor. This was the first time he'd been on a mission of such clandestine nature and he lacked the composure currently displayed by his captain Benoit Dejant. He and the three other knights sat atop their horses waiting patiently as Dejant raised his visor and briefly spoke with the guard at the castle gates.

"Tyrane Beldor of Guathane to see his majesty King Lector," Dejant barked at the guard, almost as though he were giving an order rather than making a request.

"We have word of your arrival and you are granted passage," the guard replied in the disinterested monotone of a man who had spent too many hours awake.

The gate opened slowly as Dejant slammed down his visor, gently tapping his horse with the reins. The party followed closely behind the three-guard escort into the castle grounds. It was midnight and there was scarcely a soul about. The poverty stricken outer districts were lit by the occasional fire and there was a stench of manure in the air. It wasn't a particularly warm night but Jean was sweating profusely, partly due to nerves, partly due to the heavy plate mail. As they moved through the city, the smell slowly began to dissipate and the surroundings became gradually more pleasant. The wooden, thatch roof buildings slowly gave way to more and more stone constructions until they reached the inner city, where grand monuments of stone and precious metal adorned the abodes of the affluent. In front of them rose a grand stairway leading to a pyramid like structure.

The party dismounted their horses as did the guardsman. Dejant scanned the area through the thin slit in his visor. There was no one else about, everything was going to plan. As he moved to ascend the stairs he tripped on the first step, the metal of his armour making a soft clang as it hit the stone. Jean immediately removed the small knife from his wrist guard and thrust it with all his might into the gap between the closest guard's helm and shoulder piece, the unsuspecting victim momentarily turning to observe the clumsy knight. Jean heard the sound of gurgling blood as he was hit with arterial spray from another of the ill-fated guards whom his companions had dispatched. Dejant leapt to his feet as quickly as he could in the cumbersome plate mail while the others swiftly shed their armour, changing into the attire of the now deceased guards. Jean pulled a few handfuls of cloth from a pack on his horse and handed some to the others so they could clean as much blood as possible from the new armour. The party moved up the stairs with haste. There was no time to hide the bodies. With any luck, they'd be done and out before anyone noticed. The top of the stairs adjoined a large plateau connecting them with the entrance to the pyramid like structure they knew to be the palace. Upon crossing the plateau, they were met by a small army of palace guards.

"Halt, who goes there?" came the call from two armoured men guarding the massive wooden doors that led to the King's chambers.

"Captain of the city guard bearing a message from Tyrane Beldor of Guathane to be received by his majesty King Lector with utmost urgency," replied Dejant.

"Enter," replied the guard, motioning them through with a wave of his armoured hand.

Jean noted that the tired, disinterested body language was similar to the previous guards they had encountered. This reassured him somewhat, as someone who had any notion of their intentions would not act in such a manner, especially if it broke up the monotony of standing next to a gate all night.

The party entered what Jean surmised to be the throne room. In the dim light of but a few candles, its potential grandeur was lost.

From what he could make out, the room was similar in design to many of the great churches he had visited during his travels. The high ceiling was supported by arching pillars of stone. Golden sculptures adorned the flanks, other excess existing unseen, hidden by the poor light. Instead of steps, there was a raised platform upon which sat the throne. Jean could just make it out as the candle light bounced off and cast a shadow upon the wall.

A tired looking rotund man in a vibrant robe that was certainly at odds with his mood shuffled towards them. As the large man emerged from the shadows Dejant immediately knelt, bowing his head as he did, Jean and the others following suit. The King appeared bleary eyed, as though his sleep had been interrupted for the occasion.

"Do you have the scroll?" asked the King, not realising the man knelt before him was not in fact the captain of the city guard.

"Yes your majesty," said Dejant.

Jean Pierre stood and took the scroll from Dejant, making sure to keep the end facing the King. He took the 15 steps to King Lector then promptly knelt at his feet, holding the scroll in two hands. As he knelt he made sure his right leg, the one whose shin was parallel to the floor, was further forward than usual, his toes curled against the floor, like a sprinter at the start of a race. As Lector came within a yard of the kneeling guardsman, a flicker of light from one of the nearby torches passed through something in the area, a strange formation appearing on the ground as though the light had just passed through a piece of glass. It registered subconsciously with the King and as Jean heard the slight shuffle, the change in the pattern of Lector's footsteps, his heart began to race. To make matters worse, Jean's head was bowed, the knight unable see Lector's approach. He stayed as he was and listened intently for any other indicators that something was amiss. Fortunately for Jean, it seemed Lector had ignored his instincts, a pair of finely crafted leather shoes appearing in front of him.

Now was his chance! Jean used his right leg as a spring to lunge forward with the scroll at the king. As he did, his hands let go of the scroll as one grabbed the back of the King's head the other going across his mouth. Blood began to trickle from Lector's neck around the thin transparent glass spike protruding from the end of the scroll that had just punctured his throat. Jean lowered the writhing body to the ground. Its kicks and protests at its inevitable death becoming weaker with each second. He detached the transparent spike from the underside of his gauntlet as Dejant and the others raced past into Lector's bedroom. There was a soft clang of steel on steel and a moment later Dejant and the others returned carrying another scroll. As they left the room, Jean picked up the scroll he had dropped from its resting place next to the King's now lifeless body and gave it to Dejant. Unbeknownst to the other members of his group, Jean dropped an object next to the body, the consequence of which would result in thousands of unnecessary deaths.

Finally, the four knights made their way swiftly out of the castle, changing back into their original armour as they escaped. When they were safely out of earshot, Dejant spoke.

"I thank you my friends. This night your courageous deeds have saved our beloved homeland."

A much more relaxed Jean thought sinisterly to himself. "Not exactly."

CHAPTER 2 - ALISTAIR

Light flickered about the walls as Alistair slowly regained consciousness. As the world came into focus he became aware of his dark, dank surrounds. His arms were outstretched and bound to the ceiling.

"Awake then is he eh?" came a voice to the right.

Looking towards the sound, Alistair observed an extremely ugly fat man in chain mail waddle towards him. His face was like a soft round piece of jelly and his chins wobbled with each step. The gaoler proceeded to punch Alistair in the ribs, his arms being extended making it all the more painful. The only consolation was that the impact made the fat man wobble like some gelatinous monster.

"This one's for the Baron's dog you son of a whore," the gaoler snapped as he drove his fist into the prisoner's ribs once more.

"Enough," came an authoritarian voice from the shadows.

The gaoler stepped back at once, fading into darkness as he sniggered, "Plenty more where that came from boy."

The authoritarian voice's owner manifested into reality as he stepped into the flickering torch light. Alistair observed him to be of slim build wearing the uniform of the Barathax Royal Guard. He could just make out the green tunic in the darkness. The man was taller than Alistair, by about half a foot. His hair was all but hidden by a hat that looked like a cross between a jester's and a beret. Alistair had always thought the Barathax Royal Guard hats strange, almost comical, but now definitely wasn't the time to give voice to his opinion.

"Greetings, I am George, commander of the royal guard and I think it's time we had a little chat. Bring him down but leave the cuffs on, you know what he's like."

"Yessir," replied the gaoler, obediently reappearing from the shadows.

The gaoler cuffed Alistair's hands with two rings of steel that had a solid telescopic bar between them long enough to be applied while his arms where outstretched and chained to the ceiling. The gaoler then proceeded to undo the ceiling chains causing Alistair's arms to fall down to his legs with a thud. The gaoler pressed something on the cuffs and the telescopic bar retracted, the prisoners hands now approximately a foot apart. Alistair supposed he'd been in the dungeon for some time now as he had lost feeling in his arms due to them being chained above his head. George beckoned and he followed. There was nothing else he could do for now. George led him to a table by the fireplace.

"Sit," he motioned.

As the two sat down, George rested his right hand upon the table. The skin was smooth, like that of a man who had spent his life drinking wine and entertaining fine conversation as opposed to those of a man Alistair thought would have seen more than enough battles for a few lifetimes in service of the Barathax Royal Guard. Apparently, the role of commander was more title than job, his suspicions confirmed when George's face came into view. He was hardly the portrait of a man that had led a hard, physical life. George told the gaoler to fetch some food and water. His accent wasn't high born but it wasn't completely common either - somewhere in between.

"Right then, you're going to tell me everything that happened. Firstly, when were you hired to kill the baron?"

"I didn't kill the baron and that's not the question you should be asking."

"Well, assuming you didn't kill him, which unless you have a mighty convincing story you'll hang for, who did, and what is the question I should be asking?"

"I hope you're comfortable, it's a long story."

"Better be interesting then, or I'll just tell them to send you back to your cell and we'll see you swinging in the wind tomorrow morning."

Alistair gave a wry smile as he began.

CHAPTER 3 - ALISTAIR

9pm two days prior:
The Flaming Ferret was the local Barathax tavern. As Alistair stepped through the doors he was greeted by the sound of lively music radiating from the far corner. The ale was flowing and the tavern goers, it seemed, were having a merry old time, no doubt aided by the presence of copious amounts of ale. It felt good to escape the cold night air. The tavern had a musty feel to it and a not so pleasant smell, but the large fire place was roaring, giving off a warmth that seemed to carry about the room and then be amplified by the bodies of the patrons.

"Just the man I need to see," said the barkeep as he spotted Alistair approaching the bar. The old man had been running the Flaming Ferret for as long as Alistair could remember and as such he had come to know him well. "I've got a couple of casks needs looking at down in the basement," Gerard said.

"Fantastic, just finished a hard day's work and not only do you deny me a drink, you want me to fix your bloody casks." The barkeep grinned as Alistair followed him down to the basement.

"Good to see you remembered the secret reply," Gerard said sarcastically.

"Damn Aris and his spy games. I've no idea why he insists we continue to play out these silly routines. I mean, why do they bother, you must know the entire guild by now anyway."

Gerard stuck his nose in the air and spoke in a stuffy upper class tone mocking Aris, "It is to the benefit of us all that we stick to protocol. Remember, a chain is only as strong as its weakest link."

Alistair laughed, "I suppose they have members in from out of town occasionally so it's probably technically necessary then, but not between old friends."

The barkeep removed two bottles of wine and the stone wall slid open revealing a secret passage.

"Enter my house of doom," Gerard said in a foreboding voice, laughing at his own joke.

Alistair shook his head, wondering if the old man would ever get tired of saying that. Proceeding into the dark passageway, Alistair continued on alone until he came to the end of the passageway, stopping as he stood in the secret meeting place of the Guild of Balance. The Guild of Balance was founded by the aristocracy hundreds of years ago as a covert political weapon. Alistair supposed the fact the royal family's line hadn't been broken since the guild's inception meant they were probably doing something right. The fact that they had only ever dealt with one royal family was probably also the reason they managed to remain a covert organisation for so long. They were supposed to be a political tool for the furtherance of the realm and protection of the royal family, however, more often than not, they ended up carrying out tasks of trivial importance to the realm but of great importance to the pride or amusement of their high-born masters. Tonight, it seemed, as Alistair was going to find out, was no different.

Aris entered the room from the shadows of another secret passage. As his form manifested from the darkness, Alistair thought back to the comment King Bastion of Barathax had made the last time they were both in his presence.

"I'll be damned Aris, that man is the living embodiment of you if you'd not led a high-born life."

Bastion may not have been the most perceptive man in Barathax, but his observation that day couldn't have been closer to the truth. Aris and Alistair were of almost identical height and build, both having dark brown eyes and the same jet black hair. They were both lean but muscular, the sort of build that was meant for endurance not brute force, but still with enough bulk to hold their own if the situation called for it. The contrast however, was in the finer aspects of their appearance and spoke volumes of the life each man had led. Aris's smooth pale skin, neatly trimmed hair and nails, fine attire and aristocratic accent couldn't be further removed from the shoulder length mop of black straw, tanned, worn and scarred skin, middle of the road accent and common attire of the man that stood before him.

"Greetings Alistair," Aris said as he entered the room.

"So what troubles his majesty tonight?"

"Straight to business as always I see. It seems our Baron Smythe has gotten himself into a bit of an embarrassing situation yet again."

"Let me guess, he's stolen the heart of yet another high-born lady who's been promised to a noble someone else."

"More or less," Aris shrugged. "As you know, King Ervoule III of Eboda is here to arrange the marriage of his daughter Princess Imogin with our own Prince Allan. I think I need not mention the importance of this marriage in ensuring strong relations between Eboda and Barathax, an alliance that will prove invaluable if ever Trescot make good on their threat to invade."

"The marriage is common knowledge about town now so I'm guessing there's more to this story. Our philandering friend Mr Smythe up to something mischievous?"

"How intuitive of you. Unfortunately, it seems that this time, the Baron has taken a liking to our Prince's soon to be wife. He's been engaging in a 'secret' fling with Princess Imogin and her father has become suspicious. If he were to find credible proof of this it would no doubt jeopardise the marriage and hence the alliance with Eboda. I need not say what is likely to transpire if Trescot discovers our alliance with Eboda is not so strong after all."

"Fantastic" Alistair said sarcastically. "So you want me to babysit the Baron and make sure Ervoule doesn't discover his little romance?"

"That would be the obvious choice, however I think this situation can be manipulated to yield an amazing opportunity. If King Ervoule were to somehow discover that Trescot had been framing the Baron with the intention to break the potential alliance between our two nations, I'd chance a guess Ervoule would be rather easily convinced to join forces and invade Trescot. With our combined strength, I'd dare say we could eliminate the Trescot threat once and for all."

"You never fail to amaze Aris. Trust you to actually find a use for that ever annoying Smythe's antics. That being said, what sounds good in theory is usually far more complex in practice. I wait with baited breath to hear how you plan to bring this to fruition and what role you've devised for me in your grand scheme."

"Well you'll be glad to know you get to play the part of the treacherous Trescot spy."

"Committing treason? I'm already not liking the sound of this."

"Our sources tell us the Baron has written to Imogin and that Ervoule has intercepted the letter. Ervoule has not yet said anything to Imogin but is going to confront the Baron tomorrow night. We need you to plant a fake letter responding to the Baron, written in the Princess's hand. The Baron has a window on the first floor of his mansion that leads to his study. A man of your specific talents should have no trouble scaling the wall and picking the lock, all of which will be observed by the King, as by random chance he will just happen to be reaching the peak of a nearby hill that grants vision of the Baron's window."

"So you're saying you want King Ervoule to see me, the supposed courier, delivering the letter in a rather unusual fashion."

"Precisely! King Ervoule will then be escorted to the Baron's residence where you will leave via the window just as Ervoule's men are arriving. You will then proceed to flee on horseback as Ervoule sends some of his escort after you. Your horse is the fastest I know of in all of Barathax and should easily outpace Ervoule's heavily armoured guard. You are then to make your way to Wanes River, where the man we have in Ervoule's guard will meet you. Meanwhile, we have arranged the Baron's affairs in such a manner that he shan't be present during your little incursion. Ervoule shall read the letter in the study and no doubt be furious. A squad of our King Bastion's guard will then make an appearance, stating they had been anonymously informed the Princess had sent correspondence to the Baron. It is then that the man we have in Ervoule's guard will return with you as his captive and proof, in the form of the sealed letter granting entry to Trescot, that you were attempting to escape to said Kingdom. Our man then presents you to Ervoule with the evidence of you acting as a Trescot spy. Ervoule puts the pieces together and realises the letter was planted with the intention it be found by King Bastion's guard, a now obvious Trescot ploy to sabotage the marriage and - Voila! We get to destroy Trescot once and for all with Eboda's help."

"I see... that sounds like it will probably go fantastically for all parties involved minus myself and Trescot. Correct me if I'm wrong, but you want me to attempt to mislead a King and incite war then get caught red handed doing it. I don't suppose the punishment for that is a slap on the wrists?"

"Not exactly, but you won't be hanging any time soon, be assured, we've a plan for your escape. You will have to disappear for good though. If you do this for Barathax, we'll set you up with a title, as much gold as you can spend in seven lifetimes and a brand new identity. The only condition is it will have to be anywhere but here and if Ervoule ever visits, you'll obviously have to make yourself discrete."

"Hmm," Alistair replied thoughtfully, hand on chin as his head tilted upwards and to the left. "I think Earl of Cabbon somewhat suits me. A nice castle, women, telling the minions what to do for once instead of being ordered about like the King's dirty henchman... Very well then, so what happens to Imogin and the Baron after this? Have they been informed of the plan?"

"Yes, it seems that their little fling has blossomed into something more than the Baron's usual flash in the pan romances, and as they really have no other way out of this predicament, they have agreed to play along with the assurance that after Trescot has been 'liberated' we will help them elope."

"What about our King Bastion? Does he know anything?"

"No. To keep any potential engagement between the two Kings as authentic as possible and to guarantee the Baron's safety, we've decided to maintain his ignorance. If only he knew of half the things that have occurred in the background to keep him where he is today..."

"I don't think I want to know."

Aris laughed, "Probably not my friend. Anyway, you'd best be off. You'll meet your contact on the far eastern end of the castle wall at eight. He'll provide you with all your equipment. A wolf howl will signal when it's time to start moving to the Baron's residence, followed by a second howl, indicating you should begin climbing the wall. Good luck, Gerard will let you out, Earl of Cabbon!"

Alistair laughed as he departed.

CHAPTER 4 - ALISTAIR

The grass outside Castle Brin was wet with dew. The night air was crisp, the temperature being a little on the cool side but nothing too chilly. "The perfect night for a stroll," thought Alistair. He walked around to the east side of the Castle observing the towering walls to his left, wondering how many men had spent their lives building this thing. Although he couldn't see anyone, he knew if he just kept walking something would happen. Sure enough, a moment later a rock hit the castle wall to his left. He moved towards the location of the impact and discovered a small leather satchel, barely visible from the road. Looking inside, he noted it contained the sealed letter of safe passage into Trescot and the letter he needed to plant in the Baron's study. He thought for a moment about reading it but quickly decided better of it. All he wanted was to get this over and done with and get on with the good life. He left the safe passage documents, hiding them under some foliage. He'd retrieve them after he'd outrun Ervoule's men. Any spy worth half his salt knew not to go into a theft operation with anything incriminating on their person, the risk of capture ever present, even for a man of Alistair's specific talents. There was a neigh to his right as a midnight black courser slowly trotted out of the shadows towards him. Taking the reins in his hands, the horse followed obediently. Aris hadn't been liberal with the facts when it came to his transport. Even a man who knew nothing of the equine species would instantly be able to tell that the proud creature that stood before him was built for speed.

Like clockwork, Alistair heard the howl of a wolf and knew it was time to embark on the short walk to the Baron's residence. It was only about a mile and the terrain was nothing difficult. He'd be there in no time even at a leisurely pace. Alistair tried to make the short walk look as natural as possible, resisting the urge to constantly look behind him to see if he could catch a glimpse of Ervoule and his party in the distance. The path he took was flanked by trees on each side and a stream of water glistened in the moonlight to his right. Any other time this would be a most relaxing walk through some quite pleasant scenery. Tonight it was a little more stressful, but exciting none the less. Alistair kept trying to suppress the thoughts of negative outcomes. What if his timing was off? What if the Baron's guards saw him? What if he failed to escape? He'd been in this situation enough times before to be able to recognise and ignore these thoughts, but there was still a niggling bit of nervousness. Just enough, he thought, that the adrenalin gave him an edge without rendering him too unstable to complete the mission. About a hundred yards from the Baron's residence he came to a clearing, spying the ever familiar mansion in the distance. Tying the horse to a nearby tree, Alistair thought he was probably one of the Baron's most frequent guests, albeit uninvited. The Baron however, wouldn't know Alistair from the next man in the street.

The Baron's residence comprised a three story mansion built near the stream which ended at the clearing. It was a stone monolith designed and constructed in the 1300's by Atec Leman, a renowned architect of the period, or at least that's what the history books said. Alistair had explored the many rooms and always noted the strange obsession the Baron had with bare stone walls and red carpet. He knew exactly where the study window was that Aris mentioned and this wasn't the first time he'd picked that lock. It was however, the first time he was going to be caught. A wooden lattice covered in ivy led up to about a foot below the window sill where the old worn cobblestone of the building took over, making excellent foot and handholds for a skilled climber.

The second wolf howl sounded... It was now or never. He looked about diligently to see if anyone was watching, partly show for the King on the ridge nearby and partly to make sure that no unintended parties were going to see what was about to unfold. The climb to the window almost felt routine now. Less than a minute later he began to pick the old lock which really presented no challenge at all, even if he hadn't memorised the pin positions from previous attempts. As he felt it give way to the makeshift tension wrench, he made sure to open the latch slowly and silently so as not to alert anyone who might have strayed into the study. He held his breath and listened to see if he could pick up any noise on the other side of the window. He couldn't hear anything, which didn't necessarily mean there was no one in the room, but there were only so many precautions one could take. Alistair slowly pushed the window open and peeked through the crack. Seeing no one, he proceeded to climb into the room. As he dropped silently from the window sill, he observed an old medieval style room that wouldn't have been out of place in one of the many castles of Barathax. The study had not escaped the Baron's obsession with red carpet, every inch of floor covered in the luxurious material. At least in this room however, it seemed someone had stopped him covering the walls in it as well, the smooth, bare pine spared his poor taste. Alistair saw the solid oak desk opposite the fire place which had a rather unrealistically flattering portrait of the Baron above it. He began to move as slowly as possible towards the desk. Moving this slowly was actually more tiring than moving quickly, each of the muscles having to hold their positions for a much greater length of time. Alistair thought he could have probably just walked at a regular pace to the desk as the thick red carpet would render his footsteps inaudible. He was in no rush however, and would therefore take as many precautions as possible.

"Hmm, what's that?" Alistair thought as he observed a trickle of thick liquid snaking around the corner near the desk. "Oh shit!" Alistair half thought, half whispered in shock. There, sprawled on the floor in front of him, was Baron Smythe, a stream of thick red blood attempting to camouflage with the carpet as it flowed from his lifeless body.

CHAPTER 5 - ALISTAIR

Anticipating what was going to happen next, Alistair instinctively ducked and turned, covering his face as he did, starting back towards the window like a sprinter completing a 180 degree swivel at the starting blocks. And then came the starting gun. Milliseconds proceeding his turn, the door he had been facing blasted into a million pieces with an almighty boom and a cloud of smoke. Splinters came off the door like miniature knives exploding towards him. They weren't big enough to do serious damage but it sure hurt as tiny pieces of wood attempted to burrow into any exposed flesh they found. Any other man who did not possess as swift a reflex could have been blinded. There was no stealth about it now, Alistair going straight for the window. He could just make out yelling over the ringing in his ears but concentrating on what they were saying was not the best use of his mental faculties now. His mind became singular, one hundred percent occupied with the sequence: get out of the window as fast as possible without falling and injuring oneself too much as to render escape impossible. As his first foot touched the window sill he acquired his target in less than a second. A guard was covering any escape attempt back through the window. However, the devious soul that planned this ambush didn't count on the guard, who was stunned for a brief moment from the loud bang, being used as a landing pad. Alistair directed his leap so that he crashed into the guard with enough forward momentum to knock the man on his back, landing on top of him to cushion his fall. The guard yelped in pain to the cracking sound as Alistair landed on top of him knees and shins first, breaking at least one of the man's ribs. Alistair immediately mounted the injured guard's horse and made his getaway into the night.

CHAPTER 6 - MORAN

Moran Cheldor gazed out the window of the Baron's study, observing the faint outline of a man on horseback disappearing into the night. He stood silently in a combination of disbelief and awe at the fact that someone could react that quickly and not hurt themself in the fall. Noticing the groaning guard, Moran cursed the person who placed such incompetence under his command.

"Sir, I think he's escaped sir," reported the mercenary next to him in a hurried tone. "Really...?" Moran said sarcastically. "Did you also know that it's night time?"

"Sorry sir," the guard apologised, feeling a little foolish.

Moran wasn't exceptionally tall, there being very little exceptional about his appearance. He was of medium build with short greying hair. Until one spoke to him, the thin scar running down the right side of his face was probably the only hint this man had not lead a peaceful life. Even more deceiving was his extremely average attire. He wore a bland green tunic and black pants in stark contrast to the bizarre and exquisite uniforms preferred by the mages of Bledith. This often worked in his favour, his foes underestimating his magical command based upon his attire alone. He was also an extremely intelligent tactician, although most who met him would not tolerate his arrogant, impersonal manner long enough to discover this fact. He garnered respect from those under him, not via any charismatic personality traits, but instead through their admiration of his raw skill.

The guard examined the smoking wreck where there once stood a solid pine door.

"I've heard of mages conjuring fireballs before, but god, you could have warned me it was going to be like that, I still can't hear properly."

Ignoring the comment Moran muttered, "They send me to catch a master of espionage and this is who they supply. Farmers would have performed more aptly than these supposedly 'hardened soldiers'."

The guard decided conversation with Moran probably wasn't a good idea at the moment and so went downstairs to aid his injured comrade.

Alistair had put a fair distance between himself and the Baron's residence now.

"Fucking Aris!" he said out loud.

How to proceed? He could no longer trust the man, of that he was certain. If the fact one of the most powerful men in Barathax wanted him dead wasn't bad enough, the entire kingdom would now like nothing more than to see his head on a pike for treason. His only real option was to disappear. Alistair had had to live off the land for extended periods of time previously and so decided he would do precisely that while he devised a plan to escape Barathax. Thinking about it a little more, Alistair was suddenly overcome with a wave of exhaustion. Feeling uncontrollably drowsy, the world in front of him began to blur as his surrounds faded to black.

CHAPTER 7 - ALISTAIR

"Leave us," George commanded the guards that had brought the food. As soon as the door had shut George leaned backwards in his chair, looked to the ceiling, tilted his head and brought his hand to his chin as if a major revelation had just dawned upon him. "It all makes sense now," George said more to himself than to Alistair, a grin slowly making its way across his face. "This is going to sound ridiculous, but we have to get you out of here."

"Aren't the dungeon staff supposed to keep the prisoners in the dungeon as opposed to getting them out?" Alistair asked sarcastically.

"Normally yes, but Commander of the Barathax Royal Guard isn't my only role in life. I'll explain later as we don't have much time. We BOTH have to get out! NOW! Wait here for the time being, I'm going to get the others and we'll make our escape."

"I'm obviously not going anywhere," Alistair said raising his chained hands above the table.

"Of course, I got so excited I forgot you were a prisoner for a second. Just a moment, I'll be back soon."

With that, George left the chamber and returned with two other guards, a man and woman whom Alistair had not yet seen.

"This is Terra and Augustus, they can be trusted and will be accompanying us."

"Not exactly how I imagined a dungeon works but I'm not going to complain," Alistair replied.

George shut the door and began to dictate the plan of escape.

"Just follow me and play along."

"Mind taking these off?" Alistair said raising his cuffed hands once more.

"Sorry, you need to look the prisoner if this is to work."

"The traitor's confessed like the weak Trescot dog he is," George said to the guard on the party's right as they exited the room.

The guard smiled sinisterly, making a throat slitting gesture at Alistair with his hand.

"Come on you scum," George said as he pushed Alistair forward from behind, "get moving." Alistair stumbled bare foot across the cold stone floor. Windows had been cut from the hallway's walls at irregular intervals, the moonlight shining through alluding to the fact it was night out. As he was ushered past the grim, featureless walls, he noted a surprising lack of guards. Alistair deduced he was probably in a castle as he could make out what seemed to be a moat in the distance, shining in the moonlight through one of the windows. Eventually they reached the end of the corridor, a gate of solid steel in front of them. The gate was flanked by a glowing green light on either side. Terra and Augustus both moved to the green lights and looked into them. There was a humming sound and the gates began to part. As they parted, Alistair noticed they were actually as thick as the walls they resided in, approximately a yard. He exited the tower into the cold night air which made its presence known on his bare skin. Taking stock of his surrounds, it turned out his castle suspicion wasn't quite correct, the reality being much more grim. He had been housed in a stone tower on an island. It seemed there were actually two towers, Alistair having exited the taller one coming out onto a connecting bridge of sorts. The tower behind him was massive compared to the one across the bridge and he noticed there seemed to be no windows below the level of the bridge itself. A shudder snaked down his spine as he suddenly recalled a place similar to this. It was approximately 5 years ago when he was assigned to catch a criminal who seemed to be quite the accomplished escape artist, having successfully broken out of the last four dungeons he had been incarcerated in. He remembered Aris talking about sending the criminal to 'The Silent Twins'. Inquiring further of Aris, he was later told the Silent Twins were a secret jail built a century ago to house the worst of the worst criminals, which really meant those who the royal family or other powerful figures couldn't kill but wanted to disappear. He remembered Aris mentioning that it got its name from the two towers on the Island. The first contained a winding stairwell that led up to a bridge connecting the two. The second was essentially a solid stone base up until the bridge level where the solid cylinder of stone was hollowed out to make the second tower that housed the prisoners. The doors at either end of the bridge were impenetrable. Aris also spoke briefly of a beast that lived in the surrounding waters they had somehow tamed and could convince to give free passage to certain vessels.

"Even our slippery friend is going to find his stay in the silent twins a rather prolonged experience," Aris said. "First he would have to escape his cell, then get through an impenetrable door. Next he'd need to get across the bridge, through another impenetrable door, down 50 levels of stairwell in the second tower, secure a ship and then get past our not so friendly sea dweller Korrigan."

According to Aris, no one had even made it past the impenetrable door. Only a hand full of people in the Kingdoms knew of its existence and fewer still, its location.

Two guards saluted George as Terra and Augustus pushed Alistair outside.

"Looks like an easy night lads," George said to the two guards. "This one squealed like the rat he is".

"Off to the mainland for quarterin'?" asked the first guard. "I do like me a good quarterin'."

"Here we are, stuck up on this rock, while them lucky town's folk get a bloody quarterin'," said the second guard. "Why, I haven't seen a good execution in at least a week." George laughed and pointed at a boat that was moored on the beach.

"Is it prepared?"

"Aye sir," replied the guard.

"Call sign?"

"The fish are few when the pig is fat," replied the guardsman.

"Unbelievable, who comes up with this rot?" said George shaking his head... "Alright, carry on."

The guard saluted and Alistair was ushered across the bridge to the second tower and through the next set of steel doors. It was just as Aris had described, a winding spiral stairwell that seemed to go on forever. When forever ended they came to a steel lattice door. George banged on it till the guard on the other side started turning a wheel, the door beginning to rise. Alistair's feet went from cold, to cold and wet as he stepped out onto the dew covered grass outside. The group walked the 80 odd yards across the grass and sand to the docked boat. It was a medium sized boat with a large sail and what seemed like enough room for three crew below deck. As they boarded, Alistair noticed another glowing green light similar to those he'd observed earlier in the Silent Twins. This one was positioned at head height on the mast. Instead of staring into it this time, George spoke at it.

George sighed, "The fish are few when the pig is fat." The light went out, Alistair now just able to perceive a very low pitched humming.

"Plot a course for Raven's Contact," George told Terra and Augustus.

They promptly raised the sails and the boat began to move. They hadn't sailed more than 100 yards when Alistair became aware of a pungent odour filling the air.

"God, what is that awful smell?" Alistair asked George.

"What?" George replied confused.

"Can't you smell that?"

"Smell what," George replied again as the boat started to rock gently to-and-fro. George proceeded to sniff the air. "Oh God," he exclaimed, a look of terror spreading across his face.

Taking the cabin stairs two by two he leapt onto the deck as he reached the top. Not a moment later the ocean parted in front of them, an enormous tentacle breaking the water's surface writhing to-and-fro against the dark backdrop of the night sky. Without warning, the tentacle darted forward, impaling Augustus as he turned to run. Terra stood frozen in fear as Alistair noticed amongst the chaos that the small green light on the mast had come back on. What seemed to be the head of the beast reared out of the water revealing row upon row of razor sharp teeth covered in slime and moss. At least six eyes surrounded the mouth as Augustus's still writhing body was thrown into the belly of the beast.

CHAPTER 8 - ALISTAIR

George immediately rushed towards the glowing light on the mast, yelling, "The fish are few when the pig is fat!" madly as he got closer.

Upon swallowing Augustus, the creature suddenly reeled as if hit by some unseen physical force, disappearing below the surface.

"Fuck!" George cursed the night sky as the water began to calm. "Cheap rubbish," he muttered as he walked back to Alistair. Terra, now released from her state of shock, was looking over the edge at the water below. "There's nothing we can do for him now," George said shaking his head.

"What the hell just happened!?" Terra exclaimed. "You speak the words they tell us and we get safe passage, that's how it's supposed to work, right?"

"Looks like it's not as reliable as they would have us believe," George replied. "Alistair, I need you to keep an eye on that light, if it comes back on, speak the call sign immediately."

"OK..." Alistair replied, more than a little confused by what had just transpired. "Can someone please let me know what the hell is going on here?"

George sat on a barrel that was strapped to the deck, looking like someone who thought they were having a heart attack only to be informed a minute later it was heartburn.

"Where to start... hmm?"

"Right, firstly," Alistair said. "What the hell was that and why did it retreat?"

"That my friend, is the beast of the Silent Twins, otherwise known as Korrigan The Foul. That ridiculous call sign is supposed to activate something on this ship that repels it. The deterrent should be active whenever that light on the mast is out."

"So that dungeon WAS the Silent Twins," Alistair replied, his eyebrows raising ever so slightly. "Aris you bastard..." he said looking out to sea before turning back to George. "You were saying this thing on the ship repels Korrigan so the boat can make safe passage?"

"That's the idea, only this one doesn't seem to work perfectly well."

"Do you get many that don't, 'work perfectly well'?"

"This is the first time I've ever seen it happen, else there'd be no way I'd make this voyage."

"Lucky me," Alistair muttered.

"Not so lucky for some though," George thought as he looked down at the water.

"Second question, assuming you are helping me, why?"

"Now that is a good question. Things in this world are not quite as they seem. Like you, I work for the Guild of Balance. Up until recently, I, like you, was a loyal member. Aris knows you're not from here. The Guild of Balance seeks to prevent any more of us coming through. They see us as a threat to the covert sway they've held for so long and the technology trade not worth the implicit risk they perceive to their power."

"What the hell are you on about?" Alistair asked confused.

"Look Alistair, you can play the fool all you like, but I know the truth. This boat contains a signal generator that creates electronic pulses tuned to a certain frequency. We lost a lot of men to gain some of Korrigan's DNA, but we got it eventually. Turns out that foul smell is due to the spores it sheds constantly. The scientists back home analysed some of those spores and discovered a pulse frequency that interrupts Korrigan's brain waves. The light being off signals the boat is emitting the pulse at the discovered frequency. They tell me the pulse blocks the signal in the Korrigan's brain that tells it to attack anything that moves and as such we gain safe passage."

"So there were others!" Alistair exclaimed. "I thought my DNA was the only set compatible with the gateway."

"That's almost true. It's actually 98% compatible. Once the

threshold drops below 97% the gateway won't allow passage."

"So you're obviously from Earth as well."

"That I am."

"Well, as interesting as this revelation is, it still doesn't explain why the Baron is dead, or my current predicament."

"The Baron was from Earth as well Alistair. Aris cannot eliminate us overtly lest he risk the attention of King Bastion. His majesty strongly supports the trade between the two realms, mainly due to the fact it's the primary source of his power. Aris therefore cannot close the gateway down on this end, so has decided to seek out and covertly eliminate anyone who comes through. The situation arose where Aris had the Baron killed. You would then take the blame and be executed. How did they say it back home, 'Killing two birds with one stone' I believe. Not only does Aris get rid of two of the outsiders as he calls us, he also strengthens his argument for shutting down the inter-realm trade. One outsider murdering another while attempting to incite war with Trescot doesn't portray Earth in the best light. Unfortunately for Aris, there are a few of us spread throughout the land he doesn't know of, myself included. King Bastion hasn't closed the gateway yet, so it's likely Aris will choose a target closer to the King this time. We think he may be going after Princess Imogin or Prince Allan. Bastion would think Earth has joined forces with Trescot in Prince Allan's case or have inflicted irrevocable damage to an ally in Imogin's and would have no choice but to close the gateway and shut down the trade."

"Would he really go that far?"

"I believe so, yes."

"Jesus," exclaimed Alistair.

"We need to get to Aris and soon."

"Agreed," replied Alistair. "Have you ever wondered why Earth is so interested in this world though? They are centuries behind us technologically and most of their magic, we can recreate in one way or another through science."

"I have indeed asked myself the same question, but I think that could be, how did they say it back on Earth, 'above my pay grade'." A smile cracked across Alistair's face.

"After what I've heard just now I don't think anything is beyond my pay grade. So what's the plan to get to Aris? If you wanted to slot anyone in Barathax, the target doesn't come much more difficult."

"I hear that," George moaned. "First things first. When I came through five years ago, I brought some equipment with me. It's stored at a safe location not far from here, an island we called Raven's Contact."

"I thought they could only send *people* through the gateway," Alistair said.

"You went through a bit before me Alistair. Around the time I came through they had just figured out how to send non-biological items. Something to do with coating the items in some kind of biological material that would mask their true identity. Sadly, a contact of mine that came through about a year after me said the technique no longer worked. Something about the gateway having some sort of sophisticated A.I. that had figured out what we were doing and no longer allowed passage."

Terra came back from below deck, some of the colour having returned to her face.

"Sorry about your friend," Alistair offered, "were the two of you close?"

Terra focused, "Not at all, he was a pig of a man and I rue the day they put me on guard detail with him. What happened was probably a godsend, but it's still rather shocking to say the least. I'll be OK. Oh look, seems we're almost there."

It was a clear night and the shape of a small island was beginning to manifest itself upon the horizon.

CHAPTER 9 - ALISTAIR

After a short walk across the sand, George and Alistair crossed the tree line. All manner of palm and tropical flora covered the island's landmass. After continuing on through the foliage for a short while, they came to a large boulder that seemed somewhat out of place. As they neared the approximately 10 foot tall piece of stone Alistair noticed a section of steel on the front face, smooth and shiny in stark contrast to the weather beaten sediment that housed it. George muttered something and the steel parted, proceeding to slide open to the sound of stone grinding on metal. The large cloud of dust led Alistair to believe no one had been here for quite some time. Within was a storage room about 8 feet cubed in size, packed full of military storage crates. George wiped the dust off one of them and then opened the crate.

"Still know how to use these?" he asked as Alistair walked over to see what he was referring to. Seeing the objects the crate housed brought forth a flood of memories from his time on Earth. It was almost like viewing a photograph of a long lost relative. Packed neatly inside the crate were four M4A1 assault rifles.

"So you said they can't send equipment through anymore? Does that mean when we run out of ammo, that's it?"

"Not exactly," George said as a smile crept across his face. "Had three dimensional printers caught on around the time you were leaving?"

"Yeah I remember those. People could download a design for some kind of small objects, feed the 3D printer a chunk of plastic and it would fashion the object for them. What on earth does that have to do with anything though?"

"Did you also know about the larger machines being able to print in other materials, ie metals, ceramics etc?"

"Vaguely, something like that".

"One of the drawbacks 3D printing opponents often quoted when comparing to traditional manufacturing was the slow production time, which wasn't an issue for prototypes, but not ideal for mass production. Traditional manufacturing processes would create a mould and then be able to churn the same object out using that mould over and over, cost efficiently and quickly.

Then came the man that many believe could be 3D printing's saviour, Doctor Roberto Enzo. Doctor Roberto ran a project funded by the military to produce a portable multiple material capable printer that could produce objects at speeds comparable to traditional manufacturing. Achieving said objective, the PMF or Portable Munitions Factory was born," George said, pointing at a small briefcase like object to the right of the munitions case.

"Sounds great... but I still don't see the relevance to our current situation?"

"This printer is currently programmed to make bullet shaped objects out of almost any material. You could feed it sand, stones, metal, even wood but I don't think that would make the best projectile."

"So you're trying to tell me that thing essentially means unlimited ammo. If that's true... then whoa..." Alistair said trailing off.

Suddenly focusing as though he'd just thought of something critical, he continued. "But wait, I think you're forgetting that you need some kind of propellant to actually make the bullet move, unless we're going to be using bloody air rifles."

"Just a moment Alistair, the PMF is only half the package. Another team headed by the same man was simultaneously working on a rail gun small enough to be carried by a man."

"A rail gun? I thought they were science fiction?"

"This way please." George motioned to a second, longer crate marked RG32. As he opened it, Alistair observed what he could only describe as something out of a Star Wars movie. The object in the crate resembled some kind of chunky futuristic long range rifle.

The barrel was about four feet long and contained all the usual pieces that would help one identify it as a gun. There were however, some stark differences between the RG32 and a conventional rifle. It had grooves running down either side of the barrel and a large box between the barrel and the stock. Atop the box was a squashed cylindrical object that Alistair later discovered was the sight.

"This my friend, is the RG32," George said, unable to contain the involuntary grin that had now spread from ear to ear. "From what I understand of what they told me, which isn't much, it works on the same principles as a rail gun. There's two parallel rails inside the barrel a small distance apart traversed by a piece of metal running perpendicular that connects them." George made a U shape with his hands. "The round sits in front of the connecting piece of metal and when you pull the trigger, a strong charge is sent through the two rails, creating a force that acts on the connecting metal, propelling it forward towards the muzzle of the barrel, driving the projectile as it does."

"So kind of like a high-tech sling shot then?"

"In a manner of speaking, yes," George said, a little dejected at the comparison with something dated BC.

"So that's how you get around the propellant issue too then. Well, before I was impressed, but this IS amazing George. One more question though, what happens to the connecting piece of steel? Wouldn't the force needed to get it to decelerate in time to stop it shooting out with the projectile break the connector?"

"That's what these grooves are for," George said running his finger down the side of the barrel. "The connector is actually two pieces of metal touching each other. So when they get to the end of the barrel they come apart and each one continues on its track around the muzzle of the gun and slows down on its way around the outside of the barrel." George made two oval shapes in the air with his fingers.

"Seems they thought of everything," Alistair replied. "Just out of curiosity, what happens if you have a hand on the barrel when you shoot the thing. The connecting pieces of metal would be coming around the barrel at speeds that might result in a few less fingers wouldn't they?"

"The rifle has sensors all the way along the outside of the barrel. This lets it know if there will be an obstruction to firing and it won't fire if this is the case."

"Got an answer for everything now then don't you. One more then. I heard they had problems ever implementing a rail gun because of the wear and tear on the components created by the extreme forces that are at play. Any idea on how many times this thing is going to fire before it breaks?" Alistair asked.

"I had the same question but all they told me was that they had found a way to guarantee unlimited firing attempts and deal with the wear and tear. They wouldn't tell me how though. Said it was over my head, which is surprising considering everything else they let me know."

"Right, so I've got a weapon that has no ammo problems. How does it effectively compare to a conventional sniper rifle?"

"Range and stopping power wise it's better than anything you can imagine due to the extreme muzzle velocity. For example, the M4 over there has a muzzle velocity of approximately 880m/s whereas this has a muzzle velocity of up to 4000m/s."

"God, it must hit like a freight train. I suppose that means less bullet drop and therefore higher accuracy over long distances?"

"Right you are. It's effective from a million miles away and it hits like a Mack truck when it connects."

"I'd better try out this Portable Munitions Factory as it sounds kind of complex," Alistair said.

George found a rock and handed it to him.

"Put it in there," George said as he pointed to an alcove in the briefcase looking device.

Alistair placed the rock in the PMF and then George had him press a green button that said 'manufacture'. A cover slid over the alcove as the PMF made a slight whirring noise. A green digital display above the alcove showed a progress bar. Seconds later, the cover slid open and 3 bullet shaped pieces of stone fell out along with what was left of the rock after the bullets had been fashioned. Alistair picked them up and quietly marvelled at the actualisation of what would have been pure science fiction not long ago. George grabbed two large packs from the back corner and handed one to Alistair. He then proceeded to disassemble the RG32 into four pieces, placing it in Alistair's pack.

"Grab what you can mate and let's get going," he said.

Alistair picked up a silencer for the M4 and a pistol, then proceeded to stuff his pack with as much water, ammunition and canned food as it would hold. When the two had finally filled their packs to the brim, George grabbed the PMF and started back towards the boat. Alistair was just closing the door behind him when a scream of pain pierced the serenity of the island night.

CHAPTER 10 - ALISTAIR

George and Alistair readied their silenced M4's, immediately crouching just inside the door on either side, scanning the area outside the storage room as they did. It was a clear night and the unimpeded moonlight meant visibility was good. Nothing, not a move or a sound for what felt like an eternity... and then a figure appeared over the top of the sand dune in the distance, silhouetted against the moonlight. As the figure closed, it became apparent the person was being pursued, desperately running towards them.

"Hold your fire, it's Terra," George said quietly to Alistair as her outline became clearer with each passing moment.

A second figure appeared atop the dune. As Terra closed the distance the hound pursuing her slowly began to take form. She knew it was futile. The canine had started at least 600 yards away but had since reduced the gap to at most 20. It would be over in a matter of moments but she was too scared to consider the futility of persisting to flee or her impending doom. Adrenaline had taken over, her body acting on instinct, betting on the infinitely minuscule chance she might somehow evade her pursuer or experience some feat of luck whereby it tripped and broke a leg. She could hear its growls and the flicking of sand as its four legs moved in a rhythm many times faster than her own two. Suddenly, as if fate had not been cruel enough, something moved out of the shadows in front of her. She instinctively darted to the right but in doing so the hound finally closed the distance as she felt the paws upon her shoulders, knowing that in an instance the teeth would follow. Falling under its weight, she felt warm saliva on the back of her neck... But no bite came. Was it chasing her for sport? She dared not roll over to check lest it provoked the thing. There was a whisper. Was it speaking? Had she gone insane?

"Are you OK?"

She rolled over. Knelt beside her was George holding a rather strange looking object. She felt the back of her neck, there was something on it. Looking at her hand, she suddenly realised it was covered in blood. The world started to spin, her head lolling to the side as she saw the hound's lifeless corpse, its head resting in a growing pool of red. Terra felt a hand on her shoulders and barely noticed the fact she was rolling over once more.

The voice came again, "She's OK, it's not her blood."

The haze began to clear as a pair of boots came into focus.

"Alistair, George?" she asked wearily.

"You weren't bitten were you?" asked George.

She rubbed the back of her neck again then inspected her hand. There was certainly a great deal of blood, but strangely no pain.

"No, I... I think I'm OK. What... what just happened?"

Alistair attempted a reply but was cut off by Terra as she seemingly snapped back to reality. "No, there's no time now, more are coming. They know we're here. They're early."

"That can't be," George mumbled. "They weren't supposed to find out till they came to pick him up for transfer in 2 days time. How could they have known?" he said more to himself than his companions, dreading the ramifications of the night's revelation.

CHAPTER 11 - ALISTAIR

Alistair and George had noticed the hound, however neither of them had a clear line of sight as Terra was running directly towards them, blocking any potential shot as she did. George made the snap decision to move quickly from cover, scaring Terra into changing her course, relying on Alistair to seize the opportunity. Everything happened in slow motion from Alistair's perspective. He took a deep breath to steady himself. Aiming at Terra's neck he waited for what seemed like an eternity but in reality was no more than a fraction of a second, the image in the night scope changing from human neck to hound's head. As its snout crossed the centre dot he squeezed the trigger gently. A barely audible report from the silenced rifle was proceeded by a spray of blood from the hound's eye where the bullet entered. This was followed by a thud as its lifeless form came to rest next to Terra.

Alistair was released from his thoughts as voices became audible in the direction Terra had come from.

"How many are there?" George asked.

"I don't know. I saw the boat coming ashore, left a trap on the beach and was coming to warn the two of you."

"A trap. That would explain the scream then."

The voices were getting close now, so much so that they could almost make out what was being said. George motioned for them to take cover, himself and Terra finding a hiding spot in the long grass underneath the palms whilst Alistair found a large rock and peered through the night scope. The world was a wash of green.

He counted 20 men armed with crossbows and swords in the distance moving nonchalantly towards them. He motioned for George and Terra and they quickly crawled to his position.

"How many?" George whispered.

"20ish, they don't seem too concerned."

"Think we can take em?" George replied.

"Maybe, but what happens if we don't drop them all quickly enough to stop them splitting up? Then we've got the issue of having to deal with them spread out across the island. Also, we can't let the weapons cache be discovered."

"That's taken care of, once the door shuts nothing gets in without the password."

"Good to hear, I assume you have another plan then?" said Alistair as the footsteps drew closer.

"Let's just avoid them and get back to the boat. My night scope's dead so you'll have to lead the way."

Alistair looked through his night scope once more and saw that the group's formation had changed. They'd spread out and were cautiously taking each step through the palm trees and ground level foliage.

"They know something's up," whispered Alistair as he noticed the change in his pursuers pace and formation.

"Probably wondering why they haven't heard from the hound in a while," George replied.

Alistair signalled for them to move slowly and silently around the most lateral enemy. Brushing aside an enormous green leaf, Alistair's right hand suddenly flew up in a fist then flapped frantically towards the ground, signalling them to drop at once, a previously unseen enemy no more than twelve feet away. Alistair was slightly ahead of George and Terra, on his back, staring up at the night sky. There was a rustling of grass to the right as one of the militia appeared near George. George watched the man intently as the large piece of sharpened steel he was holding caught the moonlight and reflected into George's eyes for but a moment. The man continued on, none the wiser, as the trio's elevated heart rate decreased exponentially. For the next few moments the sounds of the enemy moving through the grass around them was all that they heard. The militia obviously knew something had happened as there was not a bit of conversation to be heard. As luck would have it though, they passed without incident, Alistair signaling for them to get up when he was sure they were safe. The way back to the boat seemed clear now, a wave of relief washing over them. The respite would not endure however, their brief illusion of security cut short by a yell from one of the militia behind them. The trio dropped to the ground immediately with bated breath, their hearts pounding as they listened intently for any indication they had been spotted. Alistair quickly scanned what he could from amongst the foliage with his night scope. He sighed heavily upon realising they'd just found the dog and hadn't actually seen anyone yet.

Spreading out even further, the enemy slowed to a crawl. They'd be acutely alert now, but were heading in the opposite direction, it not being long before they were out of earshot. Getting up the trio moved swiftly towards the coast. Alistair led, cautiously looking through the night scope for stragglers or anyone who had been left behind to guard the boat. The coast gradually came into a greenish focus, before fading as his night vision scope malfunctioned. Cursing silently, he removed it from the rifle. The palms and long grass gave way in front of them to the beach ahead. As expected, there was a second boat docked next to the one they had come in on. Alistair stopped and scanned the two ships before moving into the open. There didn't seem to be any movement on deck. Motioning for them to follow, they moved up and boarded the ship they had come in on. Once on board they became aware of voices below deck. George signalled for Alistair to take point. Terra watched as George followed Alistair slowly below deck seeing them disappear into the ship. There were four barely audible hissing sounds followed by two thuds. George's head reappeared above deck as he signalled to Terra that it was all clear. Now that they were relatively safe, George spoke for the first time since back on the island.

"They brought a Black Wraith," he said pointing at the ship that had moored itself not more than 50 yards from their own. "We can't outrun it and I don't have its call sign, so even if we wanted to commandeer it we wouldn't get far with Korrigan out there."

"That's not quite what I had in mind," Alistair said with a smile. He moved up on deck, unpacked and assembled the RG32. "I think it's time to try out our new toy."

Alistair mounted the rifle on the starboard bow and looked

through the scope. His left hand instinctively grabbed the barrel as his right rested on the trigger. A large red X symbol appeared in the top right corner of the display as he felt the groove that cut all the way around the barrel. He suddenly remembered that he had to hold the second grip otherwise the rifle wouldn't fire, the moving parts needing to follow the track around the barrel. The instant his left hand let go, the red X disappeared and he found himself looking through a magnified display. It wasn't a night scope though and he could hardly see anything.

George spoke quietly, not wanting to alert anyone that might be on the other ship. "I think I forgot to tell you," he pointed to a dial on the side of the scope and made a gesture for Alistair to rotate it.

Alistair clicked it one position clockwise and the world immediately turned green, similar to the night scope on his M4. He decided he'd see what the other degrees of rotation did and clicked again. This time, skeletons appeared in the image of the enemy boat moving about below deck.

"An X-ray scope," he said, more to himself than anyone else, bewildered by what he was witnessing.

He continued clicking through the different views, wondering to himself what half of them were for, until he got to a view that seemed to function like night vision with a twist. There was no green or black and white here, the world appeared as it would have in perfect daylight, perfect night vision.

Aiming at the mast, he found what he was looking for. George signalled Terra to be ready to leave as soon as he fired and Terra began making the necessary preparations. As Alistair focused on the dull green light part way up the enemy ship's mast, he noted that in the top right hand corner of the display there was some text. "Power: Full." He squeezed the trigger. A red X appeared again. He removed his head from behind the scope and turned to George.

"Great piece of equipment this is, it won't fire, there's an X appearing in the top corner."

"Oh yes that's right," said George. "What does the power setting say? If it's anything above medium you have to mount the rifle and dismount the scope which can then be used to fire the weapon remotely. Trust me, you don't want to be holding something that generates enough force to propel a projectile at 4000m/s when it fires."

"So how do you turn down the power?"

"To hell with that," said George taking the rifle from Alistair.

George pulled what looked like a block of metal from his pack and put it on the ground next to the rifle. He then put the rifle on top of the block. Three legs of steel sprouted from the block and the rifle seemed to just stick to the top of what now looked like a tripod. George proceeded to detach the scope, taking it with him back to where the others were standing, behind the weapon.

George slid his fingers across the screen of the scope, the rifle moving in unison. "You may want to stand back for this," he said as he started walking away from the rifle that was now mounted by some unknown force to the ship's deck.

Terra and Alistair followed. Someone emerged from below deck on the other boat and spotted the trio as George's finger pressed down on the screen. An almighty explosion ensued as their vessel rocked in the sea, almost capsizing from the recoil of the shot. A plume of fire erupted from the end of the RG32 following the projectile through the air. There was a second explosion as the projectile hit the mast of the other ship breaking it in two, the stream of super-hot plasma the round created as it flew through the air simultaneously setting the boat alight. The foe who had spotted them was engulfed as his vessel became a floating pyre. A few seconds later there was an almighty crash as what was left of the mast slammed into the Black Wraith's deck, effectively slicing the burning ship in two.

Alistair and Terra stood dumbstruck, still not believing what they had witnessed, the burning Wraith slowly becoming smaller and smaller as they moved out to sea. George looked back at the Island and observed some very surprised militia returning to find their only means of crossing the sea burning atop the water.

CHAPTER 12 - MORAN

Moran sat in his study, a little disappointed at the fact his quarry had been caught through pure chance rather than any skill on his part. "What a bizarre twist of fate," he thought. Sheer absent mindedness on his behalf had resulted in him leaving a satchel of sleeping powder on the horse's back. This would later lead to the capture of the man his contractors had described as "The most dangerous criminal to walk the land." Even the keenest eye wouldn't have seen the powder escape the bag and blow into the rider's nose as Alistair hurriedly jumped on the horse. At least he had the consolation of having to track his target's movement via the most inconspicuous of signs to where he found a horse grazing with this most dangerous of men unconscious upon its back. Of course, Moran professed it was all part of his plan, which would only further increase the gap between the legends of his name and the actual truth. He did not particularly like doing this, however, the greater the legend the more work and higher rate he could command. It had not done him any harm thus far he thought, as he remembered the humble lodging at the mage's quarters before his success as a bounty hunter gave him the means to acquire his current extravagant dwelling.

He was abruptly interrupted from his contradiction of guilt and pride by an image in his mirror that was not his own. This was promptly followed by an all too familiar voice. The image in the mirror was that of a jester in green and white attire. Most mirrors were used for looking at one's own reflection, however this one was used for a different purpose entirely. Moran could communicate over great distances with other parties that had the corresponding piece of glass. The voice on the other end did not like to make itself visually known and would always have the mirror facing a blank white background with a portrait of a jester in the middle.

"Moran," the mirror spoke. "It seems there has been a small problem concerning the recent apprehension of your target."

"What kind of issue could there possibly be, I delivered him to you asleep and unharmed, which I must say was quite above and beyond the contract's stipulation."

"Yes, we are aware and we are grateful. Alas, it seems the target has evaded us and we once again require your assistance in apprehending this most heinous outlaw. Your efficiency in said target's previous capture is precisely why you have been recommended for the re-apprehension of said target."

"Hmm, as I'm so highly recommended, my fee is 5,000 gold pieces this time and I choose my own men. The last group you supplied were thoroughly incompetent."

"As you wish," spoke the mirror. "But we must act quickly. The target's last known location was the Silent Twins. We have a fully crewed vessel awaiting your arrival at Callahadre docks so please make haste."

"Very well, Callahadre docks is not far. I will travel at my earliest convenience but must ask that you contact Hadron Kado, Morris Verbata, and Gerim the Butcher. Inform them that Moran Cheldore requires their assistance in this task. They are to be made aware of the situation in full and will each be paid a fee of 3,000 gold pieces. I hope it goes without saying, my fee should not be disclosed." There was a slight pause followed by the mirror replying in the affirmative.

CHAPTER 13 - MORAN

Moran was at the docks in under an hour.

A burly lad whom Moran thought was probably the skipper asked, "You thems Moran fella are ya?" in a tone so common it almost hurt his ears.

"Indeed," Moran replied haughtily, immediately wishing to part company with the burly sailor.

"Use a specshul trip todays u does," said the skipper. "Usuallys a one ways tickets this. I dares not sez moar but weez gotta puts use down unders the deck till we gets there we does. Can't ave ya seein howz wes gets wherer wes goins ya know."

"Fine," Moran replied as he walked below deck, glad to be relieved of the skipper's company.

Moran heard the skipper say something about the journey taking a few hours as the hatch door shut above him. He found himself in a small room with a bed and table. If not for the lamp hanging from the roof, the room would be pitch black. Moran decided he'd get some rest, dousing the lamp before laying down in the bed, the dark room and gentle rocking of the boat helping him fall asleep almost instantly.

The mage was woken by an all too enthusiastic poke from the skipper.

"Wez here we iz," he said almost jumping up and down as he did.

Moran didn't bother replying and followed him out of the lower deck room and onto the beach. The scene in front of him had him

42

thinking he must still be dreaming. The skipper must have noticed because he started to laugh.

"Bet you thoughts it was a just a bed timez story eh."

Moran stood speechless.

"I wouldn't try tellinz anyones abouts this place. Seemz to be badz for ya healths if ya know wats I meanz" the sailor half spoke half laughed. "This is as far as I goes, I'll leave you in the capable hands O' Mr Riley." The skipper pointed to a thin, bald man dressed in a long black coat standing about sixty yards away at the base of two massive towers. Moran was still trying to process the scene before him, his eyes telling him he was standing in front of the Silent Twins, his brain disagreeing, knowing the place to be a fairy tale. "This can't be real," he thought. "It's just supposed to be a legend designed to scare people into behaving."

Mr Riley started walking towards the dumbstruck Moran. "I had the same reaction when I first arrived," he said seemingly reading his mind. Moran came back to reality.

"Greetings Mr Riley, I'm supposed to be tracking down a lost prisoner of yours I believe."

"Yes indeed, we require a man of your extensive expertise to apprehend him."

"Firstly, enlighten me as to what's going on, then give me any information you have on his location."

"If you'd be so kind as to follow me inside I'll tell you everything you need to know."

The two walked to a small guard house sitting next to the towers.

"Food, drink?" Mr Riley offered. Moran took the bread and wine.

"This is amazing!" Moran said out loud as he tasted the wine.

"Amazing is only the beginning of what you can acquire when you work in a place that isn't supposed to exist, for people who aren't supposed to either," Mr Riley said with a smile. "But, as much as I'd love to go on about my current station, I'm not actually at leisure to, and time is of the essence."

"To business then."

"We know you can track a person's movements given an item

they have touched in the last three days. Fortunately, we have on hand a tankard the prisoner used to consume some ale prior to his departing our company.

Moran squinted at the man as though he wasn't getting the full story. "A tankard of ale? The Silent Twins, the prison no one believes exists, inescapable, and you're serving the prisoners tankards of ale? Do they have hot baths too?"

A red-faced Mr Riley replied, wishing he'd said it were water, "No we do not. It seems two of our guards disappeared along with the visiting captain of the Barathax Royal Guard. He's the one who requested the drink. The guards on the bridge said he was taking the prisoner for execution under royal decree, the man having confessed to his crimes. I'll also have you know this IS the first escape in the history of the prison."

"So he simply walks out the front door of the kingdom's most legendary prison that is supposed to be impossible to escape. Classic," Moran said with a snigger.

"I'm so pleased you find our current predicament amusing," Mr Riley said insincerely, handing the tankard to Moran.

Touching the tankard, a stream of images played out in front of Moran's eyes, a first person, fast-forward perspective of what turned out to be the Barathax Royal Guard's movements from the time he drank from the tankard till now. Moran, being the man he was, decided not to inform Mr Riley that his prisoners weren't actually drinking during their incarceration.

"Oh, I almost forgot to mention, that buffoon they had bring me here blindfolded me. My contractor has stipulated that the prisoner's destination once recaptured is not the Silent Twins. I'll require a map of the area."

"My apologies, Bodone isn't the sharpest chap, I'll get you a map now."

"Incompetence everywhere I turn," Moran mumbled, shaking his head as Mr Riley returned with the map.

"I suppose I'm off then. Where's the boat?"

Mr Riley pointed to a vessel moored on the beach as three familiar faces disembarked and made their way towards an old friend.

CHAPTER 14 - ALISTAIR

"I thought that thing was supposed to just propel something with magnets," said Alistair after some of the shock had worn off. "What's with the flaming plume of death, anyone would think you just fired a cruise missile."

"That's what occurs at full power, and as you can probably see, that's why it will only let you fire it remotely. Apparently, matter does some strange things when it's accelerated to those speeds."

"Yeah, like turn into a blazing inferno of doom," replied Alistair.

"I don't want to know what I just witnessed," Terra said. "Just don't ever point it at me."

Alistair and George laughed.

"Can you shoot it at lower power levels without the need to mount it?" Alistair asked.

"Yeah, it still packs a punch at medium but there's no trailing infernos of doom."

George disassembled the tripod and put it back in his pack, handing the rifle to Alistair.

"Alright, back to Aris then," said Alistair.

"We have to eliminate him."

"If we kill Aris, how do we know that he doesn't have someone else lined up to follow in his footsteps and continue the assassinations?"

"We don't, but it should buy us enough time to figure out a more permanent solution."

"Fair enough. So how do we get back to Barathax? I must be plastered over every wall by now with an unlimited bounty on my head," said Alistair.

"Getting into the city proper is definitely a no no. Luckily for us, Aris is travelling to Arn two days from now. The road between Arn and Barathax is as rural as it gets. We'll ambush his convoy en route. As luck would have it, I've travelled the same route and know just the spot. I'll fill you in on the details when we get there."

"You seem to know an awful lot about Aris's movements."

"I wouldn't be much good as the field commander of the Parallel Earth Expeditionary if I didn't, would I?"

"So that technically makes you my boss I suppose," Alistair said, stunned. "Even if it wasn't against standard operating procedure here I suppose it's too late to salute you now."

George laughed, "Aren't you glad you know who pulled you out of the SAS now? Best sniper in the regiment AND DNA that matched the machine, too good a combo to pass up."

Alistair shook his head, "If only I knew that was a prerequisite I could have started missing."

George walked over to speak with Terra as Alistair stared at the dark still water lit by the full moon in the night sky, a peaceful calm ensuing. Alistair started thinking back to his time on Earth. Whilst being raised in a middle-class family in Manchester, he attended a lower socio-economic school and scored mainly average grades in most subjects except maths. He excelled in maths, not genius or prodigy level, but he did manage to score the highest in the region in his final year. A tall, scrawny lad during his school years, he excelled at long distance running. After he finished school he drifted around for a while working odd jobs but not really finding one he liked, most of the time getting fired because his mind would drift off to medieval battles and tales of fantasy to escape the boring monotony of his reality. After a few years of what could best be described as a somewhat vagrant lifestyle, he decided to join the military, figuring it was the best chance he had to do something exciting and get paid for it. There were boring parts for sure, but the first time they handed him a rifle he was befit with one of those smiles that you try to contain, but like a sneeze, it happens anyway. From that day on, he knew he was in the right place. He won Manchester barracks regular infantry shooting competition in his first year enlisted, a title he retained for the duration of his service in the infantry. Word spread of the young recruit's talent and the next year Hereford secretly sent their best marksman from the SAS regiment. It was extremely windy that day so most scores were hardly praise-worthy, that is except for two of the shooters, Alistair and the SAS entrant. The competition went on 4 hours longer than usual as the two continually gained near perfect scores. In the end it came down to one final shot. The SAS entrant needed a perfect shot to win, anything else would result in a loss. It had been raining now for a good while. He flexed his fingers inside the now soggy material that comprised his gloves. How, he wondered, was this regular managing to best 20 years of military experience with 10 of those being in arguably the most elite fighting force in the world. He lined up the target, and just as his brain told his finger to retract there was an extremely loud crack of lightning. Most men would have flinched and made a complete mess of the shot given the situation. Years of training at the highest level of his discipline however had almost nullified the reflex action. Be that as it may, the reaction wasn't eliminated completely. So minute it was, there was no way it could be observed externally. Only the man firing the weapon knew of the twitch, and only because he could feel it, not because it translated into some obvious movement. The bullet smashed through the centre of the target, winning the day for the mysterious SAS contender. Alistair was disappointed, but at the same time in awe of the mystery shooter's accuracy. No one had even come close to him in the last three years, yet alone defeated him. Alistair, being a good sport, shook the shooters hand and congratulated him on an amazing shot. The shooter, modest in victory, told Alistair he had never come across anyone who possessed accuracy on par with the man he had just defeated and before leaving, subtly hinted he should try out for SAS selection. George never forgot that day. He knew he'd met his match and that if not for a gift from the heavens, Alistair would have beaten him.

CHAPTER 15 - ALISTAIR

Alistair's reminiscent trance was abruptly interrupted by something odd in the water. His subconscious seemed to think there was something subtly out of place in the picture his eyes were presenting his brain. As the ship moved gently through the ocean, it unsettled the water behind them, creating a cone like formation as it did. The odd part was that just as the ship started to turn, a break appeared in the cone of unsettled water, as though something had cut through the wake trailing their vessel. Another realisation suddenly dawned upon him. Terra said she had left a trap on the beach. He heard the scream, but when they made their way back to the boat, he didn't see any trapped militia, yet alone any signs of injury if they had escaped.

Hearing Terra's footsteps on the bare wooden deck behind him he asked, "Did you see that?"

"See what?" Terra said as she leaned on the rail looking out to sea.

Alistair had been present at many an interrogation in his time and as such had developed a keen eye for reading faces. There was a slight inconsistency in Terra's expression. He didn't think she was lying, but there was definitely a subtle unexpected nervousness in her composure as she answered.

"Listen, about the Island, the hound would have eaten me alive if not for you and George, I'd just like to let you know I'm grateful."

"Don't mention it, it's a shame we couldn't do anything for

Augustus."

"Yes, I will miss him so, he was such a good friend," replied Terra.

Terra caught the confused look on Alistair's face for the split second it was there.

"I've got to go through some things with George. I'll be back soon," Alistair said.

Terra looked on in frustration as he went below deck, silently cursing the foolishness of the remark. Moran knew that if the game wasn't up, it was certainly close to being. He made a gesture out to sea with his hand and the cloaked ship that had been following them suddenly materialised. One of the three men aboard shot an arrow with a rope attached to it that dug firmly into the mast. A piece of material was tied to the rope as the mystery ship's occupants used it to board Alistair and George's vessel. The rope connecting the two ships was dislodged, the mystery ship disappearing from view once more. A great brute of a man greeted Terra silently with a nod of the head, his scarred face completing the image of a man who instilled fear by presence alone. Moran pitied the poor souls that ended up facing Gerim on the battlefield. During the war for Imado he was rumoured to have killed a knight by crushing his skull with his bare hands. That was how the legend went anyway. Contrary to most legends the truth was even more brutal. The knight had been wearing a helmet at the time! The next to board the ship was Hadron Kado. Hadron was a slight fellow, his physical presence paling in comparison to the imposing figure of Gerim. However, looks could be deceiving, and in this case, they certainly were. To those who knew him, Hadron was a master swordsman, his speed and technique, to Moran's knowledge, unrivalled. His long black hair and ill-fitting black attire flapping in the sea breeze. Finally came the quite overweight, slovenly looking Morris Verbata, whose stench alone forced Moran back a pace. It wasn't much of a stretch to imagine him a common street beggar in his rag tag attire as opposed to one of the most 'respected' alchemists the kingdoms had ever known. It just so happened the sleeping powder that had caught Alistair previously was of Verbata's making. His nose was a large hooked thing that protruded out from between two piggish black eyes. To say his hairline was receding would be a complement, Morris being entirely bald, save a small patch of fluff at the apex of his misshapen head.

Alistair and George appeared suddenly from below deck, rifles pointed at Terra and the three other figures in front of them. Moran knew it unlikely he was still fooling anyone and was wary of what those strange weapons the two people in front of him were carrying could do. He therefore stood still and said nothing.

"Your true form please," Alistair said to Terra.

There was a grunt from Gerim as Terra turned and yelled, "No!"

Gerim thought it quite comical as he charged forth that the two puny men holding strange looking pieces of metal would be stupid enough not to cower before his might. As he ran towards the two fools, there was a brief moment of sharp pain in his chest, and then nothing as the next couple of rounds penetrated his skull. The brute was so large however, that the inertia he had built in his charge sent his dead body crashing into the two men in front of him. Alistair and George attempted to scramble to their feet but were stopped by a man pointing two swords at their throats. Hadron's footwork was other-worldly, it was almost unbelievable the speed at which he could cover a few paces without seeming to move his upper body at all. Morris stood in shock at what had just happened.

"Drop the..." Hadron paused for a second looking from George to Alistair's rifle, "whatever they are." There were two soft thuds as George and Alistair both relinquished their weapons. Morris moved to examine Gerim as Terra's body started to shake and convulse unnaturally. In a grotesque series of events, Moran's form slowly split from Terra's like two cells dividing. As his hold over her mind and body was finally relinquished, his physical form completed the phase shift, teleporting from the invisible boat he'd been controlling his host from, to the deck of the target's vessel.

Moran stretched his neck. "Well it seems your little escapade has come to an end. I must say I'm quite impressed that you managed to take down that brute of a man. Truly, the saying brains beats brawn has indeed been proven correct multiple times today," he said with an arrogant smile.

"Bastard," Alistair yelled looking at Terra's limp, lifeless body on the deck in front of him. "What the hell did you do to her!?"

"Yes I know, not a pleasant business possession, there'd be no need though if that crew of cretins hadn't just randomly appeared."

Even the cold hearted, calculating Moran Cheldore abhorred the possession process, the strong bond it created with the host's psyche having a powerful emotional reverberation on even the coldest of practitioners. When he took control of a host, it remained fully aware, however its decisions were completely at his whim, the host not realising until close to the separation that its thoughts were not its own. He shared every feeling in its entirety, the dread as Terra frantically ran to escape the hound, the sudden elevation as her body produced a last-ditch wave of adrenaline, the relief she felt when she was saved. He had no qualms with that part however. The reason he'd attempted to wipe the spell from history was the brief moments before separation when the host realised there was someone else there, someone that was about to leave, resulting in their leaving this body too. The all too real horror at the realisation they were about to die was shared by the possessor, it leaving a melancholy emotional echo upon his psyche forever more. He had the process removed from every book, tome and scroll not long after he discovered it, the result of which, to his knowledge, being that he was the only mage in the kingdoms privy to its existence. Upon realising its devastating effect soon after designing it, Moran had initially thought he'd petition the Mages Guild to outlaw it. Mulling it over at great length however, he later decided the fact he'd shared it with no one meant a better course of action was to remove all record of its existence instead. Banning it would likely just spur further interest.

"I'd still have had to kill her regardless. The moment she drew the blade it was that or let her run me through. I hardly think 'stabbed by a female deckhand' would have positive connotations for a mercenary's market value. Oh and by the way, you have my gratitude for killing the Cereon hound. I'm unable to cast anything while in possession of another and those mage hunting beasts are a species I wouldn't mind seeing extinct."

"I wouldn't mind seeing you extinct," Alistair replied.

Before Moran could react, Morris slapped the deck excitedly.

"Extraordinary!" he exclaimed as he examined the exit wounds in Gerim's head and chest. "That must have taken some force to punch through that much meat and bone. I must examine those weapons," he said, off in his own world as he picked up the M4A1 on the ground, Alistair promptly screwing up his face in reaction to the overwhelming odour.

"There will be time for that later," Moran snapped. "I need you to put these two to sleep so we don't risk any more trouble prior to their delivery."

"It would be my pleasure," Morris said with an eerie smile, as he pulled a small pouch from his belt and sprinkled some form of powder over George and Alistair's faces. Almost immediately, Alistair saw four swords pointing at him instead of one as the words and ambient noise began to meld together, the world slowly beginning to spin and give way to darkness.

CHAPTER 16 - ARIS

Aris sat in his chair pondering how the pendulum of fortune could swing so violently against him. Whoever was meddling in his affairs must be very powerful. The Guild of Balance was the second most powerful group in the kingdom, only bested by the royal family, and even that line was blurred. He simply could not rationalise how someone else could have known of his plans. The only other people who had any knowledge of the scheme were his generals, whom he trusted completely, and Alistair, which didn't make sense at all. Every discussion had occurred in the secret meeting place, a more secure location there was not in all the kingdom. Maybe some form of magic was involved? That was just as unlikely however, the meeting place having an extremely powerful magical dampening aura surrounding its perimeter. It was to this end that he'd sent the Cereon hounds, that and the state the door to the Baron's study was in. The Cereon hound was a special breed of canine that exhibited the unique ability to sense any form of magical energy within an individual. Playing a key role in capturing the outlaw band of shape shifters known as the Sletevoka Trio, the Cereon hounds had become a sought after and subsequently expensive breed used exclusively for hunting those of supernatural arts. He'd sent a hound with each of the boats and had ended up one short. The soldiers who had described the flaming wreck their ship had been left in also bore news of the hound's demise. Aris was released from his thoughts by the sound of running footsteps on the wooden corridor outside his quarters. This was promptly

53

followed by a furious knocking at his door.

"Your lordship, your humble squire Orion requests an audience bearing news most dire."

Aris had barely mouthed the word "Enter" when the door swung open and a sweat covered, panting Orion barged into the room.

"Word from the scouts, Trescot banners march on our borders, 200,000 odd men, five days at best."

"What!"

Orion knew better than to reply and so stood silently in the corner. Aris drifted back into his head. "Why now?" he thought. Nothing exceptional had happened lately to warrant an invasion. Was the planned framing leaked? But who could have done such a thing even if they wanted to. Had Trescot been responsible for helping Alistair escape The Silent Twins? Alistair certainly wouldn't be holding Aris in the highest regard after recent events. As such, he would no doubt have few qualms bringing them up to speed on said events. Would Alistair really turn informant though? There was no use trying to figure it out now. In time he'd find out which little bird had sung its treacherous song and if he managed to keep Barathax's sovereignty intact, that little bird would fall from its tree. A very tall tree at that.

There was another knock at the door.

"Enter" Aris replied.

The door opened and his three generals entered the chambers. General Tyrus was first to take a seat at the table. He was a strong man, even now in his late 40's. Exhibiting the tanned complexion of a man who didn't spend his days indoors, the combination of his weather-beaten features and emerging grey streaks in his previously jet black hair aesthetically aged Tyrus beyond his years. He'd served on Aris's war council ever since coming to his attention during the last war with Trescot. During the war, the young soldier had boldly spoken out of turn and suggested a tactic contrary to his commanding officer's at the time. The commander was about to flog him for insubordination when Aris stayed his hand. Even though the commander was probably well within his rights to do so, Aris knew the strategy suggested was far superior to the one currently being employed and as such ordered the force to follow the plan suggested. It worked brilliantly. They sacrificed the line at Dendiden, a small town to the North from whence a large portion of the enemy were invading. While doing so, they flanked the invading force, wedging themselves between the reinforcing troops and the forward attack party that had taken the town. The reinforcements, believing the main party had taken the town, became careless and moved up without even bothering to don their armour. After all, they weren't in the vanguard, or so they thought. Tyrus's squad took them by surprise and slaughtered the reinforcing Trescots while they were either drunk, whoring or passed out. Tyrus then flanked the group that had taken the town as the Barathax army attacked. A second slaughter ensued. Aris estimated the young warrior had just saved a good 10,000 Barathax lives. Aris had Tyrus knighted the next day and later personally requested he sit on his council.

The other two generals, Meab and Crowls, were of noble birth and assumed their position through inheritance rather than merit. They were, however, extremely loyal, and their diplomatic abilities more than made up for the lack of military experience. A good combination Aris thought, "Two silver tongues and a Lion."

"Aris," came the gruff voice of his first general, "I have good reason to believe King Ervoule is in danger. As you know, your lad's show has convinced him to lend assistance to Barathax and I'm willing to bet that's why we've got 200,000 red dogs coming to knock down our walls. I've no idea how they found out, but it's the only explanation I can think of. Without Eboda at our side we're done and Trescot knows it. If I were them, I'd have sent assassins to slay the king before he gets home and passes the decree. I'd also be positioning my army between Barathax and Eboda to block the King's passage if the assassins fail, just to be sure. It's a long shot, but if Trescot have anyone with even an ounce of strategical intelligence, they'll have sent some form of advance party to take him out."

"Agreed," replied Aris. "It is a long shot. But the stakes are too high not to take every precaution. King Ervoule is still here if I'm not mistaken?"

Meab spoke, "Leaving tomorrow morning I believe."

Aris interrupted, "Meab, Crowls, ready ten of your best men and tell them they're not to leave the King's side for any reason. Oh, and ready them quickly. Tyrus, with me. Let's make sure no ill befalls our guest in the meantime."

As Tyrus and Aris left the room Crowls looked up at the ceiling, tilting his head to the side as he did, as though he had remembered something.

"Aris," he called after him. "I remember speaking with the new wine server today. I thought it odd at the time that someone other than Wendy was serving wine but the new server said Wendy's mother had fallen ill. I'm not completely sure, but it seemed strange as I believe I remember Wendy mentioning her mother was dead some years ago."

Tyrus cursed, his face suddenly becoming quite a bit less tan.

"She was preparing to bring Ervoule some wine when we came to meet with you!"

"Go!" Aris shouted as he and Tyrus sprinted towards Ervoule's chambers.

CHAPTER 17 - TERRIC

The Bogmaul was a hideous creature. Its body structure was humanoid but that was where the similarities ended. It had patches of skin missing and sporadic small clumps of hair spread all over its scrawny body. If the set of needle like incisor teeth did not spark a primal fear in all those who saw one, its long, thick, razor sharp claws that sprouted from its hands and feet certainly did. They'd first been discovered in the far north by a band of knights but had since been hunted to extinction. Unknown are the number of ill-fated travellers they consumed prior to the most fortunate day a band of knights discovered their existence by inadvertently countering their main strength.

The Bogmaul's most fearsome trait was not their claws or teeth, but the innate ability to disappear from view for an extended period of time. This led to disappearances going unaccounted for for decades, no one having ever seen one and lived to tell the tale. One fateful night however, a small band of five knights were on patrol in the north. A Bogmaul had spotted the party and decided he'd follow the group till they made camp and fell asleep. He'd then proceed to slit their throats in the night and have a feast for days to come. Disappearing from view, he followed the party till they made camp. As the fire slowly became less and less fire and more and more embers he sat patiently and watched as his soon to be dinner laid down to sleep, one by one. As all but one drifted off he began to drool in anticipation. He knew the others would feel secure and rest soundly with the knowledge that one of them was keeping watch. It would be an easy task to sneak up on the watchman and kill him quietly. He could then dispose of the others without a care. It just so happened that Terric had first watch that night. Terric was a good, loyal man, but a clumsy simpleton none the less. He bored easily and would usually end up amusing himself by finding a stick or a rock to fidget with when he had to stand watch. Tonight, Terric the simpleton, started to mindlessly flick some ashes with a stick as his mind drifted to a place only Terric knows. The Bogmaul couldn't wait any longer. Without a sound, he dropped from the tree, moving silently out into the open as he salivated at the thought of his prey. Closer and closer he came. As he got within five feet of the fat fellow, the smell became overpowering. Fresh living flesh, this was it, the moment he'd been so patiently waiting for. Drawing back an invisible clawed hand, he prepared to strike when a thick cloud of smoke suddenly blew up from behind the fat human. Billowing into the Bogmaul's face, the cloud momentarily blinded him as it simultaneously formed an eerie smoke outline of his hideous form. Frantically wiping his stinging eyes in an attempt to regain vision, the Bogmaul was unaware of the silhouette the smoke cloud had created against the night sky. Very out of character and probably the only time he did so in all his life, Terric acted instantly. With great haste, he snatched up his sword from where it lay and thrust it into the middle of the smoky outline. The outline reeled backwards in pain, letting out a wretched screech as it fell to the ground dying, its true form slowly coming into view. Upon his return, Terric reported that the wind had changed direction suddenly, smoke from the camp fire revealing the beast for but a second, affording him time to run it through.

Now Terric may have been a simpleton, but he knew the old saying, "Never let the truth get in the way of a good yarn." Terric just may have left out the part about the chest of extremely dusty old treasure maps he had brought with him on patrol. They weren't really treasure maps, just old requisition forms, but Terric didn't know that, so he'd bring them along and pretend he was a treasure hunter while he took his turn to sit watch during the long nights. The chest was set on the ground behind him. As he was flicking the embers he'd accidentally set it alight. The maps were so dusty that as they caught fire they created a thick cloud of smoke that had actually saved his and the rest of the party's life.

The Bogmaul's corpse was taken back and news of its existence reported. Soldiers were henceforth equipped with special torches that created great clouds of smoke when burnt and set about hunting the once illusive breed of demon. The torches proved so successful that it is thought the species are now extinct. Some still claim however, that a certain Trescot commander, recognising the potential tactical advantage of having a soldier that could disappear from view, reached an accord with one of the last of them.

CHAPTER 18 - ERVOULE

King Ervoule III of Eboda quietly admired the lavishness of his chambers. His majesty was housed in Castle Brin's special guest chambers that sat adjacent the throne room. His host, King Bastion of Barathax, had these chambers built to house no less than royalty. Lesser dignitaries and other visitors of noble title would be housed in a separate guest house adjoining a lower section of the castle. Finery adorned every inch of the spacious lodgings, a good deal of which was taken up by a bed large enough to sleep twenty. The sheets were made of the finest silk, the pillows fat and to some extent, overly comfortable. Gold statues representing all manner of man and beast decorated the room, struck in dramatic poses for eternity. The most amazing feature the special chambers boasted however, was a strange metallic box that was cold inside. It gave certain beverages and food an entirely different taste. Not only that, food that would normally rot within a few days would take much longer to turn in this cooling box. When he had inquired, his host had told him it was a gift from the mages of Rafin More. Ervoule ruled over a great deal more subjects, however, his wealth did not come close to matching that of Barathax. He was surprised and a little concerned at how many gifts the 'mages' had bestowed upon Barathax and King Bastion.

Ervoule poured wine into a golden goblet as he walked, drink in hand to his balcony. He parted the fine white curtains, feeling something brush against him as he did. Whatever brushed against him seemed heavier than the curtains so he grabbed one of them between two of his fingers and rubbed them together. The fabric was indeed very light. "This wine must be as strong as it is delicious," he thought, feeling the warm sun on his face as he stepped onto the balcony. Gazing down upon the castle grounds, he wondered to himself how so few peasants could support such a population. Were they all hidden somewhere? There were people in the streets, blacksmiths hammering metal, merchants selling their wares, farmers tending to crops in the distant fields... but the numbers... they just weren't like anything he'd encountered before. Back home there would have been scores more common folk. "A strange land," he thought. "Maybe after we officially ally I will press Bastion on how they manage it," he mused, swilling his wine in the goblet. The only rationalisation he could think of was that their military must be a paltry few compared to Eboda as well.

There was a knock at the door and a serving woman called out. "More wine your grace?"

"Ah, these Barathaxians might not have much of an army but they surely know how to treat a guest," he thought to himself. "Enter, enter," the red-faced king said enthusiastically.

The wine servant was an average looking woman at best. She was dressed in similar attire to a common peasant but wasn't nearly as dirty. She wore a black and white dress. She bowed her head and curtsied as the King approached.

"May I pour you another your grace?" she asked as she noticed the goblet in the King's hand.

"You may," said the King with a slightly tipsy grin.

As she began to pour, the King noticed, but thought little of the smile that slowly spread across the wine servant's face. While she was pouring, Ervoule became aware of footsteps originating somewhere in the hall. The time between thuds was short enough that it seemed someone was running with utmost urgency. The woman finished pouring the wine and curtsied, rested the jug on the tabletop and began to walk backwards towards the door. The King raised the goblet as it began its journey to his mouth. The footsteps were right outside his door now and without warning the servant was knocked to the floor as Tyrus exploded through the doors followed by Aris. Seeing the goblet at the King's lips, Aris quickly grabbed the closest object he could, which as it happened, turned out to be a diamond the size of a man's fist and promptly hurled it at the hand with which Ervoule grasped the goblet. The diamond hit Ervoule's fingers and he reacted immediately, recoiling more in surprise than pain, dropping the cup of wine as he did.

"What is the meaning of this?!" Ervoule shouted angrily as he shook his sore fingers.

"Your grace, that wine is poisoned!" Aris exclaimed between breaths. "We believe the woman before you to be a Trescot assassin," Aris said pointing at the servant who was just now picking herself up off the floor.

"You could have just told me," he retorted.

"Apologies your grace, there was no time, did you consume any of it?"

"No, it seems you are rather adept at throwing valuable rocks at valuable people," the King replied, the anger slowly leaving his words. Aris was glad Ervoule saw it this way. He didn't want to think what might happen if the King had been arrogant enough to take real offence.

Tyrus grabbed the servant by the arm, spinning her to face Ervoule and Aris. She was sobbing by now and looked genuinely scared.

"Assassin and actor," Tyrus said, not being fooled by the false tears and feigned fear, although it was one of the better acts he'd seen.

Ervoule stared at her for a moment and then in a sarcastic tone said, "May I pour you a drink my lady?" as he grabbed the Goblet and the jug of wine and began to pour.

Her face suddenly transformed from one of sad confusion to pure fear. The tears stopped abruptly as she froze still. A moment later she pointed in the direction of the balcony and screamed at the top of her lungs.

"An accomplished actor indeed," the King said.

Even though the three men thought the woman seemed very genuine in her expression, none of them were going to look in the direction she was pointing. Did she really think such a ploy would be successful?

The King put the cup in front of the spy's face and gestured for her to drink. Moments before she was to take the fateful sip Tyrus interrupted.

"Your grace, we would be wise to question her first with your consent."

The King retracted the goblet. "I like this man Aris. Bold and logical." He turned to the spy. "Don't worry, I'll save you some for later 'me' lady. His majesty will see you have your fill."

CHAPTER 19 - JORGMUR

Jorgmur had a real passion for two activities. Today he'd get to indulge both. He was engaged in the first as he climbed down from the tower apex and slowly onto the balcony. The click of his talons on contact with the stone floor was barely audible as he dropped the final yard onto the balcony with the white curtains. Jorgmur approached slowly, keeping as much of his back against the ornate parapet rail as possible. Even if he were silhouetted, it was broad daylight and almost impossible to see the faint outline of his body anyway. He looked up, observing the hardly noticeable scratches in the shape of an 'X' above the archway that led from the balcony into the room. This was the one. A large man in fine attire rolled out of bed and retrieved a goblet from the table. Jorgmur began to salivate over razor sharp, needle like teeth as he wished he would have more time to indulge his second love. The most unlikely of barriers stood between him and his quarry he thought, the fat man facing him meaning there was no way through the fine curtains without alerting his prey via their movement. He'd just have to wait until the fat man turned around and then he'd make his move through the flimsy obstruction. The fat man wasn't turning around however. He was coming towards Jorgmur, cup in hand. Jorgmur's heart rate spiked as a wave of concern washed over him. He couldn't climb back up, the scratching of claws on stone and sudden movement risked too great a chance of alerting the man. "Oh well," he thought, the fat man would come through the barrier to him and he'd just have to kill him on the balcony. But no, that wouldn't work. Upon the balcony above and to the left he'd seen a guard standing watch as he descended. "Too risky to kill the fat man out here." Jorgmur was starting to fret now, the curtains giving way as the fat man walked through. Making the split decision to utilise the opportunity and slip past while the curtains were still in motion, he pressed his wretched body against the side wall and squeezed through the gap between it and the fat man, brushing ever so slightly against him as he did. The meal was so close it was all Jorgmur could do not to lash out as he slipped past. Upon entering the room, he froze, his back to the wall. The fat man had noticed. Stopping abruptly, the human rubbed the curtains between his fingers, paused for a moment, then let go of the curtains and turned to face the sun. Jorgmur breathed a silent sigh then waited for what seemed like an eternity for his prey to re-enter the room. The man eventually came back through the curtains and moved towards the chamber doors. The anticipation of the kill was building exponentially now. It was time. Jorgmur slowly inched towards his prey, a clawed hand ready to swipe. He was just about to run his claws across the man's neck when there was a noise at the door. Retreating in frustration towards the back corner of the room, he silently cursed the interruption. A woman entered, and after a brief moment, began to pour some wine. A brief discussion ensued after which the woman moved as if to leave the room. And then the madness began. The door burst open and another man came rushing in, knocking the woman over as he did. A second man then threw something at the fat man which caused him to drop the goblet of wine. Jorgmur observed as the chaos continued. Someone grabbed the woman and they were now seemingly offering her a drink. What the hell was going on? As he came to a stop in the back corner of the room, the woman, without warning, suddenly pointed towards him and screamed. "How could she see him?" he thought alarmed, a rush of adrenaline surging through his body. He froze. "She can't see me, it must be something else behind me." He was about to make a dash for the balcony, when, as if the events leading to this moment hadn't been strange enough, the men seemed to make a point of not looking where she pointed. He continued slowly towards the balcony as a precaution anyway, quickly glancing at the back of the room to try and figure out what this woman saw.

And there it was, a reflective surface in the back of the room he had heard the Trescots call mirrors. For some reason, a Bogmaul's camouflage didn't camouflage its reflection. The angle between the Bogmaul and the woman must have been such that she saw the reflection of his back and screamed. But that in no way explained why they didn't look in the direction she pointed.

The two men eventually left with the woman after which the fat man shut the door before lying down. Jorgmur briefly wondered why the fat man didn't drink his wine but only for a moment, the thought giving way to the anticipation of his meal. He would not be denied again, the fat man's skin and muscle offering little resistance to the razor-sharp claws that ran across his throat.

CHAPTER 20 - GARY

"Alright lads, we do this right and there's no more kissin arse for peanuts," came Captain Gary's Scottish brogue. "We put our lives on the line for these suit wearing, cappuccino swillin nancys so they can have a new beema every year and in return we get a few measly quid and then ye die or get a fuck off you're too old. Well I say it's time for some fair compensation."

"Aye," came a resounding affirmation from the British SAS soldiers who were in on the plan.

"Make no mistake lads, ye get caught here and ye'll get life if ye lucky."

No one flinched.

"Right, seems everyone agrees, let's get on with it then," Gary said, underscored by the soft crack of gunfire and explosions somewhere in the distance as they began on a journey that would change their lives forever.

Five days prior:
Captain Gary Anders had been a military man his entire adult life. Having joined at 18, he was now 40, a bit slower and far more cynical, but still every bit the lethal killing machine the regiment turned out. He may have been 40, but he'd put most 20 somethings to shame fitness wise. Muscular, but not overly hulking, endurance was emphasised in his role more so than brute strength. His wild, unkempt red mop of hair and bushy beard suited his persona to a

tee. Gary and his squad were usually given the most dangerous and or dirtiest jobs during their time in Iraq. During their last mission, three of his squad had been killed and they'd later discovered the government, or insurance company (they weren't sure if there was a distinction any more) had denied any payment to their families over some minor technicality in their life insurance clauses.

During the mission they'd had to retrieve some files from a computer in Basra. They'd stored it on USB drives but one of them had gotten mixed up in their equipment and hadn't made its way to HQ. Instead, HQ received some photos of Corporal Burnley's family. Corporal Burnley plugged the USB into his laptop to look at the photographs when to his surprise, intelligence detailing a certain terrorist organisation's cash storage facilities popped onto his screen. He immediately shut the computer down and decided he'd hand it in to HQ tomorrow when his squad mate Mick Renfield announced to the group the situation regarding the deceased squad member's families.

The original seven of squad Motel Whisky were now four:

Captain Gary Anders – The wild Scottish squad commander.

Trooper Len Winters – Hailing from Manchester came Motel Whiskey's scout, his slimmer build and attention to detail making him ideal for a role that required speed and precision.

Sergeant Michael Renfield – A man born into false wealth, some would argue he'd initially been given 'special consideration' upon selection at the hands of his well-connected Uncle. Whether or not this was the case it mattered not now. Michael, or Mick as he was referred to in the unit (which ran at strong odds with his upper-class English accent) had proved himself time and time again, even in the face of the eventual bankruptcy his uncle suffered, the clandestine pile of debt eventually catching up with the man who had initially greased the wheels. A testament to his actions, Renfield was promoted to Sergeant not long after, his strong character withstanding the slight on his family's name.

Finally, there was Corporal Roy Burnley from Liverpool. Burnley was somewhat of a wild card, his strong emotional character like a magnification of the Captain's. Throughout his career he'd been on the verge of promotion and dismissal many times, the net result of events thus far having favoured promotion, albeit slightly. When he was on his game, there was no one comparable, which thankfully was most of the time. Other states of mind however, would result in some less than optimal decisions. When the extremes of his mental state were factored in, he'd probably not be at all suitable to a normal unit. Motel Whiskey was no normal unit however. The tasks they were assigned required something different, an edge Burnley was more than capable of providing.

Len Winters, was sitting in the dimly lit concrete room with the others, the half dead light bulb swinging ever so slightly to and fro.

He shook his head, "That's disgusting. We risk our lives so they can sleep easy and they won't even support our families if something goes wrong. Our families deserve better."

Corporal Burnley thought for a second, "Logically, I shouldn't do this." Logic, in this case however, lost out to emotion. "So," he said quietly, "what if there was a way to right this injustice?" his dirty face barely visible in the poor light of the plain building.

"What are ye on about lad?" Gary replied as the group's attention was suddenly all eyes on Burnley.

He ushered them to his laptop, plugging in the USB drive. A schematic of Basra popped up on the screen titled, "Liquid Fund Storage." Different locations were marked, the closest of which was only ten kilometres from their current location.

"Ah stuff it," Gary said. "What do ye think lads?"

"Rod and Stephen's families are financially ruined without it," Mick's reply came.

"I'm in," came the reply from Len. "If I'm gonna die for these bastards I wanna know my family's set up."

"Hell, why not?" said Gary. "They'll probably kick me out next year and then what'll I do. Army's all I know." Burnley clicked the link to site 45. The camera image became a wire frame of the city as it proceeded to track to the specific building where the cash was presumably stored. The text "~ $100,000,000 USD – General expenses" appeared in the top of the schematic as the wire frame image revealed the exact room the cash was stored in.

"Hmm," interjected Winters. "Assuming we got the money, how would we get it out of the country?"

Mick chimed in, "Not a problem, I'm well acquainted with some of the lads in loading and they were close to Rod and Stephen. I'll offer them a cut and they'll make sure the bags get on the plane with us untouched."

"Sounds like we best get planning then," replied Gary.

CHAPTER 21 - GARY

Captain Anders paced about his cell impatiently. It was more of a room than a cell, only the door was locked from the outside. The walls were plain white in colour and the only object in the room was a thin foam mattress. They never turned out the old light that hung from the ceiling and it was too high to reach to unscrew. Gary had never been in a military prison before so he couldn't be sure, but this didn't really match his idea of one. He could feel the fleas leaping about in the infested blue jumpsuit they'd given him as his thoughts shifted to his squad. He hadn't heard any voices since he'd woken up and as such wasn't sure if they were being held separately. The clanging sound of metal on metal jolted him from his thoughts as the bolt on his door slid open. As he turned to face the door, two men in suits that could very well have been twins lumbered in, their massive, no doubt steroid assisted frames barely squeezing through the door. As he moved towards them he was abruptly reminded of the chains that bound him as they snapped taut, the steel collar digging into his neck.

The first man spoke, "You have bin very bad boy Captain Anders," he said in a mocking tone, his voice sounding Eastern European, possibly Russian or Ukrainian. "Normally you be tried for treason and have long time in prison back home."

The second man laughed, "Who are you kidding, normally he disappear."

"Lucky for you, someone needs a man of questionable ethics and certain skills. He is prepared to make you offer."

Gary said nothing. He was going to let his captors be the ones giving out the information, not the other way round.

"Let's say you accept offer. If you succeed, we let you keep that little bounty of yours. You can't tell anyone of course. If you refuse, well, let's just say Ron and Stephen's families won't have any more worries, neither will you and your band of traitor's families. Oh, and by no more worries, I mean things like breathing."

The first and second man laughed together. Gary was furious. His jaw began to tighten and veins began to appear about his temples. He took a moment to calm himself before speaking.

"Seems like I dinnay have much of choice now then do I."

"Well that was easy," the first suit said to the second as they exited the room momentarily.

Three men dressed in blue jumpsuits, hands chained behind their backs, potato sacks over their heads were marched into the room followed by the two mountains of meat Gary thought must have caused their mothers pure hell on the way out. The two men pulled the sacks off the heads of their captives and motioned for Burnley, Winters, and Renfield to sit down. Gary's spirits lifted the moment he recognised his squad mates. Sure, they'd seen better days, but they were alive. One of the suits left the room and came back in wheeling a projector on a thin wooden table with wheels. He plugged it in and turned it on as the other suit attached Burnley, Renfield and Winter's chains to the wall next to Gary.

"Did I ever tell ye you're one ugly bastard," Gary said to Burnley with a smile on his face.

They all looked ragged, having been locked up for no one knew how long with no shower facilities of any kind. One of the suits shuffled over to Gary and punched him in the ribs. Those present could hear the air being forcefully evicted from his lungs as he felt the steel collar dig into his neck when he reflexively bent forward.

"We talk, you don't," Suit 2 grunted.

Light flickered on the wall and an image slowly appeared. An image of what looked like some sort of quaint English countryside.

"Hello gentlemen," came an American voice. "We all know why you're here so I'll get straight to the point. This is going to be hard to believe, but as they say, seeing is believing, and mark my words, you are about to see. Your insertion point will be here."

The projected image switched to a forest floor. The camera then panned to an aerial view. The image became a top down

72

perspective of a forest with a red line superimposed upon it.

"This is the path you will follow, at the end of which you will come to this pyramid like structure."

The projection now showed a top down view of a large pyramid surrounded by what seemed to be some sort of village at the edge of the forest. The image on the wall then changed to a great stone archway covered in strange carvings. Some kind of dragon shaped artefact appeared on screen and the camera zoomed into a recess in the stone archway. The artefact moved into the relief.

"Everyone you see is to be considered hostile," the voice resumed. "The structure will be guarded so stealth is advisable. You will need to breach a section of the structure and as such will be supplied with the necessary equipment to do so. Enemy numbers are in the hundreds gentlemen so direct engagements are to be avoided if possible. Good luck, I need not remind you that not only your own lives rely on the outcome of this task, but your families' as well."

With that, the projector went dark, a silence ensuing as the gravity of the situation washed over the remaining members of squad Motel Whiskey.

CHAPTER 22 - ALISTAIR

Alistair felt a sharp pain in his ribs as the world came into view.

"Up," Hadron said as he gave him another kick for good measure.

Alistair stood up awkwardly noticing that his hands were tied behind his back. He was standing on the bow of the ship and could see the sandy shore getting closer. Looking to his left George moved into focus, already standing, hands tied behind his back also. There was a soft thud as the ship beached itself on the coast. Moran jumped off in front of them as Hadron and Morris gave what could best be described as an 'encouraging nudge' off the bow. George landed just past the water's edge, the fine sand cushioning his fall. Alistair wasn't so lucky and immediately felt the biting cold water seep into his clothes. He'd have to put up with soggy boots for the rest of the journey.

"You'll be home soon gents," Moran said mockingly, not bothering to turn around as the sandy beach gave way to a dense forest. As they passed the first tree Moran cheerfully pronounced, "Take solace in the knowledge that someone has indeed paid handsomely for your recapture. Hmm, I wonder what they would give me for those frightful weapons of yours?"

"Hopefully a piece of steel between your shoulders," replied Alistair.

Half expecting a kick in the back, Alistair was surprised when he heard laughter behind him.

"He's a funny one isn't he," Morris said to Hadron.

Hadron, seemingly not one for frivolities, replied with a scowl.

Their walk dragged on for what Alistair guessed was another half hour when Moran abruptly cut the idle banter and dropped into the foliage. Alistair was pulled to the ground as he saw George drop next to him. Lying in the foliage the foul smell he had smelt earlier intensified as Morris whispered in his ear to stay quiet. After at least 15 minutes of lying quietly with naught but the night sky and the sound of the wind passing through the trees, Alistair began to wonder what was going on. He was about to suggest they press on, when finally he heard something. A sort of growl interleaved with a snort that started out as nothing more than a whisper in the distance but now grew stronger and more frequent. Leaves and small twigs were crunching underfoot as something approached. Whatever is was, it couldn't be more than a few yards away now. Another snort was followed by a sniffing sound which reminded him of a dog smelling the air as it first caught the scent of meat being cooked. Whatever made Moran drop however, was definitely no man's best friend. No common dog had the lungs or snout large enough to make that much noise when it smelt food. A soft mist sprinkled down onto Alistair as finally he saw it towering above him, a wave of primal dread he didn't think possible locking him in place, his breath catching in his throat in some sort of instinctive attempt to not make a sound. The beast had the characteristics of a dog but stood on two legs instead of four and was much larger, approximately 8 feet tall. Its body was covered in coarse black fur and long sharp claws protruded from the ends of its limbs, like five small scimitars on each paw. The thing had stopped above them - it knew they were close. Alistair lay frozen in fear, his eyes locked on the underside of its throat as it sniffed the air. Without warning, the beast's head snapped downwards, two luminous yellow eyes contrasting starkly against the night sky, vertical pupils like that of a cat beginning to dilate at the sight before it. Upon spotting its prey the beast's terror inspiring facial features formed what could almost be described as a sinister grin, excitedly moving in for the kill, barking loudly as it did. Opening its mouth, Alistair was presented with two rows of carnivorous teeth, each one at least the length of a finger. Alistair resigned himself to his fate. Even without his hands tied behind his back he didn't think himself much of a chance unarmed against this otherworldly aggressor. As the teeth closed in he made one last effort and rolled to avoid the bite, simultaneously kicking out towards the side of its head. There was some resistance as his foot connected but nowhere near as much as he expected, it almost feeling like kicking a soccer ball. As he rolled over once more in anticipation of the next attack, he saw why. The head had detached from the monster's shoulders and rolled to a stop at the foot of a nearby tree, its glowing yellow eyes fading to black.

"I've heard of a glass jaw but never a papier-mache neck," Alistair thought to himself as he lay in disbelief, wondering how he'd managed to behead such a creature with his foot.

Turning to his right he noticed Hadron wiping blood off one of his swords and all became clear.

"What the hell was that!?" Alistair yelled as he rolled forward and began to stand up.

Silence ensued, captor and companion alike seemingly still in shock at what had just transpired. Staring aimlessly past Alistair in the direction of the giant bipedal wolf's headless corpse, Moran looked on as if in a trance. Alistair felt Morris brush past him as he hurried to examine the corpse. Moran eventually replied, his seemingly vacant gaze looking through a transparent Alistair as he did.

"That... I think... was Val... But it couldn't be..." he corrected himself. "There hasn't been a sighting in at least 1000 years." Some unknown force breaking his trance, Moran focused on Alistair as though the previously transparent form in front of him had become opaque.

"If you want to live to see the next sunrise you'll not harm me when I return your weapons," he said as he untied Alistair and George's hands. "I'll explain later, but all you need to know for now is that there are at least ten more of those things closing in as we speak. We can't fight them in the forest, there's too much cover. Our best chance is to retreat to the boat."

Hadron threw George the large leather bag he'd been carrying as Moran's head flicked to the left, seemingly having heard something.

"Well it seems we're not going back to the beach. Five minutes at best gentlemen," he said in an eerily calm voice that was strongly at odds with the current situation. "Morris, a perimeter, if they surround us we are doomed."

Morris took a small satchel from his belt, spreading a powdery substance in a horseshoe path a few yards behind them. George and Alistair retrieved their rifles from the bag, readying them as Morris made his way back to the group. The forest was completely silent save the sound of crunching leaves under Morris's feet. Alistair thought the absence of ambient noise strange. Nothing, not an owl hooting, a cricket sounding, silence save a gentle breeze and the rhythm of his own nervous breathing. That was about to change.

Not long after Morris re-joined the group there was an explosion behind them. Alistair could hardly believe his eyes, a mixture of terror and surprise. The pitch-black forest lit up for no more than a split second as a green flame hissed in Alistair's peripheral vision. Feeling something solid hit him in the back, he turned to observe a chunk of flaming meat roll past him, the stench of burning hair assailing his nostrils. There was no time to think about it now however. Moran lifted his arms and an almighty flash illuminated the forest as far as the eye could see. It was then that they saw them. Less than ten yards away, like copies of the horror he had observed for the first time but a moment ago, stood at least five of the beasts, shielding their eyes in reaction to the sudden flash of light. Alistair observed the closest demon's eyes fill with yellow as its cat like pupils constricted, morphing from dark circles to thin strips of black. It was during this observation that he slowly became consciously aware of what he was doing. The rifle was raised to his shoulder, his feet in a solid stance, he felt the slight recoil as the first round came out of his gun and saw the grimace of pain in the thing's face as the piece of metal made contact with its target. Two in the chest and one in the head didn't seem to apply here as it just kept coming. Three more shots to the head seemed to do it as the first one fell to the ground at his feet. He saw another fall as George switched to full automatic, shredding the beast's cranium at close range. There were grunts of pain and barking sounds coming from all around them. Moran yelled something in another language which was followed by a grey blur and a streak of blood as a wolf's body parted company with its head. One of them had actually managed to get over Morris's explosive fire trap but was met by Hadron's sword seconds before it could take advantage of the situation.

"Reloading!" came a yell from George as Hadron moved effortlessly forward, running his sword through another of the demons as George dropped to one knee and grabbed a clip from the bag. The illumination spell Moran had cast began to fade as Alistair could hear the swish of Hadron's swords moving through the air nearby accompanied by howls and gunfire. Upon hearing the clicking sound Alistair instinctively ejected the spent magazine and went to grab another from the bag as a bolt of electricity shot from Moran's hands, spreading across the body of a wolf like an incandescent spider web, causing it to convulse violently as the smell of burning flesh and hair became ever more prevalent. As the light went from dim to non-existent, Alistair caught a fleeting glimpse of them closing in. There were just too many, their growls growing stronger as the absence of light seemed to rally their spirits. George began firing short bursts in front of him, changing the angle between each burst so as to cover as much of a forward arc as possible in the once more unlit forest. Through some cruel twist of fate, as though the illumination spell expiring wasn't misfortune enough, the explosive fire wall that had shielded their back began to die down as well. Reloading, Alistair resumed firing in a similar fashion to George when without warning he abruptly lost sensation in all four of his limbs. It seemed everyone else had stopped moving also, the growls receding as well.

Feeling returned slowly, but he still had no control over his body as he felt a warm sensation at the very tips of his fingers and toes. Almost unnoticeable at first, the sensation was spreading down his arms towards his torso, getting hotter and hotter as it did. His body began to feel as though the left side was trying to pull away from the right, the slight warm sensation intensifying. What was initially a warm sensation now felt as though he was being consumed by flame, Alistair attempting to scream in pain. No sound emerged from his mouth however as he had been rendered mute. Just as he was on the verge of passing out, Alistair half dreamt he heard a voice.

"Wait," came the sound from somewhere close by. The pain wasn't getting any worse but that was of little comfort, what little colour still existed in the world around him de-saturating to a wash of black and white. A group of small lights were bobbing up and down in the distance, appearing as blurry white balls in his current monochrome vision. He could semi-consciously hear footsteps as they got closer but he was too far gone now to take much note. "Was this the afterlife?" Alistair wondered as the white of the black and white world began to give way. The strangely dressed people were carrying what looked like torches, only the torches were of intricate design with all manner of carvings and embedded jewellery. There were approximately six cloaked strangers, each adorned in long robes sewn from black and purple cloth, their hands glowing an eerie blue. The leader strayed to within arm's length of Alistair, their torch illuminating one of the beasts as they did. It was stuck in an awkward pose not more than a foot from Alistair's face. The thing's expression was a mixture of pain, anger and confusion, its large clawed hand extended into the air ready to slash Alistair's head from his shoulders.

The leader stopped next to Alistair and removed their hood, examining the person in front of them, not seeming to mind the gargantuan wolf less than a yard to the left. Her calm yet intrigued expression matched her voice as she spoke in what Alistair would have described as an upper-class English accent if he had heard it.

"You know you really shouldn't be playing in the woods at night," came a condescending tone. Her gaze moved from Alistair to Morris, past Hadron, across George and then lastly to Moran. Upon spotting the rogue mage, her expression became one of genuine surprise. "Oh I do not believe that which stands before me!" she exclaimed, shaking her head in utter disbelief, before noticing the grimace upon their faces.

"Oh, forgive me, I am truly sorry," she said before giving the order. "Reduce force for the humans, we are taking them with us. Finish the rest."

Moving quickly to the right, the mystery woman put a tree between herself and the suspended wolf. The glow emitted by the strange group of wanderer's hands intensified which was quickly proceeded by a number of popping sounds as the wolf in front of Alistair exploded in a red mist. As the light emanating from their hands dulled, Alistair and the others felt the pain recede and the heat and pressure reduce. Colour returned to Alistair's vision as a welcome respite from the pain washed over him. He tried to move against the reduced pressure, but it seemed all he could move was his mouth.

"I'd say thanks for the rescue but..."

Like someone had plucked the words from his brain, the

second half of his sentence seemed to escape him as the woman in front of him came into focus. Alistair was as surprised as he was awestruck. The face behind the hood was as hauntingly beautiful as it was pale. The skin that covered her delicate features was the whitest Alistair had seen, the wind blowing through the torch sending shadows dancing across it. The contrast in hair colour was just as striking, as long black strands disappeared below her shoulder line into her cloak. He was drawn to a pair of large round eyes that glowed the same incandescent yellow as that of the horrors he'd just faced, only her pupils were round, not slit like the wolf demons. Against the white background it made for an intriguingly attractive, yet somehow supernatural appearance.

"You are welcome. Under differing circumstances I'd let you go, but it seems you have some rather interesting friends."

Moran groaned as Morris's belly wobbled in time to his laughter. "Hell has no fury like a woman," Morris teased.

"More like hell has no fury like Adele Vergen," Moran replied.

"Oh I wouldn't worry about me," said the woman. "Father however, will be most pleased to see you."

Moran looked to the air as if trying to remember something, "Wasn't forgive and forget Ulric's motto?"

She threw back her head as she laughed, "Your memory deceives you Moran, Never Forgive, Never Forget. I wonder if you will be so cocky upon our arrival at Bledith Tower?"

CHAPTER 23 - GARY

Gary awoke to the sound of an owl hooting in the trees above. The leaf litter made a crunching sound as he rolled over onto the root of a large tree. His surrounds coming into focus, he could see by the moonlight that he was sitting in the middle of a wood. The last thing he remembered was a small prick as one of the steroid pumping thugs injected something into the side of his neck. Looking around to get his bearing, Gary was reminded of the aerial footage he'd seen while captive. There was a rustling sound to his left as Burnley rolled over and stood up, stretching his arms as he did, soon to be followed in a similar fashion by Winters and Renfield. The air was cold and crisp, a small cloud appearing in front of Gary's mouth as he whispered to them between owl hoots. "Over here."

"The fuck'd we get here mate?" said Winters, keeping his voice low as he and the others moved quietly to join their captain.

Gary was about to answer when something vibrated against his hip. He reached down and only now noticed he had been dressed in woodland camouflage, his attire matching that of his squad mates. He grabbed the vibrating object from his belt. It was a small smart phone like device with a roughly four by two inch screen. An image was flashing on the screen that read "Press when ready." Gary pressed the screen and the device suddenly came to life, satellite imagery of their current location appearing on screen, a voice proceeded.

"Hello and welcome gentlemen," came the American voice they

had heard during their detainment. The others gathered around, the message likely to be for all of them. "A few things before we get under way. The sound you can hear can only be heard by the four of you. Each of you have received an implant, courtesy of your sponsor, that receives and transmits recoded sound and light directly to your brain, bypassing the need for your eyes and ears to see and hear the information. To this end, our interactions cannot be overheard or spied upon, which means I won't be blowing your cover any time soon. It also means that the only people who can see the images appearing on the screen are yourselves. To any other observer the device will appear as no more than a piece of glass and plastic. Now that's out of the way, onto the mission. Your first objective is to secure the supplies hidden to the north of your location."

The screen displayed video footage of their current location, then proceeded to move through the forest approximately sixty yards before coming to a halt at the mouth of a large cave.

"You will follow this path and then Gary will place his hand here, each finger in the matching relief." The display zoomed in on the cave, an image of a hand overlaying some barely visible markings to the right of its entrance.

"You won't be able to see it in the darkness, so you'll just have to take my word for it, but a door will have opened in front of you. You are to cautiously walk approximately five steps and then stop immediately so as not to fall down the large ramp adjoining the storage facility. The decline is very steep, approximately 60 degrees and to this end care is advised. Once you find the ramp, slide down feet first. A thick mattress is attached to its base, however falling down the ramp awkwardly as opposed to sliding will likely result in a landing not conducive to healthy bone structure. Once you have successfully navigated the ramp, recheck the device for more instructions."

With that the device went blank.

"I've got what in my head?" Burnley exclaimed as the others tried to take stock of what they had just witnessed.

"Could be a set up," Renfield replied. "If we're the only ones in the proximity of the device how do we know that what we're seeing on the screen and the sound we're hearing isn't originating from it?"

Winters gestured with his arms, "Doesn't matter either way at the moment. There's not a lot we can do now 'cept take what he says at face value."

Gary got up, "Come on lads, let's get to it then. See if we can come up with something on the way."

They started moving quietly through the wood, roughly trying to follow the path they had seen moments earlier. As they continued forward, the landmarks seemed to match the footage, somewhat confirming they were on the right track.

"Where do you think we are?" mused Winters as he lifted his foot a bit higher to clear the roots of a tree he guessed must have been at least a hundred years old by its sheer size.

Gary was about to answer as they moved around yet another over-sized tree trunk when the cave from the footage came into view.

"There it is," Winters pointed.

The cave was inset into a large piece of stone on the forest floor about 10 feet high. Moss, grass and orange brown leaf litter covered the hollowed-out rock. As in the footage, one could not easily see inside. Gary felt the rough, weather beaten right side wall with his hand till he found the relief, placing his fingers in the indents as he did. A soft cranking sound could be heard as though a large cog were turning somewhere inside the cave. He edged forward slowly into the darkness, followed by the others. Counting cautious steps, sure enough, on five he felt the toe end of his right boot tilt over an edge.

"Stop! It's here," he said sitting down.

Swinging his feet over the edge, he felt his heels touch the ramp in the pitch black beneath them.

"Are we really going down there?" said Renfield. "Who knows what that nut job has in store for us."

"If he was gonna to kill us, I'm guessing he would have done it already," Gary said reassuringly to Renfield, not really believing the words coming out his mouth. "He obviously needs us for something, why else go to all this trouble? I'll go down and secure the area and call back when it's all clear."

Winters chimed in, "Let me go. This might not be an official Motel Whiskey operation but I'm pretty sure I was still the squad scout last time I checked."

"Right," said Gary. "Call back when we're clear to come down or if ye need backup."

They couldn't see anything in the darkness, however they did hear the sound of Winters sliding down the ramp. After about four seconds of sliding a large blue mattress came into view, Winters hitting it feet first quite comfortably. The cave was well lit here as fluorescent lights were bolted to the ceilings and walls behind metal mesh. A large steel table with flat panel seating running either side of it featured in the centre of the room. There were three adjoining areas that seemed to have been dug into the walls, rusted and worn barely legible metal signs above them labelled "Quarters," "Armoury" and "Supplies." The room may well have been silent aside from the slight hum of the fluorescent lights but he wasn't taking any chances. He sat still for a good few minutes, listening intently in case someone was home. After approximately 15 minutes he decided either no one was or they hadn't heard him as he moved to clear the room. He slipped off the mattress slowly, heading in the direction of the room to his right labelled "Supplies." Inside, he discovered a great deal of tinned food and other non-perishables, there was even a fridge and freezer in the corner. Next he moved to the room labelled "Armoury" where as expected, multiple shelves housed a large assortment of firearms and other military equipment. Lastly the room labelled "Quarters" had four bunk style beds and a door at the end of the room with an exit sign above it. Inching towards the door he put his ear to the cold steel and listened. Not hearing anything on the other side, he pressed down on the handle gently but to no avail, the exit being locked. "Dodgy bastard," he thought. "Trapped underground." Returning to the mattress, he was about to call the others, warning them of the trap when he heard a voice in his head.

"The door will be unlocked once you are all present. I need not remind you of the consequences for non-compliance."

It seemed the others had heard it too as a moment later Gary called to let Winters know they were coming down. About five seconds later Burnley, Gary and Renfield hit the mattress in front of him. Burnley had barely hit the foam when there was a scream above them followed by smacking sound not unlike that of a tomato being thrown against a brick wall. Three seconds later, a thin, oddly dressed fellow fell onto the mattress head first, an ornate looking bow clattering down after him. Their unexpected guest wasn't moving, which probably had something to do with the thick red stream of blood, the source of which being his head.

Renfield moved cautiously towards the body. He prodded it with his boot but garnered no response.

"Looks like someone forgot to tell him about the ramp," Burnley joked.

Renfield rolled him over and felt for a pulse, of which there was none. He shook his head.

"Think he was hunting?" said Burnley looking at the bow. "Poor bastard, whoever we're working for doesn't seem to be too worried about collateral health and safety."

Renfield focused his attention on the quiver of arrows on the man's back. "The American did say everyone is to be considered hostile right."

"He's just some hunter lad. Nothing we can do for him now, might as well grab his weapon," replied Gary. "Burnley, aren't ye a bit of an archery enthusiast?"

"If by enthusiast you mean getting bronze in the Olympics, then yeah, that's me."

"Well, this looks like something King Bloody Someone The Third would be holding on the history channel," Renfield said as he grabbed the bow and threw it to Burnley. Just as Renfield was turning, he noticed something peculiar about the man.

"That's a pair of ears if ever I saw some," he stated.

The others turned around, "Bloody hell, I didn't think doctor Spock's weapon of choice was a bow and arrow," said Winters as he took note of the pointed ears.

"There's some nutters in the country," Gary said shaking his head. "We're done with him lads. Let's check the rest of the room and see what our American friend's got in store for us next."

CHAPTER 24 - ALISTAIR

After having their hands tied and weapons confiscated, Alistair and Co. found they could move freely once more. Two of the cloaked strangers stood approximately five paces behind as Adele motioned for them to follow herself and the three cloaks in front, their journey resuming, albeit at the will of a different master.

"You're sure there's not something we can work out for old time's sake?" said Moran as they were led through the dark wood.

"Well, I suppose I could kill you now if you like? It would spare you the walk."

"How could anyone refuse such an offer?" he replied disingenuously. "So how is the old fellow anyway? Still pulling the strings of his aristocratic puppets?"

"Time has not dulled his influence if that is what you infer.

Still not one for conversation are you Hadron," said the woman, changing the subject.

"I beg your pardon my lady, I did not intend offence," he replied courteously to George and Alistair's surprise, Hadron having scarcely uttered a word since they met.

"As cunning with your words as your swords," replied Adele. "How ever did you end up in the company of these two?"

"When the large wolf sees naught but sheep, he becomes complacent, gifting the small wolf his victory," said Hadron.

"I have no idea what that means," she replied. "If one were so inclined they may even conclude you were trying to avoid the question, positing a phrase that at first glance seems profound but in actuality is complete nonsense, leading the mind in circles as it attempts to discern a higher meaning that simply doesn't exist."

Hadron implicitly confirmed her suspicion via the absence of a reply.

They were being marched two by two save Moran by himself at the front. He was followed by Morris and Hadron then Alistair and George at the back.

"Apprehended three times in as many days. That must be some sort of record," George said quietly to Alistair.

Smiling, Alistair replied in a more serious tone, "What the hell is going on? I've seen some strange things in this world but that was the stuff of nightmares... and this lot... a mage, a master swordsman and ... that other guy that stinks. On top of that, you've got our latest captors... am I actually still alive?"

"I'm pretty sure we're both still breathing," George said, pinching himself for good measure. "Hmm, it didn't click before, but I remember hearing some stories when I first came through about an extremely powerful Mage's Guild that were supposedly the true rulers of this realm. Later on, I discovered their power had been slightly over exaggerated, the Guild of Balance commanding the real power. Nevertheless, if I were ranking influence and power they would probably come in just behind the Royal Family and the Guild of Balance. Their chancellor is rumoured to have an exceptionally attractive and magically talented daughter. Apparently, their most powerful mage betrayed the guild and they've been frantically searching for him ever since. Some say the reason they haven't found him is that he's become too important to the official rulers of Barathax."

"You mean the story, or rather, legend of Ulric Vergen?" Alistair replied. "That's just a silly old conspiracy. Next you'll tell me they're taking us to an invisible castle."

George shrugged, "Best I can come up with. Maybe I have been away from home too long, but after tonight's events, I've got a pretty open mind."

As they reached the foot of a mountain that sprouted out of the wood, Adele commanded the group to halt. A metallic scraping sound was followed by an event that defied belief. A rectangular image of a castle courtyard slowly came into view as if a portal to another world had opened out of thin air where the foot of the mountain should be. Adele walked into the scene, passing between the forest on either side. The prisoners followed, George and Alistair in awe as they moved into a large open courtyard where but a moment ago there was naught but the solid rock of the mountain. The courtyard was lit by burning lanterns running down each perimeter wall. As Alistair passed from one scene to another he looked upwards and saw what seemed to be a transparent ceiling far above. He could only tell there was something between him and the sky because of the way the moonlight warped as it shone through. He turned for a moment, staring back at the outside world as though he hadn't walked through a doorway at all. They continued down through the courtyard and came to a large set of stone stairs. At the top, they were greeted by two armoured sentries guarding a large ornate door that was inset into the towering stone keep. Adele had only half removed her hood when the guards parted and promptly opened the ornate door, revealing what seemed a maze of hallways, the finely polished wood veneer acting as a background for the assortment of paintings that adorned the chandelier lit keep walls. Soft coloured carpet ran the length of the hallways, changing hue as one branched into another, its soft touch on Alistair's tired feet a welcome feeling as they were forced to remove their boots upon entry. Adele spoke as she led them inside.

"Ulric will see you in the morning. Jeffrey, see that the... 'guests' are fed and take them to their chambers."

One of the cloaks came forward and gestured for the group to follow him. They were led down a long hallway and entered the third door on the right. Inside was a large room consisting of smaller rooms, each containing a bed and a table. Within the main room stood a large dining table at which the cloak asked them to sit while he fetched some food and drink. A brief moment of time passed before he returned, accompanied by what Alistair supposed were three butlers carrying an assortment of breads, meats, wine, water and cheese which was then placed upon the table in front of them. The 'guests' didn't need any extra encouragement as each of them was famished after the night's events.

"Not such a bad night after all then," said Moran as he tore the leg off a chicken. Alistair and George were so exhausted they ignored the comment, barely speaking a word during the meal before promptly being shown to their quarters. Hadron was silent as expected which left Morris and Moran to banter between themselves. A satisfied hunger and a comfortable bed to sleep on, Alistair felt his worries temporarily drift away as his head hit the pillow, his consciousness slipping into a well-deserved relaxing slumber.

CHAPTER 25 - ALISTAIR

Alistair awoke to a knock on the door. He got up and for a moment couldn't for the life of him remember where he was. Was this a dream, the strange small room? As Adele moved past his door the memories of the night before came flooding back, Alistair suddenly wishing he could go back to the moment before.

"This way gentlemen," she said, herding her 'guests' towards the staircase at the end of the hall.

As Alistair shuffled groggily out of his room he took note of his bleary-eyed companions in the hallway. They were led up a narrow flight of stairs and into a sparsely decorated room at the top. Light was streaming in through a large arched window to the left, the warmth of the marble floor on Alistair's bare feet hinting it was closer to midday than sunrise. There was something odd about the bare walls, the way the light reflected off them, creating a surface that somehow seemed too shiny, like they were made of high grade polished steel rather than marble. The back wall featured a strong concave into which had been carved some large thrones. The throne at the centre of the concave was taller, wider, and more decorative than the others, as if to let anyone observing it know that this was the seat of power. Some sort of jagged lightning bolt like artefacts had been attached to its back. As they got closer, Alistair noticed a middle-aged man sitting on the large throne adorned in a long black robe. His serious expression matched the sterile ambiance of the room as he spoke.

"I could scarcely believe my daughter's words when she said she had come across the one and only Moran Cheldore," came an almost unnaturally deep English, aristocratically accented voice that seemed to reverberate around the room. "Then to hear his old friends Morris Verbata and Hadron Kado were present, well, I thought this some sort of fantasy. But here you stand, in the flesh."

"Glad to have surprised you so," replied Moran smugly.

Ulric's supernatural incandescent eyes narrowed as he seemingly ignored the comment and continued.

"I half expected to hear that oaf friend of yours would also be providing us the displeasure of his company." Ulric looked towards the ceiling, the change in head position catching the light, revealing the same extremely pale complexion Alistair had first observed when meeting Adele. "What did commoners refer to him as... ah yes, Gerim the butcher I believe."

Hadron bowed as he spoke, "Gerim is no longer of this world your majesty."

"Is that so. I would say I was sorry to hear that, but of course, I'd be lying. To think, all the time and energy I've spent trying to hunt him down and he manages to get himself killed. If only I'd known he'd planned to do the job for me, it would have saved considerable time and effort." Ulric's facial muscles suddenly contracted as though he had just caught a whiff of something foul. "My god, what is that smell, did no one show that man to the bath," he said looking at Morris in disgust.

Morris couldn't help but smile. "I put my very best perfume on for you my majesty," he replied with a snigger.

"Is that so," said Ulric, his expression changing from one of disgust back to the cold blank slate it resembled prior. "Perhaps I could bathe you in scalding oil. That might help."

The smirk on Morris's face evaporated instantly. Ulric turned to Alistair and George.

"New friends Moran? Hmm, I think not. You were never very good at that. Loyalty IS generally a prerequisite. Who, pray tell, are the two of you, and what were you doing with Moran and his motley band."

"I'm Alistair and this is George. We were on our way to speak with Aris of Barathax when Moran and his friends took us captive."

"It would seem the rumours are true then, the mighty Moran Cheldore, eking out an existence as a soldier of fortune for the highest bidder. Ulric turned back towards George and Alistair. "Aris you say?" his icy gaze seemingly piercing a hole through the two men in front of him as his brow furrowed in suspicion.

George's heartbeat elevated as he wondered how Alistair could have been foolish enough to tie Aris to them at a time like this. Apparently Alistair knew what he was doing however as Ulric seemed to calm, his gaze shifting back to Moran.

"It matters not, whatever low rent contract Moran has is now null and void. You're free to go, and do not fear, Moran shall not be troubling anyone much longer. Adele informs me you both handled yourselves quite well. I have been informed you possess fire weapons the like of which is foreign to this land. Would you mind giving a demonstration before you leave?"

"It would be our pleasure your majesty," replied George.

Moran cut in, "This little reunion slash meddling in my business affairs is all well and good, but I'm afraid we have a far more pressing issue at hand. The beasts we encountered, they carried the mark of the Val Thane."

"Lies, you expect me to believe that an ancient scourge the like of which hasn't been seen for hundreds of years has suddenly resurfaced. If you do not remember, the portal was sealed, its location known by but a handful of trusted nobles, watched over night and day by a detail of no less than 400 men who know naught of what they protect."

"Well, it seems you should have posted 500."

"Another word and I'll have your tongue Moran!" Ulric snapped. "Alistair, did you notice any strange marking on the beasts that attacked you? Scars that they shared in common perhaps?"

Alistair thought back, the image of the head of the beast Hadron had killed lying next to his face appearing in his mind. Over the right eye there was indeed a strange lightning shaped scar. He then recalled the moment the pitch-black night became day as Moran cast his illumination spell. That snapshot had been seared into his memory, the wolf demons appearing before him. At some level he must have subconsciously taken in the fact that the first foe to appear before him had a similar marking over its right eye.

"Yes, now you mention it, I do," he replied. "A lightning bolt like scar over the right eye." Ulric's expression became grim. He paused a moment before continuing.

"Alistair and George, I have granted you your freedom, however you must now do something for me. You are to make journey for Aris at first light. Travel as quickly as possible, time is of the utmost value now. Upon arrival, inform Aris the Val Thane have crossed the barrier, let him know we require Barathax's assistance in this time most dire."

"Now, you three," Ulric said turning to face Moran and his two companions once more. "As much as it pains me to do so, I'm going to give each of you a chance to redeem yourself. I'd like nothing more than to see the three of you hang tomorrow but in light of your extensive experience regarding the Val Thane I believe the realm would be better served by your life than your death. You are to stay at Bledith Tower and assist myself in matters of strategy over the no doubt trying days to come. If we survive the Val Thane, your services will be judged accordingly and the slight possibility of a pardon may present itself."

"So, strung from a pole at dawn or help save the Kingdoms? A veritably difficult decision. Mind if I consult my comrades?" Moran replied.

"Don't test my patience Moran! Your insolence wins you no favour. I'm sure you would all like some breakfast. Adele, would you show our guests to the dining hall?"

CHAPTER 26 - ALISTAIR

Alistair and George sat at the large dining table, still trying to process the events of the past days.

"How did you know Moran wouldn't spill the beans that it was Aris who initiated the contract?" George whispered to Alistair.

"Aris works through proxies with almost everyone other than me. Or at least I thought so till a few days ago. It seems he works through proxies with everyone, no exceptions."

"So Moran likely doesn't know his employer's identity?" George smiled, "This should make for an interesting get together when we find your boss."

"Yes, we'll have to think of something to do about that."

"What are you two chit-chatting about over there?" interjected Moran. "Anything the rest of us might be interested in?"

"We were just wondering how you and Ulric knew each other? I'd hazard a guess there's quite a history".

"Old drinking buddies," Moran said off the cuff.

"More like you and your band of cowards betrayed the Mages Guild in the battle that decided the realm's fate," replied Adele. "Alistair, would you like to hear the story of Moran and Co's infamous betrayal?"

"Boring tale really," quipped Moran. "Riddled with lies and not even exciting ones."

"About 1000 years ago, when I was just a small girl, someone opened what we now refer to as the portal of the damned," Adele stated.

"Wait," Alistair interjected. "You expect us to believe that you're over 1000 years old, you look about 28."

A confused expression crossed Adele's face, "You did not know that we, the descendants of Ulric Vergen are immortal? Well somewhat anyhow. We can still be killed, as you would have noticed with Gerim, but aging it seems, is a concept most foreign."

"Gerim was a relation?" exclaimed George, surprised at the lack of physical similarities.

"Ah silly me," Adele laughed, "Gerim, Moran, Morris and Hadron are, or in Gerim's case, were, my half-brothers."

"But you all look so... 'different'," Alistair said diplomatically as his eyes moved from the filthy wrinkled tub of stinking lard Morris, to the fine goddess like features of Adele.

"Why thank you Alistair," Morris said in jest, "I never tire of being known as the pretty one."

"Yes, well they are only my half-brothers. You see, there's a small problem with being the only immortal line I know of and that's the fact that unless you breed with you own kin," Adele shuddered, "your partners tend to die before you do."

"So Ulric had you each to different women?" replied George as Morris let out a loud belch that filled the air with a horrendous stench.

Adele scrunched up her face in disgust as did the others seated at the table.

"However would you have guessed?" she somehow managed between fits of coughing.

Morris carried on oblivious as he ripped a chicken leg off the cooked bird and began to chew.

"Each of Ulric's children are gifted in some way, we just had to discover it over time. Moran and I found ours in the magical arts, Gerim's was obviously his brute physical size and force, Morris has a knack for alchemy and well, if you haven't figured out what Hadron's is... then something is quite wrong. I can't be sure but have surmised that the talents come from the female side. Ulric met Moran's and then later my mother during his time spent studying and then many years later teaching in the tower of Magi. Gerim's mother was a fierce female warrior. Hadron's was a woman he met on his travels to the eastern lands who was well versed in the fine art of the curved sword. Morris's mother, well, let's just say I think Ulric had been drinking that night."

Everyone bar Morris burst into fits of laughter. Morris, not to be insulted without retort, responded promptly. The ensuing flatulence unleashed a stench so foul the table's occupants had to clear the room, including the servants. Morris was the only one laughing now, the others currently gasping for air.

"I think you'll find she was King Ervoule I's chief alchemist," stated Morris between fits of laughter.

"More like King Ervoule I's damned curse on us all," replied Moran waving a hand in front of his face.

As the stench finally cleared they returned to the table. The wine was flowing freely now and all the table's occupants were beginning to loosen up. Alistair, only just now realising he and George had gunned down the half-brother of those present, tried to reconcile their lack of emotion.

"I'm sorry about your brother, we weren't really presented with any other options."

"Don't worry about it," Moran replied nonchalantly. "I have to agree with Ulric where Gerim is concerned - he shared a father with us but that was about all. The man had zero intelligence, his prime functions were killing, sleeping, drinking and whoring, all of which he was quite adept at. However, if things ever got out of hand the killing part oft came in handy. Hence his assistance in your capture."

"If I had an 8 foot giant like that running at me I'd have done the same thing," replied Morris. "Not that many do, but Gerim especially never sent any kind words my way. I certainly shall not mourn his passing."

"Fair enough," said George, still surprised at the lack of concern over Gerim's demise.

"I never met him, but father always said the man was a mistake, a scourge on the land that he'd take back if only he could," Adele replied.

"Anyway, enough of Gerim," Adele said, taking another sip of wine, a slight red hue beginning to appear in her pale cheeks. "I believe I was explaining our unique situation to the guests. Moran was born over 2000 years ago."

"You mock me sister. Do not pretend you don't remember my age. 2020 I'll have you know and not a year older." The strong red wine seemed to have done its job where Moran's inhibitions were concerned, the information flowing freely now albeit ever so slightly slurred. "Since we're telling Aris's lackeys everything, Gerim 'was' the second oldest at 1507, then Hadron at 1398, Morris at 1189 and then my sweet baby sister, Adele at 1015."

"1007 you craven dolt," Adele retorted angrily at Moran who grinned and replied, "That'll teach you to forget my birthday."

"Anyway, where was I," said Adele looking back at George and Alistair. "Ah yes. A great plague descended upon this land approximately 1000 years ago."

CHAPTER 27 – MITSUI'S APPRENTICE

A young man wandered across the wooden drawbridge just after dinner. His muscles ached from a long days training with Master swordsman Mitsui Hendo, the cool night breeze offering a welcome relief. Just as he had crossed the final plank in the old drawbridge he felt the soft tap of water droplets hitting his neck, the beginnings of rain. Sighing at his misfortune, he turned to walk back to the castle grounds, his nightly wander cut short at the whim of the heavens. Touching the chip in the wooden rail where it had slammed into an uneven part of its housing the last time it was raised, the man thought he heard a sound. Very faint, but as it came again there was no doubt, a voice in the distance. He stood still, transfixed to the spot, deciding whether or not it was worth getting wet to investigate when he heard it once more. This time it was louder, more discernible, a sort of moaning coming from the tree line to the north. As he crossed the drawbridge once more into the open country in front of the castle, it came again. Someone or something was in pain. Without warning the soft pitter patter became a heavy downpour, attempting to drown out the moan as something near the tree line in the distance glinted, the object catching the moonlight as it streamed through a gap in the clouds. That had to be it. Jogging now, Mitsui's soaking wet apprentice would eventually make the grim discovery that would mark the beginnings of a series of events that would almost precipitate the extinction of all those who inhabited the known world. A badly wounded man lay on the ground in front of him trying in vain to reach the long sword that lay but a foot from his grasp. Kneeling over the injured fellow, the apprentice noticed the victim had incurred deep gashes at least 12 inches in length across his chest and right arm. His eyes were wide with horror, darting back and forth crazily, not focusing for more than a second on the person crouched over him.

"Just stay here, I'm going to get help," said the young man, trying unsuccessfully to hide the desperation in his voice as he turned to sprint back to the castle. The world blurred for a second as he spun on the spot then pushed off with his back foot. As the momentary rotation-induced blur receded, the world came back into focus. The scene presented however, was not quite as expected. Dark clouds loomed in the black sky over a castle of eastern architecture in the distance, a wide clearing of short wet grass leading up to the drawbridge he had crossed not more than a half hour ago. Everything was as it should be, everything that is save the large intruder positioned no more than a few feet in front of him. The beast lunged. Mitsui's apprentice barely had time to be afraid of the two rows of teeth coming towards his head, his subconscious applying the routines that had been trained into it over the years sending him diving towards the ground. His momentum carried him in a slide on his belly directly underneath the surprised abomination which crashed into a tree as the young man slid across the now muddy ground. There was no time to look back. He pushed himself back to his feet making sure he rammed his back foot into the ground to decrease the chance of slipping in the mud, setting off as fast as he could back to the castle. The beast, confused for a moment after the impact, turned and brought his prey into focus. Its brain made a split second rough calculation of the distance to the castle versus the speed at which its meal was travelling. A sudden surge of endorphins pumped through its veins upon the realisation the man had no chance of outrunning it. The 8 foot wolf demon had no problem gaining traction in the mud, its long claws digging through into the hard dirt beneath creating a strong, stable base to propel itself towards its prey. Its extremely sensitive hearing picked up every sound the man made as he ran, the noises acting as a reminder of the others it had killed, triggering a Pavlovian response. But the noises were somewhat different this time. It didn't sense as much fear in this one. No matter, this was of little import considering the rate at which the gap was closing.

The young man knew from his initial sighting of his pursuer that there was little chance of outrunning it. The large claws and strong legs meant the thing was most probably extremely fast. Looking to the castle walls, he began yelling at the top of his lungs, hoping for dear life the archers on the ramparts hadn't fallen asleep. He kept his eyes on the castle wall for any indication of movement, as the burning in his legs was numbed by the adrenaline surge keeping him alive.

"HELP! HELP! HELP!" he yelled, but to no avail.

He could hear the thud of the thing behind him now. One hundred yards to go. He'd never make it. His spirits dropped and his heart sank as his legs began to give up, slowing down as he accepted his fate. He looked up to the wall one last time. Hope! A light! The light arched above him and then began to fall. Flashing past his head it was followed by a howl and a splash of mud as the beast slid and tumbled past him, the fur on its back having caught fire. A second wind welled up inside him as his legs kicked into action once more, running for his life as the initial flaming arrow was followed by another. The thing was hit again. It stared at the fleeing man as it rolled in the mud trying to put out the flames. Another piece of flaming wood dropped next to it, hissing as it drove itself into the mud. The chase was over. Having come so close, the wolf demon was to be cheated at the final hurdle. With a howl of frustration, it rolled back onto all fours and fled back into the forest from whence it came. And so it would seem, against the odds, Hadron would live to see the next day dawn.

CHAPTER 28 - ADELE

"And that was the first we saw of them," stated Hadron, uncharacteristically interrupting, thinking himself the most qualified to tell the story.

"It was nothing however compared to what was to come, a never-ending assortment of nightmares," resumed Adele. "Demon like creatures that till then were purely the domain of legend, some even escaping the most vivid imaginations of the story tellers, began to assault our fair lands. It was just small raids at first but grew in severity as time went on, eventually culminating into the threat of extinction. Tales of villagers being slaughtered by hellish beasts turned into the butchering of entire settlements and eventually all-out war for the realm's survival. The Kingdoms united in those times most dire, sadly however, to no avail. Every man that could fight did so bravely but there were just too many. The realm would fell 100 one day but 110 would attack the next. As time went by the sighting of an enormous lizard creature that spewed green fire like a ground dwelling dragon became common, it seemingly leading the beasts on their path of destruction. There were even reports that a soldier got close enough to stab it with his pole arm only to discover its scales were thicker than any plate mail in the known lands. Our numbers dropping gradually each day while their numbers rose, we were eventually forced to retreat to this very castle to make our last stand. It was then that the betrayal occurred. Morris, Moran, Hadron and Gerim who had been instrumental in holding them off thus far, disappeared in our final moment of need. Seeing the eventuality for what it was, we had the scholars lock the most important histories of our race in vaults on the off chance that if someone were to find this land one day our story would not go untold.

Each night, another slaughter on the castle walls, thousands of Val Thane killed, just as we had the day before and the day before that. Eventually however, we had hit the breaking point. Too many men had been lost and those who remained were half starved, barely able to lift their weapons. The Val Thane would simply return each night, their numbers growing cruelly as usual. Our race had no more than a couple of weeks. Or so we thought. Usually, we'd kill two and three more would appear. It was just a small difference at first, but as each night went by we could tell their numbers were thinning, not increasing like they had in the past. The brave men sent to forage for food eventually began to return, the demon plague receding enough to allow access to the grounds surrounding the castle. The Val Thane came within but a whisker of wiping every known Kingdom in the realm off the map, their infinite numbers becoming finite just as all hope had been lost, the reason unknown to this day. Over the centuries the facts morphed into legend as those who had lived through the invasion began to pass, the terrible demons the history books spoke of never being seen again – until last night."

CHAPTER 29 - MORAN

"You seem to tell the story very well for someone who was merely a child at the time, and in the first person mind you," interjected Moran.

"Father, someone who didn't abandon his people, recites it impeccably, I know it well."

The sibling rivalry was interrupted by a knock at the door.

"The castle is under attack my lady!" said a portly little fellow as he opened the door, not waiting for a response, continuing on to the next room in the hall.

Moran looked out the window and saw a sight he hoped he'd never see again. There were thousands of them. All manner of monstrosities swarming the castle grounds. In the distance, he could just make out the enormous lizard from so long ago, towering above its minions. If there was any doubt in his mind before, it was now most certainly gone. They were back. "Who would have done such a thing?" he thought. But no, now was not the time to ponder an answer to that question.

"We need to leave now!" said Moran, more urgently than he had intended.

Adele stood up, "You will not go anywhere till father says so Moran!"

"Bloody hell, peer out this window sister and then tell me once more I'm to stay here."

They all moved towards the window, observing the horrors flooding the castle grounds as they did. A primal fear gripped

Adele. It was one thing to hear stories about it, but nothing could prepare one for the reality.

"But... but how," she murmured, "The castle is invisible to outsiders. You abandoned us once Moran you'll not do it again," she said fairly unconvincingly.

"Listen to me damn it, if we don't go now, make no mistake, in five minutes we will all be dead. Pick your battles sister. We're no use to anyone six feet under."

"I will not betray my people as you have," she replied.

Moran grabbed Adele by the arm, "Look, there's quite a bit more to that story than you know, if you come with me now, maybe you'll live long enough to hear the rest of it."

"Even if I did let you go, they've surely taken the lower levels of the castle. We have no avenue of escape."

"There is another way that you and your erroneously idolised father aren't aware of," he replied.

Screams could now be heard coming from the rooms below. George ran to the door, smashing into it with his shoulder, bolting the lock just as something thumped the other side. Whatever it was it must have been big, the solid oak door shuddering on impact.

"Fuck that!" yelled George as he slid the beam down across the lock. "We need to get out of here now!"

"I'm with him," said Morris staring at the still vibrating door.

Adele began to raise a glowing hand meekly but Moran grabbed her arm to which she didn't offer resistance.

"Come on," said Moran gently as Adele reluctantly followed him towards the door that led up to the throne room.

"Wait, you'll need your equipment," Adele sighed, defeated as she produced a key and unlocked a chest in the corner of the room.

Hadron retrieved his swords as the others grabbed their assorted gear. A cracking sound could be heard as the door George had barred splintered, an oversized clawed hand poking through, slashing the air wildly.

Quickly closing the door that led to the throne room behind them, they ran up the stairs two at a time. Moran rushed to the large throne in the centre that Ulric had previously been seated upon and pushed one of the lightning spikes backwards. There was a groaning sound as one of the smaller thrones to the left began to move, revealing a hidden stone passageway.

"Quickly now," he urged as the group filed through, Moran hitting something on the wall that closed the passage behind them, plunging the group into utter darkness.

Morris could be heard retrieving something from his backpack and a moment later his ugly face was illuminated by a green flame atop a torch.

"I think I prefer the darkness," quipped Adele as Morris led the way through the narrow passage that seemed to snake downwards forever. "Where does this lead?" she asked as they moved quickly down the path.

"We'll end up about two miles outside the castle's left perimeter," replied Moran. "Hopefully the area won't be infested with Val Thane, but it's the only chance we've got."

The passage began to get wider as they continued on down. After about five minutes they came to a T junction at which Moran hesitated for a moment.

"Hmmm, funny thing, I don't actually remember this part."

"What!" yelled Adele. "You can't be serious! You led us down a passage that shouldn't even..." She was cut off mid-sentence as the ceiling was caved in with a loud bang by a large organic tendril, separating the party into two groups on either side of the T junction.

As the dust began to clear, Alistair clambered back to his feet, coughing as he did, the underground passage filled with debris where the roof had fallen. Feeling through his pack in the darkness, his hand eventually brushed over a torch. Flicking it on, dust particles flooded through the beam of light as he spun it left and right, silently thanking his lucky stars the battery still worked. Even with the light, the visibility was terrible, the concentration of dust particles like a quasi-solid wall surrounding him. As he started to walk forward he could just make out a dark shape on the ground about ten feet away. As he got closer he made the discovery. The dark shape was Adele, her body lying motionless in the dirt. She'd been his captor, there was no doubt about that, but she was also the reason he was still alive and her father had removed any threat Moran may have posed in the future. The decision was easy. Rushing over, he felt for a pulse of which there was none. He began CPR but to no avail, at least five minutes of nothing. He could hear shouts, explosions and gunfire on the other side of the debris that had built up around the tentacle, but he had other priorities now. Dejected and about to give up, the body under his hands suddenly snapped upright, inhaling a sea of dust violently as it did. Coughing profusely, Adele rose groggily to her feet.

"You, you know the spell of revival? But how?" she said as she swayed ever so slightly.

"Revival spell? Yeah, let's call it that," Alistair said, noting that there were more pressing issues at the current moment than explaining modern medical techniques. "Are you ok?"

"Yes, I think so...thank you."

Alistair was about to reply when George yelled out from the other side of the debris to confirm everyone was OK and to let the others know that they were too.

There was a clang of steel on steel followed by Moran's voice.

"It's no use, the armoured scales are too strong, we can't cut through. Listen, you have to find Aris. I can't explain now but just know he's the key to ending all this. Follow that path and it'll lead you out of the castle grounds. I'm just not sure which side you'll end up on."

There was a roaring sound from the other side of the tentacle, followed by an explosion then gunfire and screams.

"Moran!" screamed Adele.

"Go now!" came a hurried reply from Moran between laboured breathes interleaved with gun fire and all sorts of sinister sounds.

"Come on, we can't do anything for them standing here," Alistair said as he raised his gun attaching the torch as he led the way down the passage.

Adele found herself wiping back tears as she followed. Yesterday, Moran hanging would have elicited little remorse, barely remembering him from her childhood, her father's stories painting the picture of a shameful traitor of the highest order. But after meeting him again as a grown woman, after the events that had just unfolded, she sensed there was something else to the story of his betrayal, something Ulric had left out. It was either that or being knocked unconscious was playing havoc with her emotions.

CHAPTER 30 - ALISTAIR

They had been walking a good distance in silence when Alistair spoke.

"I'm sure they'll be OK. They seem more than capable of handling themselves," he said, not really believing it himself.

"I hope you're right" replied Adele, "I so hated them for leaving as they did, but to see them again after all this time, I... I don't know." The silence resumed for a short while until Adele spoke once more. "Do you have any brothers or sisters Alistair?"

"I know this might sound unlikely but I seriously don't know. I remember back to about 10 years ago but prior to that, it's just a blank, some sort of amnesia."

"Do you know what caused it?"

"Well, I was running along the banks of the river Schwen one fine day, chasing down... Oh stuff it, I'm probably dead anyway, I might as well tell you the truth. I'm not from this world, the place I come from is called Earth."

"I thought you said you were going to tell me the truth," said Adele, her melancholy tone transitioning to one of suspicion.

"I'll admit, the first version does sound more likely, but this is one of those rare cases where truth is stranger than fiction, apparently going through the portal voids most of your prior memories."

"Then how would you know that?" she replied quickly.

"Because there's more than one of us here."

"And how would they know? You're not a very good liar. If you didn't want to tell me, you could have simply said so."

Alistair sighed, "We can bring equipment through with us," he said, "or could initially anyway. No doubt someone wrote down how it worked and sent the information through with the first."

Alistair found himself smiling as Adele observed his face quizzically, seemingly trying to decide if he was lying or not. At that moment, he thought her face quite the diamond in the rough, a thing of great beauty if only it weren't covered in dirt.

"Why do you look at me so?" she said, quite obviously trying to suppress the hint of a smile.

Alistair caught it but didn't let on.

"So let's assume that for interest's sake you are telling the truth, what brings your people here?"

"Well, there are things that exist in this world that don't in ours and vice versa."

"Such as?"

"Well the main one is magic. There's no such thing in our world, you can't just wave your arms and 'poof' a door explodes."

"I'll have you know there's a lot more to it than waving your arms," she retorted.

"No doubt," continued Alistair, "our world is more technologically advanced than yours."

Adele looked at the rifle, "So you're trying to tell me that that has no magical function, it's just some kind of machine."

"Precisely," said Alistair. "How can I explain this..?" he said, looking up and to the side. "Ah, I know, your half-brother Morris, he mixes substances. Some of those substances create explosions. Well, every time I press on this," he said tapping the trigger with his finger, "it sets off a series of events that cause a very small explosion which pushes a piece of metal," he ejected the clip, shining the light on the bullets stacked within it, "at very high speed out of here," he said touching the end of the barrel.

"Fascinating," she replied, staring intently at the odd shaped weapon he was holding. "What other technologies does your world boast?"

"Oh, lots of things, though you'd have to see them to believe me. Metal horses that move much faster than living ones, flying machines that carry people from one destination to another, small objects that let you communicate over long distances, the list goes on, and on."

"Your world sounds very exciting," she said enthusiastically, seemingly having forgotten about Moran and the others for the moment.

An internal dialogue played out in Alistair's head as Adele's eyes locked on his, "Here I am, walking through an ancient tunnel, trying to escape a horde of angry demons with the most attractive and powerful woman I've ever laid eyes upon and all I can think of to talk about is planes and cars."

Shrugging the thought off he continued, "I think the opposite really. With magic, there's a sense of mystery and adventure. With technology, while I'll be the first to admit that it allows us to live a much better life than we did long ago, breaking everything down into its logical parts removes any sense of wonder."

"I would very much like to see it someday regardless," replied Adele.

Alistair was about to list the reasons why that wasn't possible when they finally reached a ladder at the end of the tunnel, exiting into the forest above.

CHAPTER 31 - ARIS

Tyrus shoved the serving wench in the back.

"Move!" he commanded as he and Aris escorted her to the interrogation chamber. "Tell us all you know now and I'll grant you a quick death," he stated as the door to the chamber shut behind them.

The wine server observed a bleak stone room through teary eyes. There was a cross shaped hole in the wall where light shone in from outside, casting a symbol that would have great irony for the likely doomed occupants if the chamber were on Earth. In the middle of the chamber sat a large oak table with two stools, one on either side. The table had a wooden box at one end of it. Aris stood near the door, arms folded across his chest as Tyrus pushed her onto the stool furthest from the door and then proceeded to take his place on the other.

"Who are you working for?" asked Aris.

"I'm sorry me lord, I know I'm not 'sposed to serve the royals wines but Wendy said it was really easy, I just needed a little bit o' coin," she managed to relay between sobs.

Tyrus drew a dagger causing her to scream in terror. "Who sent you to kill Ervoule and why? You give answers or fingers."

"I... I... I don't even know who that is. Wendy just said she wanted a day off to see her mother, said she'd pay me whatever she'd make for the day. Said it was easy like. Just do whats they tells you. There's something horrible in that room with him I tells you. You've got to go quick!"

"I warned you," said Tyrus as he looked to Aris for permission.

Aris nodded reluctantly. Grabbing her by the wrist, Tyrus forced her hand onto the table. He spread out her fourth and fifth finger, plunging the dagger between them, the tip burying into the wood beneath. Her eyes went wide as she stared at the blade in front of her.

"NO NO NO!!!!!!" she yelled, instinctively trying to pull her hand free.

Tyrus was too strong. He pulled down on the knife, severing her finger as he did so. There was no scream, her body had instantly gone limp, her head hitting the desk as the shock rendered her unconscious. Blood began welling up from the open wound.

"Fucking marvellous," exclaimed Aris. "Now we've got to wait till she wakes up." Tyrus opened the wooden box at the end of the table retrieving some rags with which to bandage the wound. Picking up the finger he threw it in a recess that had been hollowed out in the back corner of the chamber. "Come on," said Aris, shaking his head in disappointment. "Lets go and prepare his majesty for his ride home."

"Either I'm getting old and soft in the head or these assassins are just far more dedicated to their contractors than they used to be," said Tyrus as the duo walked slowly back up the hall to the special guest chambers. "For a moment there I think I believed her."

Aris felt the same way and was more than a little worried they might have just mutilated an innocent woman. He couldn't let Tyrus see that however. There was too much at stake to be leaving anything to chance.

"I think you are going soft in the head. What other card does she have to play? If she tells us, she knows she's dead. Holding out means initial pain, but there's still a chance we believe her. Besides, we've got two hundred thousand Trescot's within five days march of Barathax and the only means of preventing them raping our women, enslaving our people and stringing us up too mind you, is to keep that rotund old man in the next room alive and happy."

"Point taken," said Tyrus as they neared King Ervoule's chambers.

Tyrus knocked on the door, "Would his majesty be available for a word?" There was no reply. Tyrus knocked again, louder this time. "Forgive me your majesty but it is important."

Tyrus looked to Aris. Aris ushered him out of the way and pushed the door slightly ajar. Slowly, he opened the door and looked inside. To his horror he saw the King's corpse atop the bed being straddled by a filthy creature he knew could only be a bogmaul.

"NO!" Aris shouted as he pushed the door open with all his might, charging into the room, Tyrus in tow, drawing their swords as they did.

The creature had been too enraptured in its meal to notice the knocking on the door but the yelling and flashing steel soon kicked its mind into action. Aris hurled his sword at the retreating creature but Jorgmur was too fast. The foul being leapt straight for the open balcony he had entered from, vanishing into thin air as he camouflaged, scrambling up the castle wall never to be seen again. Tyrus rushed to the parapet and looked over the balcony but saw naught. Jorgmur stared down at him, indistinguishable from the rocky wall to which he clung five yards above. He was almost amused that this man with the shiny steel thought he, Jorgmur, would have jumped to his death. Turning back towards the wall, Jorgmur made his way to the roof as Tyrus re-entered the guest room.

"Gone," he said, not hiding his frustrated mood.

Aris didn't even turn to acknowledge him. Instead he stood in a catatonic like state, staring at the half-eaten corpse of King Ervoule III.

"What the hell was that?" Tyrus asked, more to himself than Aris. He'd fought many a man in his time but had never seen a monstrosity the likes of the one that had just murdered the King of Eboda.

"That," said Aris, continuing to stare blankly at the king, "was a bogmaul, and that," said Aris, gesturing towards the half-eaten king, "is the doom of us all."

CHAPTER 32 - ARIS

They stood together in silence, contemplating the ramifications of King Ervoule's death. At best, news of his demise wouldn't reach Eboda till the war with Trescot was over, which they both knew they couldn't win without Eboda's support. At worst, Eboda would think Barathax killed Ervoule and would no doubt ally with Trescot.

Tyrus spoke slowly, "Maybe there's another option. Eboda was to ally with Barathax due to the deception concerning the Baron. The current situation, an assassinated king, could be an even stronger opportunity. I met Ervoule's son Tormin, a strong-willed lad, but simple none the less. If we were to send convincing enough word that Trescot was behind his death, we'd gain the support of Eboda, and if we can hold out long enough, they might just arrive in time to get us out of this mess."

"In what light does that cast us?" responded Aris. "A bunch of incompetent fools that can't even protect their royal guests."

"Better to look the fool than the enemy."

"I suppose you're right," said Aris. "What if they ask to see the body? I don't think they're going to take too kindly to their King having bite shaped chunks missing, they'll think we left him outside for the wolves to chew on."

Tyrus knew he shouldn't but started to smile regardless. Aris thought he might find it humorous as well if the situation weren't so dire.

Aris sighed, "Summon that freak Mortimer. Hopefully he'll

know how to turn this corpse into something resembling a death by the sword. Oh, and I hope it goes without saying, no one comes near this room till we get this cleaned up. I have my doubts in regards to convincing Tormin, but I suppose it's the best and only chance we've got. Summon your fastest messenger and summon him 5 minutes ago. We have no time to waste."

"As you wish," Tyrus replied, turning to take his leave.

"Now we just have to hold them at bay till Tormin's men get here," thought Aris, "if they decide to come to at all."

Tyrus turned back as he reached the door. "The wine servant..."

"I'll do it," Aris replied quietly looking at the floor as he did, silently acknowledging she knew too much to be allowed to let live.

Tyrus nodded, then turned and exited the room slowly, making sure there was no one in the hallway. Making his way back to the interrogation chamber, Aris could think of nothing other than how much he hated this part of his job.

CHAPTER 33 - ARIS

Mortimer was Aris's reluctant first choice when it came to cleaning up a murder scene or making it seem as though something else had happened entirely. He was a twisted up old hunchback who wore an eyeglass over his right eye and always insisted on carrying a chain for some unbeknownst reason that eluded everyone other than himself. Three strands of hair popped out of his speckled old head as he shuffled along smelling of old stew.

"Feeding royalty to the wolves eh Aris?" came the old man's croaky voice. "That's a new one, even for you."

"I see you're a jester AND a freak, how about a cartwheel then?"

The old man stared at Aris for a moment angrily.

Aris, ignoring the old man's hostility, continued, "I need this to look like he was assassinated with a blade, not eaten in the wilds."

"Maybe 'twas one of those rogue bears," Mortimer said as he looked the corpse up and down. "Can never be too careful with those bears you know. They've got ulterior motives."

Aris couldn't tell if the old man was mocking him or if it was just more of his crazy babble. "If you're quite done old man..."

"Ah, yes yes, I know of a potion that can regrow flesh. Doesn't reanimate a dead man, but should be able to make him whole again. Then we can slash him however you fancy. I'd be able to brew some up..." he blathered semi incoherently, "but I can't seem to find any of my scrolls lately. I'm getting old you know."

"Hogwash, you're getting poor because you spend all your

money on booze and women far too young for a man of your age. How bloody much do you want this time?"

"Well I seem to remember about 10 gold pieces helped bolster my spirits around the time of that Baron job, so I'd say 100 pieces could very well do the trick."

"100 pieces!" Aris yelled, forgetting for a moment that the current situation warranted a lower tone. "100 pieces," he said again, this time in no more than a whisper but no less frustrated. "I'll cut you into 100 bloody pieces before I pay you that."

"I may be old, but I'm not stupid. Even considering the fact something has had a good chew on him, I know who that is. I also know you're royally, pardon the pun, screwed, if old King Ervoule here goes home looking like you gave the hounds a lunch time treat."

Aris stared at the wretched thing in front of him, wanting nothing more than to twist the head that sat atop its baggy neck 180 degrees, stemming the flow of rage inducing syllables emanating from the hole in its face.

Mortimer blinked multiple times in quick succession, his tongue licking his lips as he stuttered once more, "100 gold pieces."

Aris continued to stare at him in silence for a good 5 minutes, somehow resisting the urge to see if the old man could fly, the tongue movement combined with the blinking only serving to enrage him more.

"Well?" Mortimer half spat out between nervous twitches.

Finally Aris replied, "Very well, but for 100 gold pieces you'd better do a good enough job that even I forget what I've seen here today."

"Of course, of course sir," Mortimer said, his eyes suddenly glowing a little brighter at the promise of 100 gold pieces.

"Just get on with it." With that, Mortimer hobbled out of the room to prepare his potion.

CHAPTER 34 - DAGATH

"I'm getting mighty bored of this march!" Dagath yelled, loud enough that at least half the 200,000 strong Trescot troop could hear it. "I think I might kill me some Barathaxian swine!"

The men cheered, hammering their weapons against their shields as a moment later, thousands more, caught up in the sudden excitement, followed suit. It was like a Mexican wave of battle rally cries. There was one word that back on Earth would have described Dagath physically to a tee. Neanderthal. His body was hairier than most humans, but not freakishly so. A strong protruding forehead protected his skull and eyes, the man's thick bone structure lending a sturdiness to his frame not typically seen in homo sapiens. The strong frame provided an excellent platform to support an incredible volume of muscle, his height to breadth ratio skewed in abnormal favour of breadth even though he stood six feet tall. Dagath was no genius, but he was certainly more intelligent than most observer's preconceived stereotype of his physical form, a fact that had led more than one would be swindler to an early grave. A better field commander there was not, the unique combination of extreme physical presence and at least average intelligence rendering Dagath the perfect soldier's commander, one of the few the men followed by example rather than obligation. Reaching the top of the hill, he observed the famed stretch of land commonly referred to as 'The Last March', a sea of lush green grass stretching approximately a mile till it was abruptly cut off by an also famed cluster of stone. Most would refer to that cluster of stone as Castle Brin.

"Your time of reckoning is at hand Aris!" he shouted, not really expecting Aris to hear him from over a mile away, tucked safely behind those thick stone walls. Still shouting, he exclaimed, "They say Castle Brin is to fortresses what Excalibur is to swords, the stuff of legend and impossible to break! Well, today men, we prove that legend a fairy tale!" Another round of shouts and shield banging ensued as the first five ranks pushed up over the crest of the hill. Dagath knew all too well that the impenetrability of Castle Brin was in fact not a fairy tale. The structure was nestled in a valley with two mountains at its flanks and the sea at its back. This meant the walls could never be effectively surrounded by land as the terrain either side of it was too steep to station any large number of troops. Due to the extremely high cliff and sheer walls at its rear, an incursion from the sea was impossible, rendering the only avenue of attack a direct assault at its front. Irrespective of the walls, the fact it was nestled in the valley meant far less surface area to defend than most other castles. The walls were 200 feet high and the greater castle grounds housed some 100,000 residents. The city of Barathax proper was contained within and was self-sufficient enough that starving it out would take in the order of years not months. One man on Castle Brin's walls was worth an innumerable amount on the ground. Dagath estimated the military inside the walls to be somewhere around 20,000, maybe 30,000 if they used militia. Dagath was a brave man, but not a stupid one. In an equal numbers fight, this attack would be certain suicide. This battle certainly wouldn't be an equal numbers fight, Trescot fielding the vastly superior force. Even so, under normal circumstances, he'd lean towards starving the castle out rather than initiating a risky frontal attack. The position was just too defensible. This night, however, was not under normal circumstances. This night, they came with more than just sword and shield, Trebuchet and bow. Dagath didn't trust the alchemists, but they assured him this new weapon would relegate Brin's famed walls to the history books. The crazy old men had somehow gained the favour of Trescot's King Bartomere III, which meant it was neither here nor there if he trusted them, he couldn't refuse even if he wanted to. As more and more of them pushed over the crest the upbeat mood began to sour, becoming eerily sombre at the sight of the castle they were to breach. Dagath could hear the chatter around him. There was no shortage of words such as "madness" and "suicide" being thrown about.

"Siege crew forward!" he yelled, ignoring the naysayers.

The sea of rattled soldiers parted as the siege crew came forth, mounted upon strong draught horses towing something covered in a shroud.

"Prepare the weapon!"

The siege crew dismounted, untied their horses and ushered them away. Removing the shroud, they unveiled something the likes of which Dagath had never seen before.

CHAPTER 35 - ARIS

Aris looked out across the sea of green, lit by the gentle moonlight. At least it was a beautiful night if it were to be his last. He looked to his left then right at the thousands of men manning the ramparts, bows in hand, awaiting orders. Their armour shone against the night sky, partly reflection from the moon and partly from the flaming bowls positioned every few yards that they would use to light the tips of their arrows. Upon notifying King Bastion of the situation, he received near enough what he expected. The obese drunk was in one of his stupors, blabbering something as he swayed to-and-fro. Aris wasn't even convinced the man could appreciate the gravity of the situation sober, so he certainly wasn't going to now. The meeting with Bastion didn't play out completely as expected however as the King, seemingly snapping out of his haze just long enough to produce a coherent sentence, ordered Aris to command the defence. Sure that he had heard incorrectly, Aris asked politely if the King would repeat himself. Once more but much firmer this time, Bastion charged Aris with Barathax's defence. Aris was shocked. He'd commanded companies of knights in the field for a brief period but that was years ago. Tyrus was the field commander now, Aris was just supposed to take care of events in the background. The sudden change of scenery in the distance wrenched him violently from his thoughts as his heart began to race. Silhouetted on the horizon, the shape of a banner, followed by the head and body of a man mounted atop a warhorse. The beginnings of the legion of red that was to follow. Trescot were here and Aris knew their intentions were not conducive to Barathax's longevity. The tension in the air was suddenly amplified by the stark reality of the enormous army approaching their walls.

"Look there men!" he shouted. "For there stands the threat to your peace. For centuries, we have lived in fear of assassination, terror and depravity, all at the hands of those you see before you. Tonight, that fear ends, snap off and wrench out the arrow that has been in our side for so long. Tonight we end Trescot and assure peace forever more!"

There was a cheer from the men either side as he drew his sword, pointing it towards the approaching army. Aris turned to look over his walls at the bulk of the Barathax force standing on the ground behind the gates. He took solace in the fact they'd been convinced of the advantage the walls provided. They'd only need a few hundred men on the ramparts. The real threat were any breaches on the ground level which they could easily handle if they kept the breach small, thereby creating a choke point. The truth however, was a truth that Aris had not seen fit to tell. He'd heard rumours that those from the other side had begun to engage in trade with Trescot as well. Apparently they'd acquired a weapon that could challenge the centuries old protection Castle Brin's walls had provided. Having seen first-hand the power of the things the ones from the other side possessed he didn't doubt for a second this mystery weapon would live up to the rumour. The man to Aris's left looked at his commander quizzically as Aris raised a pair of binoculars to his eyes. Trescot weren't the only ones who had some new toys he thought. Through them he observed the Trescot siege crew pull a large cloth shroud from atop something the likes of which he had never seen. A large shiny metal object with glowing pipes running to-and-fro mounted on a wooden platform with solid wooden wheels, not dissimilar to a catapult platform. A large metal cylinder with a small hole in the end pointed towards them as a thin beam of bright orange light shot out, stretching the length of The Last March, carrying on into the night sky behind them as far as the eye could see. The beam then began its descent, momentarily being cut off as it made contact with the top of the castle wall, the man in its path moving to the side to avoid it just in time. Without warning, the beam somehow pushed through the wall, shooting out into the distance once more as smoke began to rise where it made contact, a small way to the left of the main gate.

Aris turned to look at his army on the ground as the beam made its descent.

"Second company, five paces left, third company, five paces right!"

Two blocks of soldiers separated moments before the beam of light reached them, it cutting through the houses to their rear as though they weren't even there. Those manning the wall turned to observe the strange occurrence. The beam had cut through everything in its path and could be seen continuing out to sea. Aris turned to the men on the gate who had seemingly become catatonic, staring awestruck at the orange beam.

"Every man above the gate, form up on me, everyone else, hold position!"

All troops currently stationed above the gate that was housed in the middle of the wall moved to Aris's side, leaving the ramparts directly above unmanned. Aris then commanded the troops on the ground to split either side of the gate, a loud metal clanging proceeding as thousands of heavily armoured soldiers changed formation. As the beam neared the bottom of the wall it started to move laterally to the right, cutting through the wall, then the base of the gate and anything in its path as it did. There was a great clatter behind them as structures collapsed, the beam slicing horizontally through the base of anything it touched. Aris's thoughts suddenly shifted to people he'd evacuated to the ocean side of the castle. He hoped they'd be okay. Well, everyone save Bastion that was. A King was supposed to lead people in times of peril, not get drunk and assign it to others. Admittedly, King Bastion wouldn't be much use in the fight, his years of decadence rendering him barely fit to walk up a flight of stairs yet alone wield a sword. Even considering his physical state, if he'd not been such a drunkard craven, his presence may have at least boosted morale. But no, he'd assigned Aris to the defence, Bastion joining the subjects deemed unfit for battle, namely the elderly, most of the woman folk, and the young. Prince Allan was a far better candidate. He was fit, possessed a kind heart and his unquestioned devotion to his people sometimes made Aris wonder whether Bastion was actually his father. He'd seen the shame in the young man's eyes on multiple occasions as he observed his father's drunken antics.

The beam continued on its path of destruction, the ambient mood amongst the soldiers transitioning from awe to fear as nervous mutterings began. It was all too much for one of the infantry men on the ground. Losing his nerve, he broke rank and started to run. Tyrus turned to the massive brute standing beside to him. Grabbing the large man's oversized Great Sword he lifted it above his head with both hands then threw it with all his might at the deserter, splitting his helm and head in two on contact. The brute fetched his sword as Tyrus turned nonchalantly back towards the wall in front of him as though nothing had happened. Seemingly having the desired effect, the scared, timid murmurings hushed for the moment at least. The beam had now cut an L shape in the wall, down the gate's left side and across its base. Aris's forces could only look on as it reached the right side of the gate and began its journey upwards from the bottom of the wall.

"Hold!" yelled Tyrus as he sensed the men itching to take action.

The beam finished a second vertical pass up the other side of the gate, separating it and a small section of wall either side that housed it from the rest of the wall by two very thin slices vertically. The horizontal slice in the bottom of the wall and gate meant that although the assaulted portion of wall still stood, it was only doing so by its sheer weight alone, essentially resting on its base rather than being one continual structure whose base stretched deep underground. "The wall still stands," Aris thought confused, "what was the point?" Looking through his binoculars once more to try and ascertain Trescot's next move, the scene presented brought forth a sudden unexpected rush of hope.

CHAPTER 36 - DAGATH

Dagath's men looked on, initially in awe of the bright beam and fancy contraption but then in disdain at the seemingly pathetic 'weapon'.

"We gonna kill Aris's lads with pretty lights," one of the pikemen said to the man beside him.

"Dazzle em to death," mocked another, precipitating infectious laughter from his companions that seemed to spread throughout the ranks like fire on oil.

The entire army was laughing now, all except Dagath and the siege crew who looked on stoically. From where they were positioned, the soldiers who found the 'advanced weapon' so amusing couldn't see that the beam had cut cleanly through the wall. To them, it just seemed as though a beam of light had moved down one side of the gate. The laughter waned a little as the beam stopped just above the ground but resumed again wholeheartedly as it started to move to the right, the soldiers finding the silly light show all in all rather humorous. By the time the beam had completed half its pass up the other side of the wall, Dagath and the siege crew were the only ones not enthralled. As it neared the top of the wall a beeping sound began to emanate from the machine which was accompanied by a flashing light. This only served to add further fuel to the laughter as the men broke out in an uncontrollable guffaw. The look on the lead siege engineer's face however was in no way jovial as he hastily moved to turn the machine off. One of the heavy infantry, not realising his weight in full plate armour, slapped the engineer on the back, congratulating him on a good show.

"I thought you engineers wouldn't know funny if it punched you in the face," he said smiling as his hand made contact with the engineer's back.

His well-meaning but overly enthusiastic back slap sent the scrawny engineer, who was adorned in naught more than light leather armour face first into the mud. With that, the laughter became so loud that Dagath began to wonder if Aris's men might hear it up on the wall, hardened soldiers collapsing about him in hysterics.

"Sorry lad," said the soldier between fits of laughter as he stumbled over and pulled the engineer out of the dirt.

Meanwhile, the beeping sound only increased in frequency and volume.

The engineer didn't even look at the solider retrieving him from the mud as he yelled "Fool!" turning and running towards the machine.

He was too late. A massive explosion ensued, a huge blue fire ball melting anything within a twenty yard radius, including the engineers. Within a thirty yard radius, the laughter instantly turned to screams as the intense heat of the fireball superheated the unfortunate soldiers plate armour, cooking them inside. Dagath looked coldly at the scene to his right. No one was laughing now. Dismounting his horse, he opened the chest it had been carrying. Fortunately for Trescot, the weapon had completed its purpose moments before the explosion allowing Dagath to proceed with the next phase of the plan. Grabbing the pipe like object from the chest, he raised it atop his shoulder. Looking through the glass screen attached to the pipe, he aligned the section of stone wall above the gate with the dashed marks and squeezed the trigger. A trail of smoke careened behind a bright object as it flew at incredible speed towards the section of wall above the gate. There was a loud bang as it made contact followed by an eerie silence. That was the second strange event the men had seen today, only this time, no one found it humorous. Just as the chatter began to start once more, it suddenly became clear to the soldiers what the events they had just witnessed were attempting to accomplish. The impenetrable walls of castle Brin were falling.

CHAPTER 37 - ARIS

A vibration radiated out across the wall as a large flat chunk of steel smashed into and then ricocheted off the section of stone wall above the now separated gate. This was followed by a creaking sound and then, to the horror of the men, the U-shaped portion of wall that had been separated falling backwards towards the city. The soldiers on the ground were already out of the way as Aris had had the foresight to move them. The remaining buildings in the area however, did not fare so well, the falling section of gate and wall crushing everything it fell on. As the dust settled, Tyrus immediately formed the ground squadron into an arc a small way back from the now gaping hole in the wall. "I chose the right man for that job," thought Aris as he noticed the formation from above. When Trescot's forces did come through the gap it would act as a funnel, meaning all Tyrus's archers could fire on those coming through, whereas Dagath's effective forces would be limited to the number of men that could fit side by side through the gap. He couldn't admire the tactic for long though, the sound of a horn blasting through the air being followed by two hundred thousand Trescot soldiers charging the castle. As if the fact they were massively outnumbered and without an intact wall wasn't bad enough, just as Aris called for the archers to light their arrows, it began to rain.

"Fantastic," Aris muttered to himself as the fire bowls hissed and began to extinguish upon contact with the curse from the heavens. "Ready!" he yelled as a Mexican wave of bows pointed skywards. He waited until the bulk of the advancing Trescot force was in range so as to maximise the casualties and then gave the order to fire.

It wasn't just water raining down on Dagath's men now, but a much deadlier addition. Dagath had expected fire arrows, but upon noticing the sudden onset of rain, couldn't believe his luck as the lights atop the walls began to extinguish. As he'd seen time and time before, there were heavy casualties, but as he had also thought to himself time and time before, it was a necessary sacrifice to get through the first barrage. The men carried on till they reached the gap in the wall, the cavalry having to dismount as they did, the uneven rubble too much for the heavily armoured warhorses. Volley after volley of arrows rained down on them as they rushed the wall, but they continued on, feeding on the adrenalin of the moment. The first group to make it to the wall moved through the gap on foot only to be felled the moment they crossed the boundary, a barrage of arrows piercing their armour at close range. The second group met a similar fate. The third group saw the archers disappear behind a wall of footmen as they clashed at the gap. Tyrus's ground defence were killing two for every man they lost solely due to the choke point and arc formation. Regardless, it made little difference to the outcome, the Trescot forces seemingly never ending, Tyrus eventually forced to give the command to fall back. They were being overrun now. Having to give up their advantageous position, the two to one kill ratio began to swing the other way, Tyrus's forces no longer possessing a geometrical edge. As the battle became a slaughter, Barathax soldiers began to throw down their weapons in surrender. Unfortunately for them, Trescot had no interest in taking prisoners, the centuries old animosities running too deep between the two Kingdoms, they promptly butchered armed and unarmed man alike. Realising there was no surrender, Tyrus ordered the remaining men to fall back to the still standing houses, their only option to fight a cloak and dagger war, the overwhelming Trescot numbers rendering a fair fight suicide. Tyrus knew deep down that it was just prolonging the inevitable. They might hold out a little longer this way, hiding in the ruined houses and alleyways then striking from the shadows when an unsuspecting Trescot attempted to clear the region. The end result would be the same however. Barathax had lost this war along with its sovereignty. Finishing it this way might not do them any favours in the history books, but it damn sure meant there'd be a few less Trescot scum left to rape their women. If he was going to die this day he'd take his fair share of Trescot dogs with him Tyrus thought as he performed a perfect riposte, the receiver coating his armour in blood. Breathing heavily, Tyrus stared at the rectangle of light that composed the open doorway of the still intact inn he'd taken cover in. The screams of the man he'd just cut down would no doubt have drawn the attention of the Trescot forces that were now scouring ever building for Barathax survivors. There was a yell at the door, the body of a soldier momentarily blocking out the moonlight as he crossed the doorway. Tyrus knew what was to come. He said a silent goodbye to the land he'd watched over his entire life as a torch was lit just outside the doorway, the heavens seemingly playing out a cruel jest as the rain stopped abruptly the moment its presence would render assistance to Barathax. He'd be damned if he'd let them burn him to death. Tyrus chose his fate, the general knowing full well there'd be at least five archers outside, their bows trained on the doorway as the flaming torch came hurtling in, immediately setting the dry old wooden floor alight. "One last charge," he thought as he ran for the door screaming, hoping he could at least take one of them with him before the barrage of arrows extinguished his life. He was right about the archers. Pushing through the door in a blind rage, an arc of Trescot bowman stood ready to receive him. There was one final whooshing sound as six arrows cut through the night air, every one hitting their target with utmost precision. Instead of a spray of arrows however, Tyrus was hit with a spray of muddy water as the five archers in front of him collapsed into a puddle, wooden shafts protruding from the back of their exposed un-armoured necks. Looking to the top of wall above, Tyrus returned Aris's nod as the saviour atop the wall and his closest archers resumed their hopeless battle against the Trescot forces that were now swarming the ramparts.

Then it happened, everything changed in an instant.

Over the screams of pain and steel on steel, Tyrus could just make out Aris's voice, "Eboda! Tormin came, hold Tyrus, hold!"

Dagath yelled something he couldn't quite make out in response, which was followed by the Trescot army, who were but hours from crushing Barathax once and for all, falling back through the gap in the wall, turning tail to run. Confusion spread amongst the remaining Barathax forces which quickly turned to overwhelming joy and finally frenzied blood-lust as they realised that by some miracle of fate their certain doom had been allayed. A cheer rose as the sight of the retreating Trescot forces whipped the men into a crazed state. Barathax soldiers gave chase wildly, surging forward wantonly after their vastly superior in number fleeing opponents.

"Halt! Tyrus screamed, wary of a trap on the other side of the wall.

As he did so he felt a sudden, sharp stabbing pain in his side. Looking down he noticed the thin wooden shaft protruding from his right armpit, it somehow having found its way between the gap in his armour where the shoulder piece connected with the main torso region.

From a top his perch, Aris observed a sea of yellow upon the horizon, the sun rising behind them like a flaming ball of hope, the heavens seemingly having changed their mind, a horde of yellow angels crossing the Last March, Barathax's salvation was at hand. Dagath's forces were fleeing as quickly as possible, attempting to cross the aptly named stretch of land before being caught up between the castle and the encroaching Ebodan army.

"It worked!" Aris accidentally yelled out loud between tears of joy. Even if he weren't so overcome with emotion, he would never have heard the sound of splattering mud on the grounds below him as Tyrus slumped to his knees, the wall in front of the weary General denying him one final sunrise as he breathed his final breath.

CHAPTER 38 - LUDWIG

Ludwig Steiner was puzzled by the smoking hole in the ground surrounded by burnt corpses as he and his hundred and fifty thousand strong army, yellow banners flapping in the dawn breeze, mounted the top of the hill. In the distance, he saw a sea of red attempting to pour through the gap where castle Brin's gate had once stood.

"Forward!" he yelled, as his troop set off at a charge towards the walls, the guttural accent of his birthplace still as prevalent as it was the day he left Ghotine twenty years prior. A far cry from the wandering vagabond of his youth, the 45 year old had risen through the Ebodan ranks the hard way. His blue eyes and close cut blonde hair might not have been quite as vibrant as they were in his youth, but whatever he'd lost physically over the years, he'd made up in spades mentally. Near genius level intelligence combined with an extreme machine like calculating, cold, logical nature even when it came to the most emotionally charged decisions had earned him respect and contempt in equal parts. Ludwig also possessed a trait that when combined with a man of his personality, resulted in a character set that was almost certainly unrepeated across all the Kingdoms of the realm. There were others who possessed above average intelligence, there were other extremely logical emotional voids, and there were their opposite, the socially and politically adept. Logical intelligence, lack of empathy and social graces almost never went hand in hand. However, it seemed Ludwig had broken the mould. In actual truth, he hadn't broken any moulds, Ludwig thinking social customs and emotional irrationality an inefficient bore. The differentiating factor that had caused Ludwig to rise so quickly from nothing in a foreign land, was his ability to see the weaknesses these customs and mood swings created and capitalise on them with appropriate action. Pulling the reins of his heavily armoured destrier, he set off towards the sea of red.

Dagath, commanding from the rear, was closer to Ludwig's army than most of the other Trescot soldiers. Upon noticing the line of yellow atop the hill behind him, he called for an immediate retreat, hoping they could make it out of the valley before they were crushed against Castle Brin's walls by the approaching Ebodan army. Sadly for Trescot, they were not fast enough. What proceeded should not be described as a battle, but rather a slaughter, as Dagath's troops were cut down from both sides, sheer numbers on the Ebodan flank and a wall of arrows from the Barathax side. Dagath himself fought well but to no avail, eventually being disarmed and taken prisoner. There were cheers from the soldiers on either side as the last remnants of the Trescot force gave up and surrendered to the combined strength of their foes. As Aris came rushing down from the battlements, his extreme elation turned to utter horror. The sun was just beginning to peak over the wall, the very first rays casting a shadow as they struck the slumped head of the man on his knees.

"NOOO!!!!" Aris yelled as he took the stairs two by two, rushing towards Tyrus, his body still slumped upright as his armour had dug into the mud, a thin shaft sticking out of the gap in the joint of his armour under his arm.

Getting stuck and falling over as he sprinted into the mud, he looked up towards the man he had known for so long. Tyrus was like family, a brother. The two had been to hell and back over the decades. Now he was dead, at the hands of the red scum. As Aris lay hopelessly in the mud, a primal anger boiled up inside him, a wild rage that a man of his high birth should never display. They'd gone too far this time. Getting to his feet as he pulled Tyrus's sword out of the mud, he started yelling madly.

"Where the fuck is he! Dagath! If someone's felled him I'll have their guts for garters! Dagath!"

"Greetings Aris," Ludwig said in his usual stern voice, his

heavily armoured horse cantering through the rubble of what remained of the gate as Aris staggered about in a drunken like rage, his wild eyes not taking any notice of the Ebodan commander. "My condolences for your losses," Ludwig continued as he surveyed the heavy casualties that had befallen the ground troop.

The archers on the wall had now come down to thank their Ebodan saviours, their losses not nearly as great. Aris still took no notice, his wild eyes darting left and right, he continued to yell the Trescot commander's name.

"Aris!" Ludwig yelled grabbing the crazed man by the shoulders, shaking him as he did.

The sudden shaking seemingly brought Aris back, his eyes beginning to focus as his **highly civilised** upbringing began to fight back against raw instinct.

"King Torman brings a gift," Ludwig said as he nodded to one of his captains.

A knight adorned in bright yellow kicked a bloodied Dagath forward into the castle grounds, the sight of the man almost tilting Aris back towards madness. It took all his willpower to not give in and slay the primitive man where he stood. Seemingly having calmed down, Aris turned to Ludwig.

"My condolences to you also for the loss of his majesty," Aris said, his head bowed.

"Ah yes, that," replied Ludwig as his soldiers poured into the city and began to mount the ramparts. Aris sensed something wasn't right. "I thought it interesting that just a single day after our scouts leaked information of the approaching Trescot army our King was suddenly assassinated. **Murdered by the hand of Trescot you say?** Sadly, I think not. I've never really trusted you Aris, I don't think many do as a matter of fact. To this end we made sure Ervoule was well watched during his time in your lands. It seems we weren't quite careful enough as his demise would demonstrate. We do however, have it on the word of one Mortimer Cornish, your most trusted alchemist if I'm not mistaken, that you had King Ervoule killed. Not content with that, you then tasked him with making it seem an assassination by a bogmaul of all things, a species the remains of which are rumoured to be under the control of Trescot. The obvious aim of this despicable act being a desperate alliance with Eboda, the purpose of which being to not only fore stay the impending invasion, but to later wipe Trescot from the map once and for all."

"That is a complete and utter lie, I did nothing of the sort!" retorted Aris. "How much did that treasonous old worm demand for his blatant falsehoods?"

"I knew you were ruthless Aris," Ludwig said, ignoring his attempted rebuttal, "but I didn't think you'd go this far." Turning to face the surviving Barathax army Ludwig spoke once more. "Hear me now all ye present, as of this day, Barathax ceases to exist in any of its sovereignty, its lands and titles to be redistributed as King Tormin, rightful and just ruler of Eboda sees fit as recompense for the most grievous act of regicide." He turned to face Aris once more before continuing. "Aris Treycartheon of the land formerly known as Barathax, by the power vested in me by the righteous King Tormin, I hereby sentence you to death by hanging, for the crime of regicide against his majesty, the late King Ervoule III of Eboda."

CHAPTER 39 - GARY

Gary and company moved to the room marked 'Armoury'. The rusty metal door scraped on the ground as it opened. It was a small room with three rows of racking, one on either side of the room and one running down the middle. Stored within the racking was various military equipment.

"S'pose we might as well gear up," said Gary. At that moment, he felt the device vibrate. Grabbing it out of his pocket, he signalled the others to gather round.

"I see you've managed to navigate your first obstacle," came the now all too familiar voice. "It seems my faith in your skills may be warranted after all, that is, I suppose, if ALL of you managed to make it down there uninjured." The voice paused to laugh. "As you can see, we're well stocked for your little adventure. Grab what you fancy but make sure to get some suppressors. They're in a box in the back corner. Stealth will be of the utmost importance. When you've got what you need, and I can't emphasise this enough, you must also take the bag marked XM-41'. It's right next to the suppressors. Without it you have no way to complete your mission and we all know what that means. Once you have everything, the door marked exit... gosh, I made this too easy," the voice laughed. "Open the door that says exit. Oh, and I almost forgot, you'll probably want to take as many of those ration packs as you can because that conveniently marked exit door locks on the way out. I'd hate for anyone to go hungry. As always, stay tuned for more updates." The device went blank. Burnley was already digging through the ration pack box.

"This crap's best before date was two years ago. And here I was thinking they'd have cooked us a five-star meal."

"It's the least that psychopath could have done," replied Renfield.

Gary had a look at the ration pack. He started reading the contents listed on the side out loud. "Chocolate, chilli paste, cheese, biscuits, tinned chicken and ham, vegetable soup."

"Sounds delicious," Renfield added sarcastically.

"Alright lads, lets gear up and get on with it then. The sooner we get this done the sooner we get to slot this tosser."

Gary grabbed a large carry bag off the shelf and threw it to Renfield, then another to Burnley and Winters as they proceeded to stock up. When they'd finished collecting the gear they'd need, Gary spoke once more. "Everybody ready?" he asked as he threw the bag over his shoulder and moved towards the door marked exit. "Don't forget anything aye, doubt this pillock's lying about the door."

"What a stupid idea. Why don't we just put something in the gap and leave the door ajar?" said Burnley.

Gary smiled as he pulled down on the handle and pushed as the door gave way.

Sunshine burst into the room as they stepped out into the daylight. The group was presented with a lush landscape of dense forest similar to the one in which they had awoken. Golden light was striking through the canopy and hitting the ground in pieces ahead of them. The door made a slight noise as it attempted to shut behind them, Winters having left a spare ration pack against the frame to keep it ajar. Gary looked over his shoulder to see that they had come out of a hole in a rock face at the base of a cliff. The door had been made to look just like the rock face and had no handle on this side.

The device vibrated.

"Morning gentlemen. Now the real fun begins."

An aerial map appeared on the device, a marker taking the place of their group. A red line appeared showing a path from their current position, through the wood, ending at what resembled a large stone monument.

"You have twelve hours to travel the 50 miles to forest's end," the voice said.

There was a sudden whooshing sound as Renfield opened his mouth to speak, a yelp of pain coming out instead as an arrow smashed into his left shoulder.

"Contact!" yelled Gary as the others scattered to find cover.

Gary slid behind a large pine tree with Renfield who was clutching at the arrow protruding from his shoulder. There was an eerie silence in the forest now. "Who the hell uses a crossbow?" said Renfield between quick short breaths, gritting his teeth as he did.

"Best not take it out, it'll be stopping most of the bleeding being lodged in there," replied Gary reassuringly.

Renfield snapped the end of the arrow off just before his shoulder with a grimace of pain. "Hand me a pistol, will you? The bastard didn't get my strong arm but I'm not going to be any use with a rifle."

Gary handed Renfield his glock. "You gonna be alright till we get the fuckers?"

"Yeah, it's not too bad."

Burnley was five trees to the left. He stuck his head out for but a second to see if he could see any of the would-be attackers. Ducking back into cover he turned to the others, shrugging his shoulders and shaking his head as if to say he couldn't see where the attack had come from. The device vibrated. Gary took it out and heard the now familiar voice.

"Need some help there? The screen lit up with a black and white aerial view of the forest. The camera was moving over the trees. "Sorry it's not armed gentlemen, it should however provide some useful reconnaissance."

"The bastard's got a bloody drone," Gary said as he moved the device so Renfield could see.

Four blurry images came into view amongst the dull grey of the trees which Gary recognised as himself and his squad. "Alright, lets see where ye are then," he said more to himself than Renfield as he held up his hand to signal the others to hold position.

The drone passed over the group and about one hundred yards away, four heat signatures appeared. He could just make out based on the blurry images he was viewing that they were probably in the trees. He signalled to Burnley and Winters as best he could that they had a drone in the sky. It began circling the area, eventually confirming there were no more than four enemies. Just as he was about to slide the device to Burnley something strange caught his eye. One of the heat signatures suddenly began to grow at an exponential rate until it was just a massive blotch on the screen about three times the size of a person. Moments later, it suddenly shot towards them. Three loud snapping sounds occurred in quick succession followed by what felt like the heat you feel when you get too close to a fire as a huge flaming ball crashed through the trees between Gary and Burnley, smacking into the cliff face they had come out of. Burnley could hardly believe his eyes but wasn't given long to process the events, an almighty din ensuing as three great pine trees came crashing down around them. Gary wasn't going to pass up this much of an opportunity, the trees crashing into the ground kicking up a large enough dust cloud to temporarily obscure their movements. Gary set off laterally in an attempt to flank the enemy. He sprinted through the dust to his right and took cover behind a tree fifty yards from his original position. Renfield and the others knew the tactic and reacted accordingly. Renfield, still kneeling behind the tree, raised his gun to its side and started blind firing while Burnley and Winters ran to the left, retaking cover twenty five and fifty yards away. Once Burnley had re-established cover, he glanced out for a moment longer than before and this time he saw a thin looking man perched in the tree about 100 yards away with a bow and arrow aimed directly at Renfield's tree. He quickly brought the AK-47 to his shoulder, lining up the aggressor's head in its iron sights and squeezing the trigger. Pulling back into cover almost instantly, he had just enough time to observe the figure's head snap back in a cloud of red. Renfield moved forward and to the right to another tree the second he heard the shot, knowing it would have drawn the enemy's attention. The wounded Motel Whiskey member reached new cover without a moment to spare, an arrow coming within a half inch of his head as he dropped to his knees in front of the tree. Gary looked into the device. He saw one of the figures fall from its perch as Winters shot him down. The images were blurry but he was pretty sure they weren't facing his direction. He crouched down and moved quietly through the trees, closer and closer to the two remaining enemies. He could hear the occasional crack of gunfire as he got into position, Renfield and the others drawing their attention. The drone circled to the right and Gary could now see himself and the remaining two enemies on screen. There was another sudden glow of light as the heat signature increased in size again followed by a second roaring fireball which headed towards Renfield and Burnley. He hoped they'd be OK but now wasn't the time to check. He screwed the silencer onto the muzzle of the AK-47 and then slowly poked out from around the tree. It was then he got his first real glimpse of their assailants. They were about fifty yards away sitting silently, high up in the trees. One was a rather skinny fellow that looked very similar to the chap they'd met in the cave with the same oddly pointed ears. The other stood out far more, not because of his heavier build but more so the way he was dressed, the bizarrely extravagant attire not at all suitable for the current situation. He was wearing some sort of bright red and gold embroidered tunic underneath a dazzling green cloak with a strange golden slouching hood over his head. The thin one was dressed in a tattered sleeveless jacket and a baggy pair of pants that seemed to sport sporadic holes. His bow was trained and ready to release, more or less in the direction of where Gary had been moments ago. The other was waving about some kind of staff. Something that looked not dissimilar to heat distortion atop a tin roof on a hot day manifesting in front of him. Gary took aim, held his breath and squeezed the trigger, then moved the rifle the few degrees to the left and squeezed again, all in the matter of a seconds. The two figures dropped from the trees before either realised what was happening.

Looking at the device, he confirmed there were no more hostiles and yelled "Clear!" as he moved cautiously towards the bodies on the ground.

Burnley and Renfield emerged from the tree line as he kicked one of the bodies, forcing it face up.

"What the hell's going on, some pointy eared nutters taking pot shots with bows and arrows then fireballs to boot," said Winters.

"Have any of you ever seen something like that?" asked Burnley, visibly shocked by the flaming balls of death that had come so close to killing them all.

"Nope, maybe some kind of experimental weapon?" replied Gary.

"Shit, I hope it's not radioactive," Burnley replied.

"Check their bodies and see if ye can find the weapon," Gary said, ignoring Burnley's concern.

They proceeded to search the bodies but to their disbelief found nothing but a staff and some bows and arrows.

"It's like they conjured them with their bare hands," said Renfield disbelievingly.

The device vibrated. "Gentlemen, congratulations on your victory, but may I remind you that the clock is still ticking. I suggest you make haste. You may also wish to take the opportunity to sample some local attire. Sneaking through town will be much easier if you look the part."

Burnley walked towards the device. "I'm not doing shit till you tell us what the hell is going on here."

"You're in no position to bargain, unless, I suppose, you think your family's lives are worth an explanation."

"Fuck you!" yelled Burnley frustratedly as he retrieved a first aid kit from one of the bags.

"I'll take that as a sign you're ready to continue. Good luck."

With that, the device went silent.

CHAPTER 40 - GARY

Renfield hadn't shown it, but Gary knew it must have hurt like hell as he pulled what was left of the arrow from his shoulder. Luckily, it didn't seem to have hit anything major. Gary finished applying the bandage and they pressed on. It was nightfall when they got to the checkpoint as Gary felt the now familiar vibration of the device.

"Just in time, well done gentlemen. On to the next order of business then. One hundred yards north of here the forest ends and gives way to the village of Alman. In the centre of the village there is a pyramid like structure. Trust me, you'll know it when you see it. There are three plateaus that surround the pyramid. On the second plateau you will find a large archway that looks not dissimilar to a door. In the bag you're carrying marked 'XM-41', you'll find a good deal of thermite amongst other mission critical equipment. When you get to the archway, place the thermite in the recess above the dragon and ignite it. The archway will then recede and grant access to the chamber beyond. Again, I must emphasise, discretion is of utmost importance and it is to this end that the bag contains a light dampening device. The device will absorb any bright sparks created on ignition, minimising your chance of detection. Once inside the chamber, you will place the stone dragon key that is also contained in the bag into the recess in the wall and then extract to the RV two miles north of the city."

"Light dampening device? What the hell is that?" Burnley asked.

"You expect no one to notice ignited thermite in the middle of the night? You fool. Just do as you're told and you will be reunited with your families soon," replied the voice in an annoyed tone. "Oh and those clothes you 'liberated' earlier, I think it goes without saying, now would be a good time to change." With that, the device went silent once more.

"Do you think this guy's the full quid?" asked Winters. "If we ignite some thermite in the middle of the night like he says there's no way no one's gonna see it."

"Alright then," said Gary, "let's see if he's telling porkies." He rummaged through the bag, sorting through the various items inside. There was a cube like object with the letters 'LD' engraved into the front of it with two flick switches at the top and what looked like a camera lens on one side. Gary set the box down on the ground and flicked his lighter on.

"Alright, activate it then," he said to Renfield.

Renfield looked at the two switches. One had 'Capture' engraved underneath it, the other 'Release'. Renfield flicked the switch on the box that said Capture and the flame disappeared almost instantly. Gary moved his finger just above the lighter where the flame would normally be, a second later retracting it in pain.

"It's still burning!" he said in amazement as he flicked his burnt finger to-and-fro beside him. Renfield noticed a small LED counter had lit up on the side of the box. Its green dot matrix read '0%'.

"Ah, I think I get it now," he said.

He flicked the capture switch off and the flame from the lighter reappeared. Next he flicked the release switch. A dim, barely visible flash that lasted naught but the briefest of moments appeared in the lens.

"I'm pretty sure this device actually captures light and stores it!" Renfield said excitedly.

"Well whatever it does, let's hope it works as well with thermite as it does a lighter," replied Gary.

"Do you realise the potential of something like this!" Renfield stammered excitedly. "Just imagine having this on a stealth mission. A more powerful version that had an effect over a greater area might be able to capture enough light to render objects invisible! I suppose the lighter itself didn't disappear though, it must have to be a certain intensity?... Hmm, maybe that doesn't make sense... I actually have no idea," he said confused. The remaining members of Motel Whiskey looked at their companion, wondering when he was going to stop rambling.

"If you're quite done..." Gary said, regaining Renfield's attention.

Renfield was about to respond when he was stopped mid thought. "Wait, we'd better be careful releasing the light. It was just a small glow at 0% but I don't think anyone's eyes would thank them if they were looking at a 100% release."

"Let's let our American friend worry about releasing it. With any luck, the fucker 'ill blind himself," said Winters. "Come on, time to get changed," replied Gary.

"Dibs not wearing the pansy outfit," said Burnley as he grabbed the tunic and pants one of the archers had been clothed in."

Before Gary could react Renfield and Winters had grabbed the other archers attire leaving just the bright red and green cloak/tunic combo that he now noticed was covered in embedded gold floral embroidery. Burnley made a coughing sound as he tried to stifle a laugh at the sight of his commander in the floral cloak the fireball conjurer had been wearing.

"Very funny," he said grabbing the bag, slinging it over his shoulder. Try as he might, Burnley could no longer contain it, proceeding to break out in uncontrollable laughter, it seemingly spreading like a contagion to the others.

"Say, that's a nice cloak sir," Winters said between fits of laughter, "do they make them for men?"

"Yeah, go on, have a laugh ye bastards, at least I dinnay look like I just crawled out of a sewer."

Burnley, Winter's and Renfield's attire was admittedly very shabby. They both wore sleeveless shirts composed of some very old, worn, dirty leather. The pants were in a similar state, a dull brown colour, holes throughout. Notwithstanding the lack of fashion, they made their way through the remainder of the forest. As they neared its edge the trees gave way to a small lake straddled by a thin wooden bridge, the village of Alman located on the other side. Old stone buildings and a mish mash of huts were chequered throughout, lit sporadically by straw torches attached to the walls. On first impression, the village appeared empty, a far cry from the dire warning they'd been given. The group made their way cautiously towards the village. As they got closer it became apparent that the village was not in fact empty. Noise and light were emanating from a large thatched building across the way, further down the dirt path that wove in front of them between the buildings. As they got closer still, what at first had been a murmur transformed slowly into the sound of music and people talking. Burnley prodded Renfield,"It's like we've been sent back in time to some medieval village, the bows and arrows, these thatched little cottages..." The sound of a violin and drums could be heard over a rabble of lively voices. There was definitely some sort of party going on inside. Just as they were passing, the doors suddenly swung open, a wave of hot musty air hitting Gary in the face soon to be accompanied by the stench of a drunk who obviously hadn't showered in a good while. The man stumbled out a few paces, holding a pitcher of what they assumed was ale before promptly falling face first into the mud. His clothes were of similar style and quality to Renfield, Burnley, and Winters. The drunken man groaned as he pushed himself up out of the mud.

"Top O the morning to ya," he slurred as he wavered to the left, somehow defying the odds, keeping most of the ale in his pitcher throughout the whole process. He began to laugh but was stopped short as he suddenly threw up where he'd been lying but a moment ago. They carried on past the drunk, hoping he wouldn't draw too much attention. Fortunately, it soon seemed he'd forgotten about them as he began to talk to the tavern wall.

Burnley pointed into the distance. "There," he said.

The others directed their gaze to where his finger was pointed. The pinnacle of an enormous pyramid jutted out above the buildings in the distance. The dusty paths between the buildings were now littered with puddles of god knows what. The road became muddy and foul smelling as it seemed the people here simply dumped all of their waste to the sides of the dirt paths that ran between the buildings. They came to a cul-de-sac, an approximately six foot wall between them and their passage to the pyramid as three filthy hobos manifested from the shadows. Gary thought he could almost smell them before he saw them. The first one smiled revealing a checker board of black and orange teeth. He then produced a rusty old dagger from his tattered belt.

"What have we here lads?" sneered the man.

"You ever seen a high-born out here Victor?" he said to the second man.

"Think he's lost his way he has," Victor replied. "We'll kindly help you find your way again me lord, but I think you'll be better off without all that gold. Weighs you down you see." The third man laughed as he drew a sword.

"What the fuck is wrong with you people, I dinnay have any bloody gold," Gary replied.

"Come on, fancy cloak like that and you've got no gold?"

"That's a right shame then isn't it," said the man with the dagger. "In that case, we'll just have ta gut ya then," he said, a sinister smile spreading across his face as the three started to advance.

Gary was semi-conscious of a blur to his right followed by three hissing sounds as the trio of would be mugger's heads kicked backed on collision with the bullets from Renfield's pistol. He'd reached into the bag Winters was holding, slowly attaching the silencer while they were talking.

"Thank Christ for that," said Gary, "Who knows what freaks we'd have drawn the attention of if that wasn't done quietly?"

"Never thought I'd end up getting mugged by a bunch of clowns playing medieval dress ups when I signed up," said Burnley.

"Come on lads, we'd better hurry now before anyone finds the bodies."

With that they climbed the wall and continued on towards the pyramid. Gary signalled for the group to stop behind a small hedge. In front of them stood a monolithic construction that stretched at least ten roughly twelve-foot-tall levels into the sky. It had steps running up the front side and just as the voice had said, there were three plateaus incrementally as you ascended the stairs. Seemingly abandoned, Gary and the others approached with caution regardless.

"Hmm," whispered Winters, "so why did he need us to do this, I don't see any guards."

"I'm guessing they're having a few back at the tavern with the wall whisperer, seems it's our lucky night," replied Winters.

"Just stay sharp," Gary said as the group began to tentatively climb the stairs to the first plateau.

Upon reaching it, Gary signalled for them to halt so he could stop and listen. Nothing. They began to climb again. As they reached the second plateau Gary pointed to a complex on the ground at the base of the pyramid. There was a stone wall with a palisade fence arrangement on top surrounding a compound. From this height, they could see into the grounds and noted that there were a number of sectioned off areas with what looked like scarecrows in them. Burnley spotted a rack of axes and swords in the middle of the compound.

"Where the hell are we? It's like some kind of dark ages barracks," Renfield said, shaking his head. "Do you think it's really wise to have no roof on the grounds like that, anyone that comes up here could see in," replied Winters.

"Yeah but how are you supposed to get in there genius," said Burnley.

"Ah good point."

"Well at least now we know if we mess up there'll be a friendly welcoming party nearby," said Renfield.

Gary walked around the plateau ignoring the others. The sides of the pyramid were giant blocks of stone and he had to admire the feats of engineering it must have taken to get them up here. He continued around the plateau to the next face of the pyramid and there, just as the voice had said, was a carving of an archway a little taller than himself. He motioned to the others and they quickly moved to the archway.

"I feel like a Pharaoh," said Burnley as Renfield grabbed the light dampener and thermite from the bag.

"Reckon there's secret rooms and what not?" said Winters as Renfield handed the thermite to Gary and set the light dampener on the stone floor, flicking the capture switch as he did.

"I suppose this is what we light it with?" said Renfield, grabbing a small blowtorch from the bag.

Gary poured the powdered thermite into the recess above the dragon figure that had been carved into the stone and then engaged the blowtorch. Confused for a moment, Gary could hear the roar of the flame but couldn't see anything at the end of the nozzle. Almost instantly remembering the light dampener, he silently marvelled at the amazing piece of technology. The group stared in silent awe as the recess in the wall turned black, getting progressively larger in front of their eyes as if it were being eaten away by some invisible force. As it burnt through the rock a steel bar came into view. This slowly dissolved and with a sound of stone grinding on stone, an archway began to slide down in front of them, revealing a hidden room behind it. The LED display on the light dampener stabilised at 25% as they waited a few more seconds just to be sure the thermite had fully burned out before turning it off. They stepped into the secret room that had just been revealed in front of them. The inner linings of the room were comprised of shiny smooth steel, not the harsh weather beaten rock that made up the outside of the pyramid. The light dancing across the walls from Gary's lighter illuminated etchings of all sorts of hideous creatures devouring their poor human victims. There were shapes of what Gary thought resembled werewolves, ogres, dragons, and all manner of other demons that Gary and the others weren't familiar with.

"Whoever did these seems like a fun chap," quipped Burnley as Gary searched for the recess. Moving along the wall to the left, he found it in the mouth of a something or other stone carving, whatever it was seemingly having been sculpted by the same being responsible for the etchings, similar grim themes evidenced in its demon like features. He grabbed the dragon shaped artefact from his bag and placed it into the thing's mouth.

"Well that wasn't so hard," said Burnley. "Some wanker sends us to crazyville to complete a bloody sculpture."

"Whatever," replied Gary, "we've done our bit, time to get the hell out of here."

The pyramid however, seemed to have other ideas, the ground at its base lighting up an electric blue as a deafening roar began from somewhere deep within.

CHAPTER 41 - GARY

Sprinting out of the secret chamber onto the plateau, their attention was suddenly drawn skywards. A great beam of blue light was shooting out of the apex as the roaring sound from deep within grew louder, something akin to an enormous flowing flame, not unlike a blowtorch, only thousands of times more intense.

"So much for stealth!" yelled Burnley over the roar as Gary hurriedly bagged up all the equipment.

"Let's get the fuck out of here now!" replied Winters moving to the edge of the plateau to check for any movement from the barracks.

"Wait," said Gary. "We can't go down that way, there's no way someone hasn't noticed. Let's circle around to the back of the pyramid and climb down."

Renfield and the others didn't need telling twice as they set off in a sprint across the plateau around to the back face.

There were no steps on the other side meaning they had to drop down the large stone blocks one by one. Noises could be heard originating from the barracks now as the soldiers were no doubt wondering what in the world was going on. The group were about half way down the pyramid when the device vibrated. A face appeared on the screen for a second but then the picture began to distort as though something was interfering with the signal. Cringing as he felt a short sharp pain in his head, Gary noticed the screen had gone blank a moment later as the pain receded. This was certainly not the time to be looking for an aspirin however,

Gary thought as he vaulted off the last block and onto the ground, soon to be followed by Renfield and company. They hit the ground running, hearing shouts from what was probably some very surprised towns folk. The shouts however, were promptly followed by something unexpected - screams of horror. "What the hell is going on back there," thought Burnley as he came alongside Gary, their rapid steps aligning. Breaking the tree line on the back side of the pyramid they kept pace a little longer before slowing down to assess the situation behind them. Gary grabbed a pair of night vision goggles out of the pack and looked back into the night. Strangely enough, it didn't seem as though anyone was chasing them, and stranger still, the sounds they could hear coming from the town sounded more like a medieval battle than a pursuit, the sound of steel on steel interspersed with yelps of agony.

"That bastard never said anything about setting off fireworks," Burnley exclaimed in an annoyed tone.

"Yeah, I think we've been played pretty hard," replied Winters.

"Can you hear the screams?" said Renfield. "No doubt we set off a bit of a light show and probably broke someone's sacred something, but that sounds like they're hacking each other to pieces."

"Maybe one of those rocks fell on someone?" offered Burnley half-heartedly.

"Any contact from that joker?" asked Winters. "We've done our bit, it's time we got out of this freak show."

"That's the thing," said Gary, "as we left it activated but then I'm pretty sure it broke."

"It broke!?" exclaimed Burnley. "What do you mean it broke!?"

"The screen went all swervey and then it just went black. Wait, did any of ye feel a short sharp pain in your head as we were coming down the pyramid?"

"Yeah, how did you know?" replied Burnley.

"Me too," said Renfield and Winters.

"I think the stuff he put in our heads just got fried along with the device by whatever it was that pyramid just did."

"Oh dear," said Burnley, "so the good news ladies and gentlemen is we don't have some psycho's tech toy in our brain any more, the minor, insignificant, not important at all, bad news... WE CAN'T EVER GET HOME NOW!?"

"You've got to be shitting me, the signal probably just got

interrupted, maybe it'll come back on later," offered Winters.

"All I know," said Renfield, "is that the evac point is a few miles north of here and that I'm not sticking around for the next sixty years of my life."

"Hmm, think about it lads, if you were in his shoes what would you do. Bring the people you kidnapped home and risk them telling their story, bizarre as it may be, or option two, leave them wherever it was you sent them and not have to worry at all."

"I'd take option three," said Burnley, "set up an ambush at the evac site and kill them all. There has to be someone else here that knows what's going on, otherwise how does he have satellite images of the terrain and access to a drone. If I were him I'd make sure those two parties never met up."

"Look," said Gary, "I know it's dangerous, but let's go check the evac point and hope the devices in our head aren't tracking us anymore. We'll assume it's an ambush, do some reconnaissance, then take the fuckers. We just might be able to get someone to talk."

"Sounds like a plan if ever I heard one," said Renfield as the squad made their way towards the evacuation zone.

CHAPTER 42 - GARY

After a couple of hours spent clearing every square foot of land surrounding the evac zone it became apparent they'd been had. Just a clearing in the forest with naught to suggest any sort of rendezvous or ambush for that matter.

"Looks like they took option two," said Winters in a depressed tone.

"SHIT! SHIT! SHIT!" yelled Burnley at the top of his lungs, kicking the tree in front of him as the realisation slowly set in that he'd never see his family again.

Renfield stood silent, staring blankly into the night as Winters shook his head. Gary wasn't sure he really meant it but said it anyway. "Settle down lads, it's not over yet, we just go back to the village and start asking around. We'll get back, I promise ye, and when we do that fucker's gonna die slow."

"Bollocks!" replied Burnley. "Those nutters are completely mad. Why the hell couldn't he have just shot me and been done with it rather than let me live knowing I'm never getting home."

Gary slapped Burnley across the face. "Quit your fucking whining, we're going back to the village and we're gonna get some answers. I'm going home and the three of ye are coming with me!"

Seemingly having the desired effect, Burnley stopped complaining for the time being.

Winters had a strange look on his face as he turned to Gary, "Um, where's Renfield?"

Gary looked to his left and right, then scanned the area with his night vision goggles. Renfield did indeed seem to have disappeared.

"Oh great, just what we need now," said Gary as he began quietly calling Renfield's name.

A response came in the form of some branches cracking underfoot somewhere in the darkness ahead. Gary, Winters and Burnley drew their weapons as they moved silently towards the origin of the noise. The world was awash with the glowing green of his night vision as the sound came again. Cracking twigs, not more than ten yards ahead, just audible over the soft sound of his now rapid breathing. They moved ever closer, inch by inch. Gary could now make out an odd black splodge in the world of green, possibly the shape of a boot. Signalling caution to the others, he slowed down so much so that he was barely moving, not daring to make a sound. And then he saw it. His heart skipped a beat as the night vision goggles died. The night vision however, was not the main cause for concern. Moments before the world of green faded to black, he was able to discern a figure that looked about the same size as Renfield propped against the base of a tree. The image stuck in his head like a photograph as he slowly removed the goggles, not moving a muscle as he waited silently for his eyes to adjust to the lack of light.

"Renfield," he whispered, as his eyes adjusted. Something moved to the right of the body. As Gary's head snapped to the right in perfect synchronicity with his weapon, his concerned expression turned to one of pure horror. In front of him, crouching over the lifeless body of Renfield, was a creature the likes of which Gary and the others knew didn't exist. From behind it looked like a gorilla, but as it turned they observed its pointed fangs and long claws as the moonlight reflected off them. Its eyes glowed a strange orange glow as its slit pupils dilated at the sight of them. Gary squeezed the trigger a moment before the other two, the three of them sending a shower of bullets smashing into the abominations head. The thing was dead before it had time to make a sound.

"Oh god no!" cried Burnley in shock as he moved forward to check Renfield for vital signs. Gary heard a clicking sound to his left, not unlike someone clicking their tongue. Turning, he was immediately faced with another of the things. He promptly unloaded three rounds into its head. Winters spun around and began firing at yet another as the clicking sounds started to come from all directions. Burnley spun from Renfield's corpse as he joined the fight. The brief flashes of light from his AK47 illuminated the area just enough to render all hope lost, their impending doom now evident. It wasn't just three or four, there was a pack of the things, the likes of which had surrounded the three remaining members of Motel Whiskey. Ejecting an empty clip and reloading, he started firing again.

"They're everywhere!" screamed Burnley, more to the night sky then to anyone in particular.

Moving towards each other slowly, they fired short bursts into the forest at the horrific attackers.

"There's just too many," said Burnley, defeat and fear in his voice.

"Don't make me fucking slap ye again!" replied Gary. "Just kill the bastards!"

The trio had brought down a not insignificant number of their would-be assailants, but it wasn't enough, the pack seemingly never ending. Gary heard the slightly different click of Winter's gun running out of ammunition, a scream following in short order.

"Winters no!" There was no reply as Gary turned to see one of them dig its teeth into Winter's throat. Burnley turned to run but as he did he was caught in the chest by a clawed palm, dying almost instantly. They'd closed ranks now, every set of glowing eyes transfixed on Gary as the fateful click of his magazine running empty confirmed the inevitable. His spirits sank only to lift a moment later, Gary being taken on an emotional roller coaster as he remembered the light dampener. Quickly prising it out of the bag, he covered his eyes and hit the release switch.

CHAPTER 43 - ARIS

As Aris and Dagath were marched down the long hall of cells, the expected jeers came from their soon to be fellow inmates. These were promptly followed by the mutterings of those who'd been here for too long or those whose minds had simply broken under the less than hospitable conditions. There were no windows or ventilation in the underground prison, the air so musty as a result it was almost unbreathable. Aris had been down here on more than one occasion and as such was no stranger to the filthy conditions and occupants that comprised the dungeon. It wasn't pleasant but he could deal with that. The one aspect that made a trip to the bowels of Castle Brin something he avoided like the plague, was the smell. There was no real sewage system and water was something you drank gratefully whenever it was rationed, it wasn't a commodity you wasted on washing. These conditions combined with the lack of ventilation made for an environment conducive to madness even if you weren't surrounded by the realm's most twisted and depraved. As he was pushed into his cell, Ludwig whispered in his ear.

"Just quietly between you and I, you have my utmost regard for the most kind donation of both the kingdoms Barathax and Trescot. Under normal circumstances I seldom reward such stupidity. However, considering the decade or so you have just advanced my career, I shall leave you with one parting gesture of thanks. He's a big fellow but without the use of his hands I'm sure you'll manage," Ludwig said with a parting smile as he undid the stained ropes that bound Aris's wrists before pushing him into an open cell. The grimy walls that were to accompany him for his last few days were all too familiar, the only difference being he was usually on the other side of the bars. The iron gate slammed shut behind him as his captor turned the key, locking the gate in place. The old, rusted lock made a loud clunking sound, the internal pieces oversized and indelicate. Observing the figure to his left, Aris began to realise what Ludwig meant by 'gift'. They'd locked Dagath in the same cell, only his hands were tightly bound. Almost instantly, Aris lost control, some primitive force possessing him as he lunged at Dagath, his fist connecting with the Neanderthal's face as he did. The big man stumbled backwards as Aris felt a spike of pain run across his knuckles and up his forearm. The man's skull was indeed not homo sapiens, and although Dagath had reeled from the blow, Aris felt like he'd punched a stone wall. Flicking his hand as he cursed in pain, Aris suddenly became acutely aware of an eerie silence. The jeers had dissipated, naught but the drip of a leak somewhere in the dungeon could be heard. Aris had put a great deal of the men he'd just walked past in here and it was only now that the realisation was dawning upon them. It wasn't just Dagath being locked up, their captor was also to be housed alongside them. When the revelation finally clicked in their heads the howl of frenzied excitement became deafening. The prisoners began banging on their bars, yelling all manner of threats and taunts. The mad ones did what they had been doing all along just with a greater intensity, one man even tearing out what was left of his hair. The prisoner in the cell next to Aris slammed into the bars. The only thing worse than his crooked, yellow, rotting three teeth being his stench. "Come to join us 'ave you Aris?" his face forming a sinister grin. "It's ok, you can come and 'ave a talk to 'ol Boris if you get lonely. I promise I won't gut you, really."

"You better fucking not, came a deep booming voice from further down the corridor. I'm gonna kill him s-l-o-w and any man who takes that's gonna join him."

The taunts continued on as Aris tried his best to ignore them for now while there was still iron between them.

Dagath spoke as he shook his head in an attempt to clear his watery eyes caused by the blow to his nose.

"The mighty Aris, locked in his own dungeon. Seems you're

quite the star down here. You know we would have had you if those poncey yellow pansies hadn't shown up."

"200000 soldiers against 30000 militia? You pick your battles well," sneered Aris. "If it weren't for your little lights display you wouldn't have stood a chance even with those numbers. Oh, and do tell, was it part of your elegant battle strategy to engulf your own siege weapon in flame along with the men around it?"

"Oh you caught that? Say, did you like our little toy? It certainly made an 'impression' on your famed wall."

"Somehow I think that impression is going to be the last."

"Maybe so, but you know what they say, it's first impressions that count. Half the efficacy of those walls was the legend surrounding them."

Aris sighed, "God I'd like nothing more than to stick both my thumbs deep into your eyeballs, but I'm not even sure they'd find a brain in that empty case atop your neck."

"Why don't you find out then, or is killing a bound and unarmed man below your station?"

"It's certainly not below yours."

"Ah yes, that's right, always taking the high road. You're no more civilised than I, you just prefer to hide that fact behind pretentious talk of King and Country and fancy clothes. You're a craven backstabber Aris, the only reason I'm still breathing is your audience."

It took every last bit of restraint Aris possessed to not kill the brutish man there and then. He knew he'd need Dagath if he were to live longer than the next three days, logic eventually winning out over emotion as Aris replied.

"Well then, since we're discussing what we have in common, how about the fact we're both locked in a cell that we'd much rather be on the other side of, and the fact that if we temporarily put our differences aside we might just get out of here with our heads still attached."

"Oh, and how do you suppose we do that."

"It goes without saying, this truce is temporary, the only reason you still draw breath is that this will require two people."

"Just shut up, cut the drama and I might not kill you till we're free," replied Dagath.

"That goes double for me," said Aris, looking down the passageway to see if anyone was watching. Aris removed his right boot and then took off the sock, turning it inside out as he did. Two small pieces of metal fell to the ground. Dagath lunged forward at Aris the moment he saw the two keys drop only to feel something connect with his throat as he started to wheeze, unable to breathe. Aris, not keen on punching a brick wall twice, had this time employed a more technical approach. Upon seeing the big man charge, he'd brought his fingers together in a knife hand like formation then struck him just under the chin in the Adam's apple with the bone dense region where hand joined forearm. He could very well have killed Dagath if he struck with enough force, but Aris needed him alive. He then followed up with an open palm strike to Dagath's nose. Precious little air reaching his lungs, his vision blurred, blood streaming down his shirt, Dagath instinctively covered the location of the sudden pain with his hands. Through watery eyes he watched as Aris cocked his head, ushering him to follow.

"Now, if only you could have been an honest fellow, there would have been no need for that. Oh yes, I'm afraid that after that little show, you won't be ridding yourself of those ropes any time soon my friend. Now, come on, fortunately for you, I still need you in one piece."

Dagath, his breath returning, spat out some blood that had run from his nose into his mouth in a gesture of disapproval.

"You first," said Aris pushing Dagath from behind, manoeuvring him down the ancient hall.

As soon as they left the cell the howling from the other prisoners went into overdrive, the dungeon's occupants realising the very real prospect of Aris escaping their 'convict justice'. Some started screaming at the top of their lungs, calling to the guards, trying to alert them to the ensuing escape. Aris knew it didn't matter how loud they screamed.

"Great plan," said Dagath. "Surely this little din won't render our freedom a brief affair." Aris ignored the sarcasm and Dagath began to wonder as Aris strayed a little too close to one of the cell walls deeper in the dungeon. Turning his back on Dagath, he stood up close to the iron bars, his face not more than a few inches from the cell in front of him. A pair of arms burst forth from the cell, clawing at Aris's throat as they did. Aris reacted so quickly that Dagath guessed it must have been planned. Grabbing one of the assailant's arms just below the hand he swivelled 180 degrees on the spot, dropping his body weight as he did, pulling the arm with all his force away from the cell towards the dungeon hallway. There was a loud ding as the head that went with the pair of arms smashed into the metal bars. Aris then pushed with all his weight to the right which was followed by the sickening sound of bone breaking in two. The arm that had grabbed at Aris moments ago was now horrifically bent at the elbow 90 degrees in the wrong direction. There was a scream as the arm's owner recoiled only to get his now broken limb stuck in bars on the way through. Aris turned and although in the lack of light he couldn't see the prisoner, he pushed where he guessed the centre body mass would be, sending the would-be assailant screaming backwards into his cell. Aris then calmly instructed Dagath to unlock the cell, the large man fumbling with the lock, the clunk of its large components eventually slipping into place, signalling success. Upon entering, he immediately moved to the screaming man, promptly twisting his neck in such a way that Castle Brin's prisoner count was instantly reduced by one. He then handed Dagath a key.

"You've become very trusting all of a sudden," said Dagath.

"The hole in the wall over there, we need to turn the keys at the same time," Aris said pointing to the cell's back wall. Dagath walked over to the wall. "On three," said Aris. "One, Two, Th...."

"What's that?" Dagath interrupted as he cocked his head back the way they'd come. Aris heard it too now, the sound of rapid clinking footsteps, someone in armour running their way.

CHAPTER 44 - ALISTAIR

Alistair and Adele had emerged from the secret passage about a mile north of Bledith Tower. Fortunately for them, it seemed the Val Thane were quite preoccupied with their former lodgings, allowing them to slip away without too much hassle. The journey to Castle Brin took no more than a couple of days, the two fortresses not being separated by a great deal of landmass.

Alistair looked out over the top of the mountain, taking in the sprawling city of Barathax below him. As he surveyed the region he'd called home for the last few years, he noticed something odd had happened to the main wall. He removed the RG32 from his pack not bothering to assemble the rifle, instead using the scope to get a better look. As he focused on the city walls, he noticed that where the front gate used to be there was now a gaping hole in the wall. The magnified image revealed the gate had been destroyed, the area directly behind it reduced to rubble, seemingly as though it had fallen backwards onto the buildings below. As if this weren't strange enough, something else caught his eye. The banners flying on the ramparts were yellow in colour as opposed to Barathax's green and the town was swarming with armed men in the unmistakeable yellow of the Ebodan army.

"What do you make of that?" he asked Adele as he passed her the scope.

Taking the scope, she put it to her eye. Alistair noticed the confused look on her face then realised she still had both eyes open.

"Close your other eye," he instructed.

"Oh, much better. Eboda it seems," she said as she noted the yellow flags and large number of armed men. "Now there is a face I have not seen in quite some time... Ludwig Steiner."

"Ludwig Steiner?" Alistair said thoughtfully, trying to remember where he had heard the name before. "He's the high commander of the Ebodan army isn't he? I suppose Aris's plan must have worked out after all."

"I'm not so sure," said Adele, looking from rampart to rampart at the yellow flags. "Even if Eboda had allied with Barathax, why would castle Brin be flying their banners? Flying another Kingdom's banners from your capital's ramparts is akin to relinquishing sovereignty."

"Hmm, I suppose that's true," said Alistair, puzzled by the current state of affairs.

"The large section of missing wall would also tend to imply a rather successful siege," said Adele.

"You think Eboda did this? Barathax is their closest ally."

"All signs point to the affirmative. Anyhow, whatever has happened we can worry about it later. Before we delve into too much theory crafting, the main objective is still to find Aris as Moran instructed. The Val Thane pose a far greater threat than any inter Kingdom squabbles."

Adele's expression changed as her face recoiled from the scope.

"It's doing something," she said as the image zoomed out. "Here, look." Adele passed the scope to Alistair. Alistair noticed some transparent text had appeared in the top left corner of the scope that read 'scanning' and that a small square box had appeared and was darting all over the screen. The view was gradually zooming in as the box seemed to be moving around the extremities of the scope. Without warning, the box came to a halt in the bottom left corner of the image. A moment later two boxes appeared, one with an image of Aris's face in front of a white background and the other, a wire frame image of a face that shared a similar shape to Aris's. The text at the top of the screen changed from 'scanning' to 'target located' as the scope faded in footage of Aris in a prison cell alongside a massive brute of a man. It then slowly zoomed out, displaying a path from the initial zoom perspective to that of Aris in his cell.

"I think you may have just found him," said Alistair.

"What...? How?"

"I'm guessing that when you said the main objective is to 'find Aris' it may have recognised the keywords 'find Aris' and prompted a scan function.

Looks like I'll have to leave the technology to you in future," Alistair joked as he put the scope away.

"It can hear us?" Adele whispered.

"Kind of," he replied. "Don't worry, it doesn't have a mind of its own, it just acts on certain commands."

Adele smiled wearily, not quite sure she trusted the scope regardless. "So where is he?"

"It seems our good friend Aris's location may give traction to your theory of an Ebodan invasion. According to the scope, he's in the dungeon."

"How fortunate," she said with a smile. "The fact dungeons are made to stop people getting out, not in, should make accessing Aris somewhat less complex."

"Yeah, well, I think I'll leave the bastard there once we get the information Moran was talking about."

"The two of you don't get along?"

"It's a long story," said Alistair observing the strong contingent of guards at the front of the castle. "Ever fancied yellow?"

CHAPTER 45 - ALISTAIR

Static preceded Alistair's voice, "Testing, can you hear me?"

"I hear you," Adele replied excitedly into the radio Alistair had picked up at Raven's Contact.

He pushed off the cliff face once more, his gloved hands making a whooshing sound as he slid down the rope. A few minutes later he was back where his journey started, Barathax.

Alistair wasted no time moving to the edge of the thick tree line that grew at the base of the valley adjoining the castle wall. He'd noticed soldiers occasionally straying into the trees nearby. Guessing they were using the trees as a lavatory, he'd decided it the best place to catch one alone. He sat patiently in the darkness for over an hour when suddenly there was a crackle in the radio.

"A soldier is approaching from just North of the ruined gate. He is alone, and judging by his gait, I'd chance he has probably had a little too much to drink."

"Roger that."

"Who is Roger?" Adele replied sounding confused.

"Ah... it just means I heard you ok," said Alistair thinking how silly he must sound. He didn't get long to think about it however, as the crunching of leaf litter under foot became audible. Alistair waited until the yellow man had finished his business before commandeering the attire. Fortunately for Alistair, the soldier had removed his helm, throwing it on the ground nearby until he'd finished. Also fortunate was the fact he was wearing a light suit of chain mail that was void of neck protection. Alistair caught the unsuspecting fellow from behind in a sleeper hold, locking both his forearms in such a way that his right hand could cover the soldier's mouth to stop any cries for help. As the body in his arms went limp, he proceeded to bind the unconscious man to a tree, gagging him as he did, just in case getting to Aris took longer than expected.

A nervous voice came over the radio, "There's another approaching."

"How many fucking times do I have to tell you muppets! When on duty, never go anywhere by yourself!" came an annoyed voice from the direction the now unconscious soldier had come from. "Rodney! Rodney! get the fuck out here now!" the voice yelled. Alistair could see him through the slit in his helm, another yellow fellow, only this one was in full plate armour and was carrying something. This man's head wasn't exposed as he had his helm on, the full suit of plate armour also covering his neck. Alistair reasoned that by his demeanour, this was probably an officer or sergeant.

"Bloody piss head," the officer said as he approached the man he assumed was Rodney, kicking him off the tree he was slumped against. "I'd have you flogged for this if your father and I weren't such good friends."

Alistair replied with some garbled, slurred speech.

"Come on, back to your post you bloody drunk."

Alistair stumbled to his feet and followed the officer back into the city. Through the visor he could make out a small number of guards posted at the gates and on the ramparts. He'd seen the broken wall through the RG32 scope but up close was a different thing entirely. The wall was so thick, how on earth did Ludwig's forces manage to punch such a large hole in it? Stranger still, the gap in the wall was a perfect rectangle, like someone had taken a gigantic knife and sliced a portion out of it. There was no way a catapult or trebuchet volley would create such a linear cut. Tents were beginning to spring up behind the gap in the wall where Alistair knew houses once stood. They carried on through the city. The armed men in yellow certainly gave credence to Adele's theory that Eboda had taken the city by force but the motive was still a mystery.

Then, as if by some miracle of chance, the officer led Alistair to the dungeon.

"Go on then, you can sleep it off in here," the officer whispered. "If anyone sees you hopefully they'll think it's punishment. I'll put you in the cell and make it look like the gate's locked. Come back out when you're feeling better. But don't think this is over, you'll be pulling a double shift tomorrow night and there'll be drinking for a week after that."

Alistair couldn't believe his luck as he shambled along behind the man, eventually reaching an empty cell. There was an almighty racket further down the hall as the officer pushed Alistair in and shut the gate behind him but didn't actually lock it. He'd placed him a fair number of cells from the next occupied unit but even so, Alistair could hear the banging on the bars and wails of mad men as he thanked his lucky stars. Retrieving the radio from under the yellow garment he spoke into it once more.

"Seems some luck's finally come my way, they thought I was drunk and they put me in the dungeon to sleep it off, even left the cell gate unlocked."

He heard laughter in his ear, "At least something has gone well tonight." There was a pause and then, "Are you quite sure this thing works? I'm looking at Aris now. Generally, someone locked in a dungeon doesn't walk out of their cell and go for a quaint stroll."

"Ah, what do you mean?" said Alistair as he heard a sickening cracking sound that he knew could only be that of breaking bone followed by a scream.

"Ewwww...Oh dear, it seems he just had a disagreement with a fellow inmate and is now entering another cell. Alistair, you've got to get moving, he's escaping! I think there is some sort of hidden passageway behind the cell he just entered. He is on your level, further down the corridor! Quick! Before he gets away!"

Alistair pulled the gate open, throwing off the helm as he did so he could see more clearly in the low light. He hastily fastened the radio to his belt, connecting an earpiece to free up his hands. The screaming sound ended abruptly as he drew the pistol he had tucked under the uniform and set off as fast as he could, deeper into the dungeon. As he neared the source of the scream he slowed, moving more cautiously, pistol outstretched in front of him, his eyes staring across the top of the barrel. Some garbled static came through the radio which he requested Adele repeat, but to no avail, the signal not strong enough to penetrate this far into the dungeon. The source of the screaming came into view. A filthy prisoner was slumped in the corner, his arm bent at a horrible angle at the elbow, his head seemingly hanging unnaturally to the side also. The man standing next to him, presumably responsible, swivelled and upon spotting the gun immediately raised his hands. Even in the dim light Alistair could make out the face of the man he'd been chasing, the man who'd betrayed and left him for dead. Alistair's finger squeezed ever so slightly on the trigger as he almost allowed himself to execute Aris then and there. Head won over heart moments before his finger could initiate the chain reaction that would have resulted in Aris's demise, his finger slowly relaxing.

"Hello Aris."

Whatever Aris said in reply was drowned out by a burst of loud radio static as an instant later Alistair felt something connect with his head followed by the room fading to black.

CHAPTER 46 - ARIS

The frequency of the footsteps helped Aris discern there was only one potential pursuer. He motioned with a nod of his head for Dagath to hide by the opposite cell wall. Dagath disappeared into the dark corner as a chain mail clad Ebodan soldier came running down the hall, slowing to a cautious walk about three yards from the cell. Dagath noted the guard didn't have his sword drawn but instead was holding a strange small piece of 'L' shaped metal in front of him. Aris saw it too, immediately throwing his hands into the air in surrender.

The guard spoke as he rounded the corner "Hello Aris," he said in a sarcastically jolly voice.

Not waiting for a reply, Dagath positioned himself directly behind the soldier. Leaning back as far as he could, Dagath then swung his upper body forward, head butting the yellow intruder with all his might.

"What did he think he was going to do with this silly thing," said Dagath as he crouched to grab the pistol that had fallen but a yard from the now unconscious guard.

Aris quickly reached down and snatched it off the ground before Dagath could reach it.

"This, my foolish companion, is a more powerful weapon than any sword in the kingdom."

"If I didn't know you better I'd say you've lost the plot, my sword'll best that puny thing any day. And who's this one then? Friend of yours? He seemed to know you."

"Never seen him before. Come on, time to leave."

The moment Aris and Dagath turned the keys in unison the rear wall of the cell swung backwards as if it were on hinges. The secret door revealed a passageway comprised of a not dissimilar architecture to that of the dungeon. It was too dark to tell how far it stretched but there was some dim, unknown source of light, as they could see a few yards in front of them. Aris ordered the still restrained Dagath to bring the man he had knocked unconscious with them.

"So what's the plan now we've escaped?" said Dagath, dropping the man in the darkness as Aris closed the secret passage behind them. "Your city has been sacked and my army destroyed. I hardly think we'll be launching a counter attack any time soon."

"Let me assure you, there are far bigger problems afoot than Ludwig taking Barathax and the decimation of your merry band of killers. I recently received word that the Val Thane have once again been released into this world. I might have been able to prepare if you and your cronies hadn't decided it a good time to attack."

Dagath laughed, "I thought you might have lost it when you said you'd take that rock in your hand over a sword, but now you're telling me ancient monsters from hell are spewing into the land of the living. The Val Thane? Ludwig didn't per chance slip you any goodbye flagons did he, last drinks and all that?"

Aris pointed the pistol in the air and fired. There was a flash and the sound of the bullet hitting the roof followed by that of Dagath falling over in shock.

"You may have been gifted with superhuman strength Dagath, but intelligence was surely not part of the package. Look, someone has reopened the Val Thane gateway. This is most certainly not the time for petty squabbles. And pick him back up, he's coming with us."

"Why, I thought you said you didn't know him."

Aris fired into the air once more, "Just do it!" he yelled as he began to make his way down the tunnel.

CHAPTER 47 - ALISTAIR

The body being dragged through the dirt suddenly stirred. Alistair awoke to a blinding headache. He observed what little he could of the world around him through groggy eyes. Realising his hands were tied, it all came flooding back. He put his head forward to see who it was dragging him along the ground. He observed the back of what he could just make out to be an extremely large man in the lack of light. Alistair knew he was a big fellow judging by the breadth of the hair covered forearm attached to the hand that was pulling him through what seemed to be a tunnel. He didn't think whoever was towing him had noticed he'd come to and so decided to keep it that way.

"So the bogmaul was a nice touch," said Aris. "I didn't know you Trescots had actually captured one, let alone trained it to do your dirty work."

"Ah that," said Dagath. "No sense denying it now I suppose. We managed to tame one years ago but the bloody thing got away. I think it slipped its control ring. I tell you, that thing was a silent killing machine, anyone you wanted dead died while we had it under our control. What about this regicide thing Ludwig seems to have accused you of? I know you're a ruthless bugger when no one's watching, but I never took you for a King Slayer."

"Nice try," said Aris. "I know you're behind the bogmaul that killed Ervoule."

"A bogmaul killing Ervoule? Now I'm even more convinced you've had one too many flagons. Like I said, we haven't had a bogmaul in years, and there's no way they would have assigned another without my knowledge."

"Then why conveniently attack when you knew we'd have trouble gaining support from Eboda?"

"Are you having a laugh Aris? Trescot and Barathax were never best of friends but assassinating Prince Cartian? Well, that made some folk a little angry. Me personally, I hated the arrogant fucker, but the rest of Trescot didn't see it that way."

"Prince Cartian is dead?" Aris replied.

"Unless he's got a twin I don't know about, then yes."

Not wanting to give anything away, Aris decided it prudent not to add any more till he'd had time to process these revelations.

After about five minutes of no noise other than the sound of chain mail being dragged through dirt, Aris paused for a moment and shook his head.

"It just doesn't make sense," he said more to himself than to Dagath. "The Val Thane's release and Alistair's attempted capture at the Baron's residence together point to a single definite motive - the substance. But who? Only two others knew of its existence and both of them are long since deceased. And what of the other events? The Baron's death - maybe it was necessary for Alistair but was it also a low probability bonus if it sowed some discord between Eboda and Barathax? Then a bogmaul killing Ervoule, leading us to blame Trescot while still being improbable enough to any who didn't witness it to make it seem we engineered the man's fate. Trescot's Prince Cartian being assassinated, provoking an inevitable invasion that conveniently coincided with their acquisition of a weapon strong enough to challenge Castle Brin's walls. And finally, some unknown entity, possessing more knowledge of the situation than they should, guiding Ludwig to Mortimer. The entity familiar enough with the man's emotionless ambition to know he wouldn't baulk at the opportunity to overthrow both Kingdoms irrespective of his opinion on the circumstances of Ervoule's death. Someone is seemingly quite intent on the major Kingdoms crushing each other, but to what end? A united realm means more time to harvest the substance and a possible victory, so why start a war? But then maybe there is more than one player in this game most dire. Two conflicting interests? But who would doom an entire civilisation simply to spite another's intention? Well I suppose there is one man, but he drew his last breath so long ago..."

"Are you talking to me or is there someone else here that I should know about?" replied Dagath as Aris continued talking to himself.

"It didn't go quite to plan with Alistair did it. He escaped. But maybe he was supposed to... No, that does not make sense either, else he would not be here now. Unless he escaped again?"

Aris turned back to Dagath. Having escaped the prison, he'd served his purpose. Aris reached for the pistol, a wave of emotion washing over him in anticipation of the impending justice. His hand stopped a moment as his fingers touched the cold steel. A better use and more fitting end for the prehistoric man had just crossed his mind. He'd need to subdue his lust for vengeance a little longer.

"There is a safe house about five miles from here. We will make camp there and devise a plan to stop these madmen before things get any more out of hand," said Aris.

"Whatever you say you crazy bastard. Does this safe house of yours have any food? I'm starving."

CHAPTER 48 - ALISTAIR

Alistair became aware of the rays of light streaming into the tunnel.

"Ah, a beautiful morning to not be rotting in a Barathax dungeon," said Dagath smugly, letting go of Alistair for a second to stretch his arms.

A figure in a cloak with a pack strapped across their back appeared in front of Aris a moment before he felt his whole body stiffen, unable to move a limb. Alistair sprang to his feet as quickly as was possible in the chain armour, looping his tied hands around Dagath's neck, pulling downwards with all his weight, bending his knee so it stuck into the small of the big man's back. Dagath tried to fight it, but the position Alistair had him in and the fact his hands were tied, meant he couldn't do much of anything save grab at the stained rope that was slowly choking him. Alistair manoeuvred himself and Dagath over to the rather uncomfortable looking Aris. When they were side by side he released Dagath, simultaneously kicking him in the back, sending him sprawling forward. Alistair turned and grabbed the pistol from Aris's belt. Dagath, not noticing Alistair had grabbed the pistol, spun about in a rage and immediately charged in Alistair's direction. The now familiar gunshot sound was followed by a sudden, sharp pain in Dagath's leg as it failed to take his weight, causing him to fall forward into the dirt at Alistair's feet. Clutching at his leg, he felt the warm blood flowing from the gunshot wound.

"Stop! Stop!" yelled Aris. "We surrender."

"I should shoot you in the head right now," said Alistair through gritted teeth as he walked backwards towards Adele, keeping his eyes on the duo at all times. "Why Aris? Why did you betray me?"

"I know you probably won't believe me, but I truly had no knowledge of the Baron's murder or the trap that had been set. I owe you an explanation, that is certain, but right now, the most important prisoner Ludwig will ever preside over has just escaped. No expense, be it time or gold will be spared in my recapture. If we stay here we are all in danger. There is a safe house not far away, escort us there and I will tell you everything."

"Safe house you say," replied Adele. "More likely trap! I think you will just tell us everything you know here and now and depending on what you say, your neck and limbs may remain attached to your torso."

There was a noise on the road ahead as a horse drawn carriage passed carrying farm goods, manned by an old man with a white beard. Alistair quickly put the gun to his side and waved, putting on his best 'nothing to see here' face. Once the farmer had passed out of earshot, Aris spoke.

"Think it through, if I wanted to kill you I would have done so while you were unconscious."

Alistair sighed, "Try anything tricky and I won't hesitate," he said pointing the gun at Aris's head.

Aris looked to Dagath, "He's not going to be too sprightly now you've put a bullet in him."

"Barely grazed the side of his leg, and a big leg at that. I'm sure he'll be OK."

Dagath had ripped off a piece of his clothing and wrapped it around the wound. Just as Alistair had said, he'd only just hit the side of his leg and so hadn't done any permanent damage.

"He'd best behave himself though, else the next one's in his head."

"Suits me," said Aris.

Dagath, grunting as he struggled to his feet, hobbled over next to Aris. Adele fell in beside Alistair behind the odd duo.

"Lead the way," said Alistair walking a few paces directly behind Aris, keeping the gun trained on his back at all times.

Adele whispered in his ear, "Are you sure we should do this? From what I've heard, Aris is no fool and not exactly the most trustworthy character either."

Alistair whispered back, "I understand your hesitation but Aris is right, if we stay here, Ludwig will find us before we get the information Moran was alluding to. Besides, he's the only chance I've got of clearing my name. That said, I suppose he might not be that much use now Barathax is in the hands of commander Steiner. Although he also knows where the gateway is which I need to get home.

"Oh, so you're planning on leaving are you? Things get tough and Alistair runs off home. Here I was, beginning to think you were going to help us."

"I didn't think you needed my help, you seem to be quite capable of handling yourself."

"What if I don't want to handle myself? What if I wanted someone else to handle me?" she said with a cheeky smile, knocking Alistair off guard for a moment.

He turned his head towards her wondering if he heard correctly when Aris called out "it's just here," pointing to an old overgrown ruin. Bits and pieces of stone and sections of large rock were strewn everywhere in what seemed man made shapes. Alistair could only imagine what the structures had looked like when they were complete, weather beaten debris all that remained. He and Adele followed Dagath and Aris cautiously through the ruins till they came to a large rectangular stone block about sixty yards across and again as high. It was too large to get any idea of how deep it was from the front. Aris made a gesture in front of the wall which was proceeded by the sound of stone grinding on stone and what was probably a pulley somewhere as a thin slab receded and slid to one side. They stepped inside the block to discover that it was hollow and missing a roof. What seemed a solid structure from outside was actually just four stone walls in a rectangular formation that bevelled at the top to give the illusion of solidarity from the ground.

"This is a safe house?" inquired Adele, seemingly unimpressed. "It doesn't even have a roof. A more apt description would be four walls in the middle of nowhere."

"I never said it was going to be a palace," replied Aris, as he walked back over to the door, making a similar gesture to the one he enacted on entry, the stone slab sliding back into place behind them. "No one else knows how to activate that door, we're in the middle of nowhere, and unless someone can fly, we won't be discovered. He moved to the back left corner of the compound and dusted off what turned out to be a large wooden trap door.

"There's supplies and weapons in here. Anyway, now that we're safe, I suppose I've got some explaining to do. I'll fetch some food and drink from the cellar and then I'll tell you everything you need to know."

Alistair followed him down into the cellar he'd just revealed. Aris retrieved some canned food, water and wine and returned to the surface with Alistair without issue. Making a second trip, this time he emerged with some large bags slung over his shoulders.

"Tents," he said. "We might as well make camp here tonight, and as Adele so elegantly reminded me, the safe house does in fact come with open air views."

After they'd eaten and set up camp for the night, the four of them gathered around the fire.

"Get comfortable. This is going to be a long story," Aris said as he began his tale.

CHAPTER 49 - ARIS

"A long time ago I knew a man named Benoit Dejant. Well, I knew him as Captain Dejant. He was the commander of the royal guard when I was just a young knight. The royal guard were sworn to protect the King of the time. Hand-picked by his majesty himself, the very best Barathax had to offer. I can still remember the day I was given the honour of joining, it was the proudest day of my life. Days like those would be few and far between in the years to come. There were legends about Dejant, most of them relating to his unmatched skill with a blade. They said he could cut down ten men in the time it took an average man to complete a single strike. Legends are usually just that, but let me tell you, Dejant lived up to his and then some. Picture the fastest swordsman you've seen and then try and imagine him ten-fold faster. So quick were his movements that it looked unnatural, like he was a movie in fast forward while everything else was playing at normal speed."

"A movie hey, you're not really from Barathax then are you?" interjected Alistair.

"I am," replied Aris, "but I'll get to that."

"Excuse me," interjected Adele, "but what is this 'movie' you speak of?"

"Something from Alistair's world. Just know he was faster than naturally possible," replied Aris. "Dejant's exploits eventually led him to become the most respected man in Barathax, more so than even the King. The King of the time was a devious, spiteful, cruel and jealous man, the likes of which our land has been fortunate enough to avoid in recent times. Bastion may well be a useless drunk, but he is still far preferable to King Mordren. Mordren grew envious of the respect common folk and lord alike held for Dejant, which was only further frustrated by the clandestine disdain they showed their true ruler. So the King, in a fit of jealousy, plotted not only Dejant's demise, but that of the entire nation.

Mordren's long line, stretching back centuries, had held the secret of a substance that granted one thousand extra years of life. It was created by an ancient machine the workings of which have been of great interest to some of your kin on Earth for some time Alistair. The problem was, one could not start the machine without also opening the Vale Thane gateway housed in the Alman pyramid. For those of you who do not know the legend of the Val Thane, it is thought that they are the minions of hell itself and that the Alman temple is the gateway between our two realms, much like the gateway between here and Earth. Now I don't know if the pyramid is actually the gateway to hell, but judging by the things that come through when it is opened, it's certainly a fitting description.

Mordren knew of the machine but little of its location, his predecessors believing the price paid for an extra thousand years too great to risk its allure to the sound character of generations to come. To this day I have no knowledge of how he ascertained the scroll's location, the fateful piece of transcribed knowledge that detailed the machine's location kept by another Kingdom's royal family throughout the generations. That Kingdom was Trescot."

"So wait," Alistair said, "the machine and the Val Thane gateway are in two different locations?"

"I'm afraid so. Whoever invented the machine possessed a cruel sense of irony, as to activate it, one must first open the Val Thane Gateway, a certain death to the man seeking a longer life.

Once he had discovered the scroll's location, Mordren ordered the assassination of Trescot's then ruler, King Lector, under the guise of Trescot plotting an invasion. He charged Dejant and three others with the retrieval of a certain scroll that would then prove Trescot's intention to the other Kingdoms. I went by a different name back then, but alongside Benoit Dejant, Dannick Veltross and Jean Pierre we carried out the assassination and retrieved the scroll we naively thought would prove Trescot's guilt."

Dagath interjected, "I spoke in jest previously but now I really do wonder, did you take a knock to the head in that battle? King Lector sat the throne over a thousand years ago and you're trying to make out you were there?"

"Just hear me out, it will all make sense in the end," replied Aris.

"Upon receipt of the scroll, Mordren covertly poisoned Dejant's wife Eden. He knew Dejant loved her fiercely, I'd even go so far as to say she was Dejant's reason for being at the time. A part of that man died each day as he watched her grow ever more frail. As her condition continued to worsen, Mordren cast the bait. He informed Dejant of a substance that could save her. Conniving as he was, he failed to mention that activating the machine would also all but ensure the doom of those who did and put in jeopardy the lives of countless more. He knew Dejant would not have opened the gateway if he knew it meant potential genocide, even though it would have quite literally killed him to pass up the opportunity to save his wife. Mordren planned to travel to the location of the machine set out in the scroll and wait for Dejant to activate it. Dejant would then be killed by the abominations and the King would gain his thousand years of life."

"What good is an extra thousand years of life if you're about to be hunted down and slaughtered by the demons of hell?" asked Alistair.

"Well," said Aris, "the gateway you came through Alistair, was once open freely and was well known. People could pass between this world and Earth at will. This, I suspect, is the origin of the medieval stories of magic and the like told in your realm. King Mordren was as evil as he was cunning. He planned to immediately flee through the Earth gateway, notifying them of the impending terror on the other side released by Dejant and urging them to shut it down for good. He would live the next thousand years in luxury, content in his vanity, knowing he had outsmarted the mighty Dejant and punished the people of Barathax for their insolence.

So Dejant, myself, Dannick and Jean set out once more, thinking we were going to activate a machine that would save Dejant's wife. Little did we know we were marching to our death and the death all of those we held dear."

"Something didn't quite go as predicted?" said Alistair, noting that Aris was not in fact dead.

"Indeed," replied Aris. "The King's plan didn't quite pan out as expected. Against all the odds, Dejant, myself, Jean and Dannick overpowered the things that came out of the temple that day and escaped. My god it was terrifying. Things that would make my worst nightmares up until that point seem pleasant in comparison. It still sends a chill down my spine whenever I hear someone click their tongue, that sound the ape like demons would make. There were so many of them. We knew Dejant was good, but that night he fought like something else knowing Eden's life was at stake. After an epic battle, we made our escape. Dejant had fought so hard he collapsed from exhaustion as we got within one hundred yards of the castle, Dannick having to carry him the rest of the way."

"Are you attempting to convey that yourself and three others were the cause of the legendary plague that almost decimated all life so long ago?" replied Adele.

"That is correct. We made it back to the King's hall as Dejant slipped from Dannick's shoulders, a second wind empowering him, he swayed upon his feet, half yelling at Mordren, 'Where is she!?'

I still remember Mordren's vile smirk as 20 men with crossbows stepped out of the shadows. 'Why, she's just here,' he said as he grabbed a pale Eden from behind the curtain and slit her throat in front of Dejant. Dejant's face became a mix of helplessness and rage, conveying an intention his body was too exhausted to enact, the man not even capable of lifting his sword. Mordren then had us thrown in the dungeon, while he decided how to proceed. He was an evil man, but he was also fastidiously cautious, always planning, never acting on impulse alone. In many respects, he was probably the polar opposite of the man whose wife he had murdered but a moment ago. We weren't to know until much later, and in this instance it is probably the reason I stand before you today, but one of our companions was just as devious, if not more so than Mordren himself.

Jean Pierre had been appointed to the Royal Guard mere weeks before Lector's assassination and as such, I knew little of his character. Jean Pierre, the only man I have ever known to be as morally void as Mordren, was one step ahead of everyone, the King included. Not only did he somehow have prior knowledge of the majority of the King's planned deception, he'd also been collaborating with a company on Earth - James Errol and Co.

James Errol and Co. were a finance and banking company that had existed in one form or another for hundreds of years, the control of which being passed down from generation to generation. Nepotism over meritocracy is usually a recipe for disaster when selecting a board and senior executives, however, they had so much power and influence that the company essentially ran itself, the senior officials more akin to silent partners than operators.

A small mining group in Barathax stumbled onto the now famous and very depleted 'Yellow Fields' gold deposit, one of the richest and most easily accessible concentrations of gold either world had discovered at the time. The head of the small group, Yern Tilber, was good friends with the Errol family and was hence able to secure finance to begin mining the region without any real scrutiny from James Errol and Co. An Errol family member granted the loan at an incredibly low interest rate without bothering to research the prospect, the loan being more friendly gesture than business transaction. It was an insignificant amount of money for James Errol and Co. and as such they cared naught as to whether or not they saw a return on their investment. Little did they realise, they had just given Yern Tilber the keys to a fortune that rivalled their own.

As Yern proceeded to mine the area, word of his wealth began to spread, eventually reaching the Errol family. Upon the realisation they had just given a poor friend the keys to a fortune out of pity and ignorance, the greed instinct that had been pivotal in their acquisition of such great wealth over the years reared its ugly head once more. James Errol and Co. created a new company and through this new company ordered as much gold as Yern could supply. Yern, overwhelmed by the sudden enormous order, neglected all other customers and began selling exclusively to the new company who unbeknownst to him was controlled by James Errol and Co. Yern wasn't very intellectually inclined. He was a simple man who had merely become the recipient of an incredible stroke of luck. To this end, it was a trivial task for James Errol and Co. to convince the man he should borrow a great sum so that he could excavate the precious metal faster.

All James Errol needed to do now was shut down the gateway between the two worlds for long enough that Yern would be without enough cash flow to meet a repayment. Upon the gateway's reactivation, James Errol and Co. would exercise a right detailed in the fine print of their loan agreement to repossess all assets against which the loan was secured if a payment were missed. James Errol and Co. would then own the rights to the enormous gold deposit.

The trickiest part of the scheme was shutting down the gateway between the two worlds. James Errol and Co. possessed power and influence in abundance, but that was not going to be enough if they were to cut off the only link between two worlds that had been frequented for centuries. So, they bribed Jean Pierre, a man whose moral compass was stuck pointing south, to sow discord between the Kingdoms now known as Trescot and Barathax. James Errol and Co. were counting on the war that would follow to destabilise the region enough to temporarily justify a travel embargo between the two worlds. It was years later that I discovered Jean had intentionally dropped a small knife bearing the seal of the Barathax Royal Guard the night of the assassination. For a mere 100 gold pieces, he was willing to start a war that would result in thousands of lost lives. In a karmic twist of fate, James Errol and Co. would never see their money again, the Val Thane threat resulting in Earth destroying the gateway on their end rather than simply temporarily disabling it.

So, there we were, locked in the dungeon, bemoaning the fact Mordren had escaped with his prize, leaving this realm to the horrors we had encountered earlier, when Jean Pierre produced a scroll from under his cloak with a sly grin. 'I don't think his majesty is going to be feeling too well tomorrow,' he said. 'Essence of night shade certainly isn't something I'd recommend washing your breakfast down with. A coup de grace more fitting there could not be.'

The scroll he had handed Mordren after the assassination did not lead to the elixir of life, but instead to a carefully placed vial of poison that Jean, or whoever he was working with, had placed in a remote cave.

Too consumed by the elation of karmic justice to question his methods further, we quietly revelled in the knowledge King Mordren's murderous crimes would not go unpunished.

Upon reading the information contained in the true scroll, we ascertained that the key to closing the Val Thane gateway was located alongside the substance. Escaping approximately a week later, we retrieved the substance and the Val Thane gateway key along with directions to a second gateway to Earth - one only a handful of people on either side know of to this day. We then proceeded back to the Alman temple where we closed the gateway just in time, the realm's defences having reached the breaking point.

Jean Pierre wanted to take the substance but Dejant wouldn't allow it. He thought it hardly seemed fit that the men responsible for unleashing this plague into the world be given the gift of a supernaturally long life. We were young and foolish back then and one thousand years sounded far too great an opportunity to let slip. Myself, Dannick and Jean secretly agreed that since the damage had already been done, we might as well reap the benefit now. We still had the problem of the ever stubborn and now mentally unstable Dejant however. Each day after the loss of his wife it seemed he would fall further and further into madness and none of us was game to take it against his will. The devious solution to which I must say I am not proud of, was provided by Jean Pierre.

Contacting a powerful yet very poor mage he knew in the city, he paid the struggling man to cast a control spell on Dejant. Dejant was now unknowingly subject to our will as we altered his memory to the point that he believed he was our bodyguard. In some ways, we thought it was for the best really. We released him from the pain of the loss of his wife, not to mention the fact that there was no way to know he wouldn't suffer a breakdown during a battle in the future. Over the years, we periodically had his memories altered to suit the changing situation.

The years after the Val Thane's defeat were a golden age for myself and Dejant and could have also been for the other two if they had not been so selfish. Can you imagine how much power and wealth one can attain in one thousand years when everyone else is lucky to get ninety? I'll be the first to admit I personally benefited immensely, however, I have also made it my duty to use the extra years to cement peace and prosperity throughout Barathax and the realm as best I could. Jean was of a different mindset. One thousand years for him was a chance to rule both this world and Earth. Dannick was competent but easily persuaded and as such experienced a similar fate to his devious companion.

Ulric Vergan and his kin are the only other beings I know of who enjoy such a long life. A mere 4 years after consuming the substance, Jean grew jealous of his longevity. As fate would have it, a fissure had occurred between the mages under Ulric's stewardship, two sets of differing ideologies eventually catalysing a rebellion. Jean and Dannick assisted the rebels in an attempted power grab that went horribly wrong, Ulric crushing it before it really even began, killing Dannick and Jean in the process.

I gained so much influence throughout the middle ages, the industrial revolution, the renaissance and the time that has passed less eventfully here, that for the last hundred years I have basically pulled the strings of every major ruler, be it this world or Earth. Pre-modern fire arms, having the best swordsman either world has ever known under my control also helped a great deal. This all may sound rather uncaring, but I will never forget the sacrifice that was made by the people of these lands. I've spent my very generous gift of time trying my utmost to ensure the inhabitants of this world have the very best lives possible and that what we did so long ago would never be repeated. Still, I haven't slept a guilt free night for near ten centuries now, knowing so many bore the heavy cost of my near immortality. Now it seems I have even failed in that small piece of recompense."

"That's got to be the biggest load of bollocks I've ever heard," replied Dagath. "Don't get me wrong, I know you're no spring chicken, but one thousand years? Come on!"

"I care not what you think Dagath. I would have thought you had figured that out by now," Aris said staring directly at his crooked nose.

"A fascinating story Aris," said Alistair. "I'm with our overgrown companion on this one though. It sounds like you've just made up some mumbo jumbo and concocted it into a bed time tale. What I can't understand is why you'd tell it. I can't believe you'd actually think I'd buy it, and even if I did, I don't see how it helps your predicament?"

"When I get to the end, I promise you on my life, I will prove its validity," replied Aris unfazed.

"This year will be the 999th after taking the substance. Living ten life times is a gift beyond the common man's perceivable imagination, however, if you asked me if I'd do it again I'd say no, the price paid was too dear. The problem is, I believe someone does not currently share my opinion. For the life of me, I cannot discern who though. Four people other than myself have known the full story behind the Val Thane gate. One of them has no memory of his former self, two others are deceased and the fourth is Ulric Vergan, who has no reason to see it opened. In time, the party behind this and the events that have befallen the realm over the past few months will no doubt make themselves known. Whoever they are, the priority now is to close the Val Thane gateway before this world is overrun.

Oh and Alistair, there is one other thing. Your real name is Benoit Dejant."

CHAPTER 50 - ARIS

"That's crazy talk Aris, I can clearly remember coming here through the gateway after my SAS selection."

"We made that up. Alistair, do you have recurring dreams that resemble anything I just spoke with you about. Maybe there's demons involved, maybe a beautiful woman, Eden perhaps, maybe a King you despise with all your will but don't know why, maybe I've even featured in one of them."

"That could be anything," Alistair replied. "I've had it with you and your silly games Aris, I should have killed you the moment I saw you."

"Wait! I was not lying when I said I'd prove it. If you'll just give me five minutes all will become clear. Follow me, if you will."

"No bright ideas, either of you," Alistair said as he raised his gun and escorted Dagath and Aris to the storage pit. After sorting through some of the neatly stacked equipment, Aris retrieved what seemed to be two wooden practice swords.

"You seriously expect me to partake in a sparring session with you Aris? What is this? Some kind of pretence at honour? I'm good with a rifle, but you'd have to be mad to think I hadn't heard the stories of your exploits with a blade."

Aris laughed, "Believe me Alistair, there is a reason I chose wooden swords and it is definitely not your safety I'm worried about."

"No, you seem to have a history of not worrying about other

people's safety."

"Look, if I were to attempt some form of deception I am more than confident your sorceress friend would make certain it did not end well for me. Just pick it up and all will become clear," he said, throwing one of the wooden practice swords on the ground at Alistair's feet.

"Go on Alistair," said Adele. "If he attempts any slight-of-hand he'll incur the most painful death you could imagine and then some."

"This is silly," said Alistair, "you want me to hold a sword to prove your fanciful tales?"

"Just humour me this once. If you're still not convinced, well, you can do what you will with me afterward."

Alistair reluctantly picked up the wooden sword. He grabbed its hilt, his hands squeezing in slightly against it to increase grip strength, a little taken aback by an odd sensation of familiarity but not entirely convinced, his inner sceptic still whispering notions of the subtle power of suggestion. Alistair hadn't said anything but Aris had already detected the surprised look.

"Now isn't that strange, someone who has supposedly never handled a sword knows just how to grip it. Oh dear," Aris sighed raising his own practice sword, "I know I'm going to regret this part."

Aris's look suddenly became one of pain. His face went from its usual pale white to a now bright red as every muscle in his body seemed to tense.

"Calm down," he choked out. "For me to fully prove this to you he is going to have to duel me."

"Adele, this is going to sound strange, but I think it's ok," Alistair replied, feeling a sudden unexpected surge of confidence seemingly deriving from within the sword itself.

"Are you sure?" Adele said, tightening her grip over Aris, causing the already red faced man to cough and splutter as his cheeks started to swell.

"Yes, I... I... can't explain it but something does feel right... you can let him go."

Aris keeled forwards onto the ground, wheezing and coughing as Adele released him from her grip.

"Oh that's no fun," said Dagath with a frown, "I thought I was going to see some Aris splatter."

Alistair instinctively held his sword out in front of him, its tip pointed at Aris's neck as the man rose back to his feet. "How do I know to do this?" He thought as his feet automatically moved into a stance that would be optimal for sudden acceleration.

"Be careful Alistair, I don't trust him. Remember I'm here if you need me," came Adele's voice.

Aris slowly closed the distance, his sword in a similar position to his opponent's. Alistair was now noticing random, seemingly insignificant things about how his opponent moved, how tight his grip was etc. He knew Aris was no novice with a blade. He had not only heard tales of Aris's skill, but had also, unbeknownst to Aris, seen him bring down many a man in a certain Barathax tournament. Standing here now however, his concentration razor focused on the man in front of him, his brain was registering lots of very subtle weaknesses. He also deduced from Aris's breathing and facial expression that Aris was nervous, maybe even genuinely scared. And then it happened, time slowed as Aris lunged towards him. Alistair's feet and legs instinctively moved his body backwards and to the side just enough that Aris missed, but not so far as to render him unable to capitalise on the evasion and counter. The movement resulted in Alistair ending up at a 45 degree angle to Aris's side, leaving him open to any kind of counter Alistair saw fit. What seemed like a minute to Alistair, Adele and Dagath observed in less than a second. It was just as Aris had said, the speed he moved at didn't look real. It wasn't natural, almost as if he didn't move at all, Alistair seemingly appearing to the side of Aris as he attacked. Alistair's sword cut through the air with incredible speed, coming to an abrupt stop a hair's width from the base of Aris's skull where his head joined his neck. Aris froze, his wooden practice sword falling to the ground.

"Well that was unexpected," said Alistair, as Aris threw his hands up in surrender.

CHAPTER 51 - ARIS

Adele and Dagath stood speechless as the dust began to settle where Aris's sword had hit the ground.

"You can't be serious!" said Dagath as Aris proceeded to turn, his hands still in the air. "At least give him a bit of a smack, that's twice now damn it."

Ignoring Dagath's frustration, Alistair spoke.

"Ok, assuming what you've said is true, and assuming you didn't set me up in regards to the Baron's death, who did, and more importantly, why?"

"I've been trying to figure that out for quite some time," Aris replied lowering his hands. "Well I think I know the why. There is an obstacle during the final stages of acquiring the substance that only a man of your talents can overcome. The 'who' however, remains a mystery. Whoever it was obviously wanted you in the Silent Twins. I sent multiple ships to retrieve you upon hearing of this, but it seems you had other ideas. The men tell me you slew a Cereon Hound then destroyed their transport in an almighty conflagration."

"Those men were sent by you?"

"Indeed they were."

"You had nothing to do with Moran Cheldore however?"

"No, what does that disgraced man have to do with anything?"

"He was the one who captured me after I unknowingly destroyed your ship and escaped Raven's Contact," replied Alistair. "When Adele and I were separated as The Val Thane overran

Bledith Tower he instructed us to seek you out. Said you would know what to do about the Val Thane."

"Interesting," replied Aris rubbing a hand on his chin. "I did hear a rumour he'd visited the Silent Twins not long after your incarceration. This further extends the list of possible suspects though, and I'm still not sure if the same party who is creating the havoc between the Kingdoms is the same party that has released the Val Thane."

"Yes we noticed the Yellow banners flying above Castle Brin," said Adele. "What have you been up to Aris?"

"Where do I begin?" replied Aris. "A bogmaul conveniently killed King Ervoule right around the time Trescot decided to attack, rendering our plan of a united Ebodan Barathax force almost impossible. Dagath claims to have had no prior knowledge of the assassination plan even though the only known domestication of one of those foul creatures was at the hands of Trescot. We attempted to put Ervoule's death on Trescot so that Eboda would assist us in remedying the imminent threat posed by the Trescot army marching on our borders. But alas, it seemed that once again, some unknown force conspired against us. Eboda somehow knew to bribe our lead alchemist, Mortimer Cornish, thereafter blaming us for Ervoule's death. I was initially convinced the bogmaul attack was of Trescot origin. However, it is only recently that Dagath has informed me that the catalyst for the invasion was the assassination of their Prince Cartian, supposedly at our hands. I can wholeheartedly claim Barathax had no part in Cartian's demise. Someone, it would seem, has quite eloquently turned the three nations against one another.

We fought Trescot, but with some otherworldly assistance, our walls were breached, rendering our victory an impossibility against the overwhelming numbers. As all was thought lost, lo and behold, what do we see on the horizon but yellow banners. Erroneously believing we were saved, we watched on as Trescot's forces were cut down or captured. Believing Eboda to be our saviour, we allowed them within our now broken walls, at which point we were surrounded and I was taken prisoner. Ludwig Steiner, representing Eboda, took the castle and sentenced Dagath and I to death. That is how I ended up in the dungeon. My only hypothesis is that there is someone whose interests conflict with the party who wishes to obtain the substance. They may have therefore simultaneously weakened two of the three largest Kingdoms in the land, so that when the Val Thane threat is recognised there should be much less chance of defeating them, making acquiring the substance a much more unlikely outcome."

"So you are essentially saying someone is committing this world to extinction merely to spite another party? replied Adele. "Who would be mad enough to do such a thing? I think this most unlikely."

"As unlikely as it sounds," replied Aris, "it is the only logical explanation I can think of, unless the events are some form of coincidence, which I believe even less likely. Regardless of who is responsible, we need to shut down the Val Thane portal and fast, we can figure the rest out later. I suggest we leave at first light."

Adele and Alistair walked back to their respective tents. Suddenly out of nowhere, the ropes holding Adele's tent in place all snapped at once causing it to collapse on itself. She then proceeded to perform what Alistair would describe as possibly the poorest attempt he'd seen at a surprised reaction.

"How odd," she commented, her expression one of feigned ignorance. "Oh no, I'll have to sleep out in the open and it is getting oh so cold."

"You can have mine," replied Alistair. "I'll just curl up next to the embers."

"Oh... how kind of you," replied Adele, a disappointed look on her face.

Alistair had been trying not to smile but was unable to feign ignorance any longer. Stepping forwards he embraced her, their lips meeting in the dying firelight.

CHAPTER 52 - ROBERTO

Doctor Roberto Enzo paced back and forth excitedly in his white lab coat staring directly at the ground but not really noticing it. The results of the discovery were amazing! If one could control the function of a brain through wireless signals, well, the power would be absolute. "Incredible!" he thought for but a moment, the sudden rush of enthusiasm being curbed by the afterthought of his other test subjects. It seemed the technology he had invented would only work on an individual brain by brain case. If only he could develop an intelligent algorithm to identify brain composition differences and modify "the leash" as he called its code. He was abruptly transported back into the here and now as a voice came over the intercom.

"They tell me you have good news doctor."

Roberto, annoyed at the sudden interruption, looked up at the camera in the corner of the lab through his thick glasses.

"Indeed," he replied, his gaze moving back to the hideous snake like head floating in a large containment tube.

It was the size of a small truck. When they'd first brought it in he'd been overcome with a flurry of questions, his scientific scepticism going into overdrive. They had a hard time convincing the hunched genius that something like this could be real. Now it was to him a piece of furniture in the sterile lab environment.

"A demonstration yes?" said Dr. Roberto as his dark dress shoes squeaked across the pristine metal floor on the way back to his bench.

Opening a laptop, he directed the camera's focus to the other biological materials being stored in the containment tubes to the left of the oversized snake head. The camera observed the two other heads floating in the tubes as what could only be described as extremely large wolves.

"When I simulated the theta waves here..."

"Just the results please doctor, the board has full confidence in your method," the intercom interrupted.

Roberto paused for a moment, shaking his bald head, frustrated by the lack of intelligence his superiors possessed.

"Activating the program now," he replied, pressing a button on his laptop.

The two wolf heads were moved aside by a mechanical arm and a cover slid off one of the spotless white walls revealing a tiger and a deer in a cage. Bars separated the two animals into different sections. An opaque glass panel obscured the two animals view of one another. The moment the panel was raised, the tiger, spotting the deer, ran to the dividing bars and began frantically clawing the air.

"Inhibiting aggression and hunger in subject A," said the Doctor.

The tiger slowly calmed down to a point where it didn't even seem to notice the deer. He then pressed another button and the bars between the tiger and the deer lowered. The deer ran frantically and cowered in the corner of its cell, trying to put as much distance between itself and the tiger as possible. The tiger on the other hand, seemingly completely uninterested, lay down and began licking its paws. Next, the doctor lowered a monkey into the cell. It too ran from the tiger, screaming as it went, the sterile white lab becoming more akin to a zoo. Still, the tiger showed no interest.

"I recently discovered that if I modify a certain electrical signal, I can influence thought patterns in the target's mind," said the doctor. "I will now send a signal to the tiger that identifies the monkey as a threat. Its neutral impression of the deer shall remain unchanged."

The doctor clicked another button. The tiger, having been completely docile up until now, stopped cleaning itself, stood up, bared its teeth and snarled viciously in the monkey's direction. It then proceeded to pounce on the monkey, ripping it violently to pieces as the deer passed out from shock in the corner. Having disposed of the monkey, the tiger, who would normally be expected to attack the deer, completely ignored it and finished consuming its fresh kill. Doctor Enzo turned to the camera and smiled as an approximate 30 seconds of silence ensued...

"That will be all for today Roberto."

CHAPTER 53 - ???

The man in the suit turned away from the monitor, metaphorically salivating at the potential of Dr. Enzo's research as the voice continued through the speaker.

"The first step is complete. Now all we need is our good friend Dejant, oh, I mean, what is he calling himself now? Oh yes, Alistair, to infect that god awful Lizard."

The suit swivelled in place on his generously padded leather chair, his knees moving underneath the thick oaken boardroom table until he was facing the monitor once more.

He replied, but not nearly as confidently, "Yes but are we sure the Val Thane brain works as Dr Enzo tells us?"

"Roberto is exceptional at what he does, perhaps the best I've seen in my lifetime, and as you know, that is a very long time. If he tells us that the Lizard's brain acts as a central control for the lesser Val Thane brains then that is assuredly how it is."

"I do hope your faith in Dr Enzo's abilities is justified when the time comes," said the Suit, still not entirely convinced.

"The only other option is to die of old age. If it goes wrong, we wouldn't have had much time left regardless."

"I suppose that makes sense," said the Suit reluctantly, clinking the ice in his glass as he downed another sip of whiskey. "So remind me, why do we have to use the RG32 on this thing? Couldn't we just have him use a normal rifle?"

"Yes, we could have had him use a normal rifle... if we just wanted to annoy the thing. Its armoured scales are too thick to penetrate sufficiently with a conventional gun."

"Ah yes, I seem to remember hearing something to that effect. Tell me, why exactly is it that you didn't just shoot the bloody thing yourself, or at least keep a hold of the RG32?"

"As for shooting it myself, I'm not bloody doing that! There's no telling how long it will take for it to have an effect and I don't think enraging that hungry cretin is conducive to good health in a place where the fastest means of escape is a horse. Some of those things must travel at least as fast as a car. You remember the cat like things from last time, don't you? As for losing the RG32, it's fortunately still in his possession," came the voice through the speaker.

"If you had actually secured the bag before fleeing the castle it wouldn't have been a problem."

"I thought you were supposed to," replied the Suit.

"We can debate this all day, but it doesn't change the facts."

"Agree to disagree and move on, shall we? So, what's our plan for tagging the thing?"

"Through certain channels, Moran has obtained a convenient piece of information that should lead him to reunite with our good friend soon. He's going to tell Alistair that shooting the thing with the RG32 will kill it, simultaneously triggering a chain reaction that results in the disarray of the other, interconnected Val Thane, rendering them an uncoordinated horde of demons rather than a single minded coordinated one."

"And why would he say such a thing?" replied the Suit.

The Suit could just picture the other man's sinister grin as he spoke. "It would seem that Moran has been convinced the rifle is made of the same material as the sword Dejant killed it with last time."

"That would be the same sword that was utterly destroyed and thrown into a volcano directly proceeding the last invasion?" replied the Suit.

"Fortunately for us, Moran was never privy to that, so he'll go along with it. Imagine his surprise when instead of the mortal wound he was expecting that thing shrugs it off like it's been stung by a bee."

"His reaction would be quite interesting to observe," said the Suit. "From a distance of course, a great distance."

They both laughed.

"Once we get our hands on enough of that metal and bring it back to Earth, Dr Roberto assures me he can complete his task. Just think, every living soul on Earth is no longer just implicitly but explicitly at our command."

"So let me get this clear. To get enough steel we need to keep the machine running for a good deal of time. That's why we need to control the Val Thane, so that we can safely harvest it?"

"Precisely. And on that note, I need to get some sleep," spoke the voice. "Ruining a civilisation without getting oneself killed in the process takes quite a bit of energy. I'd suggest you do the same Ulric."

CHAPTER 54 - ALISTAIR

Alistair awoke to the sound of birds chirping in the morning and for a brief moment, thought he was dreaming as he felt the warm body next to his. As the events of the previous days came rushing back, he took solace in the fact that something good had happened amongst all the bad. He closed his eyes once more, wanting to savour the moment, knowing all too well that the next few days were going to be the toughest of his life. His moment was to be a brief one however as a gun shot rang out somewhere outside. Adele jumped up, staring at Alistair, her eyes wide with shock.

"What was that?!"

Alistair was dressed in no time, joining Aris and Dagath next to the circle of black ash where the fire had burned out last night. More gunshots followed, short bursts of automatic fire interspersed with periods of silence. Without saying a word, Aris moved to the stone slab that functioned as a door and proceeded to open it, peering outside. Alistair and Dagath joined him, followed by Adele.

Two men were retreating backwards through the woods. One stopping periodically to kneel and shoot while the other retreated a small way, the other then repeating the process. It became apparent moments later that one of them was George. There was a howl as it seemed they had hit their target and the two of them slowed down.

"George it's us, don't shoot!" Alistair yelled.

George spun on his heels still aiming his rifle, adrenaline

surging through his veins. "My god you're a sight for sore eyes." George began to lower his rifle until he noticed Aris standing next to Alistair.

He instantly raised it again, his eyes glancing at Alistair then back to Aris. "What the hell is he doing here?"

"It's OK, he's helping us. Turns out he was set up to take the fall for my betrayal.

George didn't lower his rifle, "How do you know he's not just stringing you along as usual? You've a talent for that don't you Aris."

"My reputation precedes me, and as such I understand your concern. In your position, I wouldn't trust me either. All I can do is tell you that I wanted to see your friend dead no more than I want to see the sun stop shining. Either way, there is a bigger problem now as I suppose you've just found out."

The other man emerged from the wood aiming his weapon at the party.

"Who's this?" asked Alistair as a rough looking red haired man approached the group.

"This is Captain Gary Anders, he's also from Earth, we met up a few miles down the path. He was being pursued by one of those things so I helped him out."

"Greetings," came a thick Scottish accent from the new arrival.

George, seeming to have calmed down a little, spoke to Aris.

"I'm going to lower my weapon, but if I hear so much as a whisper out of your rat mouth that I don't like the sound of, you're dead."

Adele nodded, "Don't worry, you're not the only one keeping a close eye on our friend here."

"Glad to see you're safe Adele."

"It's OK," George said motioning to Gary. "They're friends... well... mostly," he said turning to Aris.

"God Aris, is there anyone who doesn't actually want to see you dead," Dagath said shaking his head.

"Gary Anders," said the man to George's left, moving forward and shaking hands with the four new faces in front of him.

"George, Moran and the others...?" asked Adele nervously.

"They should be here momentarily, they split off so as to make it more difficult for the few beasts that were chasing us to follow. We agreed to rally back together as soon as the threat was gone."

"But how will they know where to find you?"

"Morris had some sort of tracking powder, said something about when he drinks a potion he can see where anyone else who's drunk it has been."

"Can someone tell me what the hell those things are?" said Gary.

"Exactly what they seem," replied Aris.

"Forgive me for not introducing myself sooner," said Alistair. "Aris and I are from Earth too," he said looking at Gary's AK47.

"Listen, no offence laddie, but I dinnay know what the fuck's going on, what do ye mean by 'from Earth too'."

"You don't know?" said Alistair.

"I'm not sure if I even know my bloody name any more lad. The last couple of days, the things I've seen... I'm just wondering when I'm gonna finally wake up. What I do know though, is that I was captured along with my squad mates. The next day I wake up and there's pointy eared people with bows and arrows shooting at me, some freak in a floral coat throwing fireballs, nightmarish demons killing my men, all the while having some joker on a mobile telling us to place a rock in a temple in the middle of some medieval village."

"So you're the one who released the Val Thane!" Aris said aloud. He stroked his chin, "Interesting," he mumbled, more to himself than anyone else. "This is going to be hard to believe, but it's the only truth Gary. I probably wouldn't believe it if I were in your position but here it is regardless."

Aris proceeded to bring him up to speed. He couldn't tell if Gary believed him but that was of little consequence at the moment. All that mattered was he had an explanation of the situation at hand.

As Gary stood silent, still trying to decide just how mad this person in front of him was, there was a rustling in the tree line. A familiar face with a staff accompanied by a short fat fellow and someone with two swords across his back emerged from the wood.

"So you made it after all little sister," Moran said as he walked towards the group looking at Adele.

Adele brought her hand to her chest, exhaling in a sigh of relief as she spotted her brother.

"Do my eyes deceive me or is that Aris Treycartheon in the flesh?" Moran said, now walking briskly towards them, Morris and Hadron in tow.

"Hello Moran," said Aris, something in his voice hinting at the lack of regard he held for the man.

"Apologies for our earlier, less hospitable encounter," Moran said turning to Alistair and George. "Nothing personal. Just business."

"Maybe I'll make it personal later," said George, still not having forgiven Moran for kidnapping them earlier.

"I seem to recall you did kill one of my brethren. I think that makes us more than even."

George ignored the comment.

Moran turned to Aris. "I believe I have some information that may fill the final pieces of your puzzle. The Val Thane being released. No doubt you have an idea of the **why**, but the **who** I believe, may still elude you."

"What do you know?" said Aris, his brow furrowing in suspicion.

"Yourself, and most other souls who are familiar with the story of the attempted coup within the mages guild directly after the first Val Thane incident, believe the movement was quashed. This is not the case. A brief while after discovering the possession procedure, I realised its terrible potential and attempted to destroy all reference. Sadly, I was unsuccessful, a powerful mage by the name of Kereal Hawkin uncovering a scroll I missed not long after the Val Thane invasion. Your friends Dannick Veltross and Jean Pierre were successful in aiding the rebellion and as such, they overthrew Ulric, claiming control of the mages guild and all of Bledith in the process.

To make the transition of power a simpler affair and keep the status quo, instead of banishing or killing those previously in power, Kereal Hawkin adapted the procedure, causing a permanent transfer of consciousness from one physical body to another, essentially overwriting one person's soul with another's, but keeping their physical form intact. It seemed one shortcoming of the modified procedure was that although the physical characteristics of the possessed remained the same, any supernatural abilities they may have were destroyed along with their mental and spiritual sentience. All previous members of power, including Ulric Vergan, had their consciousness overwritten by the willing members of the successful coup. Your two companions from so long ago, Jean Pierre and Dannick Veltross live to this day, just in completely different bodies. Their access to Earth made them very valuable and to this end Dannick was chosen to lead Bledith in Ulric's body. This was all executed very covertly and anyone they deemed not fit to possess was silently disposed of. Myself, Hadron and Morris stayed in the city as long as we could, attempting to find a way to expose their scheme before the fateful day we were discovered. Narrowly escaping, we have to this day been branded traitors to the Kingdom, unable to set foot in our homeland ever again."

"Are you attempting to tell me the man I believed my father for all these years is an imposter," said Adele. "That's nonsense, I would have noticed... I don't even remember a coup... you lie Moran."

"It all happened when you were very young my dear, these people were extremely careful."

"But..." Adele stood speechless, the world beginning to spin as she collapsed in Alistair's arms.

As she came to she heard Aris speak. "If what you say is true, it certainly does fill in some more pieces of the puzzle. It still doesn't explain the discord someone is sowing between the major Kingdoms however."

"You have the truth of it there Aris. I have as yet no explanation for that. Something else I have discovered however, which may be of use, is that the rifle Alistair carries is capable of downing the Chimon, it being made of the same material used to fell it last time. This will render the horde feral and undisciplined, making the task of closing the Val Thane gateway a much simpler one."

"Hold on," said George. "Firstly, what is the Chimon? Secondly, the RG32 is a fine piece of engineering indeed but 'made of the same material used to fell it last time?' It's just steel."

"Oh Aris has not told you? The Chimon is that great fire breathing lizard that leads the Val Thane.

In regards to your second point you are quite incorrect," Moran replied. "The machine that produces the substance also produces a unique metal that occurs nowhere else in either world other than a sword of unknown origin that has been in my family since records were kept. The RG32 as you described it, is fashioned from this metal. The horde, being led by the Chimon, has been spotted moving towards Plester's Canyon just south of here. The canyon should provide the best possible opportunity to shoot the thing from a safe distance."

"Well then, what are we waiting for?" said Aris. "Let's get going."

CHAPTER 55 - ALISTAIR

Alistair moved slowly towards the edge of the cliff overlooking the canyon. He touched the rock with his right hand, painstakingly edging his head higher till he could just see over the top of the outcrop that bordered the cliff face. The scene presented was even more terrifying than he had imagined. The canyon was filled with them, wall to wall Val Thane, all kinds of unspeakable horrors a mere 300 hundred yards below him, passing through the valley. He was observing the dark, bony, bat like flying creatures that circled above the horde when he spotted it, the unmistakeable behemoth Aris called the Chimon. Positioned in the middle of the Val Thane sea, the Chimon's large lizard like head swung from side to side as its forked blue tongue flicked out intermittently, tasting the air as it lumbered forward. The thing was so huge and ungainly that it would occasionally crush smaller minions under its massive feet.

"Run me through the escape plan again just in case it's not all rainbows and unicorns when I shoot gigantor over there in the head."

Aris sighed, "Grab the RG32, run like hell back up that hill, then take cover in the tunnels till they give up or we die of old age. We won't have to worry about the ones on the ground but those fliers, well, they are a different story. Once we're inside the narrow tunnels though, they will have to come through single file, in the process losing any advantage the wide, open spaces afford them."

"Ok, so as soon as I shoot, I grab the RG32 and run?"

"As soon as you confirm a good effect on target," said Aris.

Alistair mounted the RG32 on the block as George had done previously, the tripod forming, wedging itself into the ground. He then detached the scope, finding a nearby boulder to take cover behind. Using the scope as a touch screen, he zoomed in until the Chimon's head filled the field of view. Transparent text appeared referencing different parts of the Chimon, a menu reading: 'Target Lock?: Eye, Nose, Head region general, Jaw, teeth...'

"Jesus, this scope takes the marksman out of marksmanship," said Alistair, marvelling at the facial structure recognition software that appeared to have broad reasoning and pattern recognition similar to that of a human.

"Lock eye," he commanded.

To his amazement the weapon started tracking the demon's eye, keeping the centre of the cross hair directly over it as it moved. A grouping of numbers and letters appeared in the top right hand corner which Alistair guessed was corrections for wind speed, temperature, humidity etc. "If this thing ever goes into mass production I might be out of a job," he thought to himself.

Taking a deep breath, he touched the screen where it said fire. A deafening roar ensued as a blazing inferno trailed the projectile. Both his ears were ringing but other than that he was ok, the boulder he had his back to shielding him from the blast. Looking into the scope, he saw blood spurting from the location where the projectile collided with the Chimon. There was an almighty roar as the beast came crashing to the ground, crushing a great number of Val Thane and sending yet more into a frenzy. Wild screeches and howls ensued as it bellowed in pain, lying on its side, its clawed feet thrashing the air, blood spraying from the open wound. Alistair rushed out from his hiding spot, retrieving the weapon and its mount from the edge of the cliff as he noticed one of the winged creatures swoop upwards in his direction. He ducked his head as quickly as possible, but was almost sure it had seen him. Not wanting to wait around and find out, he set off as fast as he could towards the tunnels.

"If it's not dead it's close to!" Alistair yelled at Aris, his words coming out at a frantic pace between breaths as his heart beat a million times a minute.

Reaching the tunnel, he took cover behind a rock next to Aris in the darkness. A screeching sound reverberated off the walls, not helping Alistair's already ringing ears as one of the flying creatures landed just outside the entrance. They crouched in silence as it paced back and forth, seemingly trying to tell if whatever had attacked its leader had made its way into this cave. After about five minutes the noise receded, the thing ceasing its incessant high pitched screeches.

Alistair's heart beat slowed to a more regular pace as it seemed whatever it was out there had given up. Looking to Aris on his right, the two of them jumped to the left in shock as a pointed limb thrust into the cave next to the rock they were behind, the flying Val Thane resuming its screaming madly as the pointed bone began thrashing about the tunnel wildly. Huddling against the rock for protection, they were trapped. To go further into the tunnel, they'd have to move out of cover to the right. Doing so however, would result in them being impaled by the bone limb. It seemed this was it. The thing knew they were there. It was just a matter of time till one of the smaller demons joined it and entered the tunnel, ensuring their doom. And then, just as suddenly as its mad frenzy had begun, the thing went silent once more. "Was it bluffing?" Alistair wondered, a glimmer of hope creeping in.

Giving one final terrifying screech, Aris and Alistair heard the flap of its bony wings, the skin webbing between its nightmarish frame lifting it into the air along with the two men's spirits.

Alistair and Aris waited in the tunnel for over four hours so as to be sure their pursuer had given up chase, not making any assumptions after the cunning it had displayed earlier. Those four hours seemed more like a day as they sat silently in the darkness, not game to make a sound. Eventually, Alistair signalled to Aris and the two moved slowly back towards the tunnel entrance they had come through. Alistair scanned the rocky plateau for any signs of lingering Val Thane.

"Looks clear," he said to Aris in a hushed tone, beckoning him to follow.

The two moved slowly back to the rocky outcrop and stared over the edge of the cliff. The scene they observed at the other end of the canyon caused their spirits to sink like a brick in a pond. The Chimon was back on its feet, lumbering on as though the events that transpired hours earlier had never occurred.

"What the hell do we do now, I thought Moran said this was supposed to kill it?" said Alistair frustratedly.

"It was," replied Aris shaking his head in disbelief. "There must be some mistake."

Just as Alistair turned to speak something caught his eye. He looked back through the scope and observed a sight most strange. "What the hell..." There was a human walking next to the Chimon, the lesser creatures having cleared a path, seemingly not showing any interest in attacking him.

"Come on Alistair," called Aris in a **defeated** tone, seemingly having come out of his trance. "We'll just have to take our chances with them at full strength."

"Aris, quick, come and have a look at this!"

Aris took the scope from Alistair. "What am I supposed to be looking at?" he said, his mood still depressed.

"Just behind the Chimon."

Aris's defeated tone suddenly turned to one of shock, "but... but... how is that possible, they kill all humans on sight."

"Do my eyes deceive me or is that Ulric Vergen mingling with the Horde?" As if it weren't bad enough that the RG32 hadn't successfully killed the Chimon, it now seemed Ulric had somehow allied with the Val Thane.

"This is bad," said Aris. "This is very bad."

CHAPTER 56 - ALISTAIR

After reuniting with the others, Aris and Alistair informed them of the failed attempt on the Chimon and the arguably more unsettling fact that it seemed Ulric was somehow in league with the Val Thane. If Adele had needed any more convincing that Ulric wasn't the man she thought he was, this was certainly it.

Not all was lost however. Aris knew the location of the substance, a location it shared with the keystone they needed to deactivate the Val Thane gateway in the Alman Temple. Having tried to explain everything he knew to the best of his abilities as quickly as possible, he'd accidentally neglected a crucial piece of the puzzle. Dannick Veltross, Aris's old acquaintance who had been secretly inhabiting the body of Ulric Vergen for close to 1000 years as well as the yet to make himself known Jean Pierre, needed Alistair. So much had happened so quickly, that he hadn't had time to spare a thought for the event that started it all - Alistair's ambush at the Baron's residence.

The journey north to the rift in the side of the mountain that housed the substance and keystone was void of trouble, be it Val Thane or human. Aris reasoned they must still be ahead of the Val Thane, the horde of demons moving up from the South. The party had stopped at a village on the way. The small folk were in the process of evacuating, tales of the devastation to the south having reached them just in time. Alistair and the others took no pleasure in commandeering the horses but they knew it had to be done. If stealing a poor soul's equine transport meant they shut down the gateway sooner, albeit at the very possible cost of the owner's life, it was sadly worth it. Each day the gateway was open cost not one, but thousands of lives. One aspect Alistair took no issue with however, was the fact that they had only managed to steal six, Adele's hands around his midsection a welcome distraction to the melancholy times.

The plateau was located approximately 250 yards above the base of the mountain, the party stepping forwards into the large triangular hole in its side. Ahead stretched a tunnel lit with torches at approximately ten yard intervals. Strange carvings were engraved into the wall. As they progressed, the theme painfully reminded Gary of his fateful journey into the Alman temple and his fallen comrades. Alistair noticed them also, the images consistently depicting a similar figure with a long, forked, snake like tongue. The figure was armed with an ornate looking sword. Almost all of the depictions were of him battling multiple foes, the forked tongue character brutally slaughtering his opponents regardless of their numbers. As they crossed an almost invisible white line, the man they had seen carved into the tunnel walls materialised from a cloud of black smoke in the centre of the hall, approximately 60 yards in front of them.

"Who will challenge?" came an unnaturally deep voice, two pitch black glassy eyes contrasting strongly with the red sockets in which they were housed.

As the humanoid like figure moved with a sinister confidence towards them, it became clear that this was not actually a man. The body shape was similar, but its skin was a dark red, a forked tongue appearing at intervals similar to the carvings they had encountered earlier. He was dressed in dark, flowing black pants and a sleeveless shirt, revealing two muscular arms covered in dark red skin. Removing his hood, it became apparent that whatever it was that stood before them had no hair.

Moran, leaned forward, scarcely able to believe his eyes. Was it actually him?

Turning to Hadron he asked, "Does that fellow look somewhat like Teren Antes to you?"

"It would seem so," replied Hadron most out of character,

conveying an unusually concerned persona.

"Who is Teren Antes?" asked Adele, her curiosity piqued by the sudden fascination.

"Oh, only the greatest swordsman to have ever lived... or have not lived... I guess?" replied Morris.

"Demon swordsman," Moran corrected. "Legend has it that he arises from the underworld whenever the Val Thane are released, the final obstacle to the acquisition of the substance. Supposedly never defeated, having killed anyone unfortunate enough to stray into his lair, the demon swordsman is confined to the 'Final Hall' as it is told. Legend states he guards something of great value and that he has never been bested in combat."

"That does not make sense at all," Adele replied. If he guards the key to closing the Val Thane gateway and has never been defeated, then how were those horrid creatures stopped last time?"

"Yes, I think the legend may be somewhat embellished. However, I heard naught of him last time, maybe they simply avoided him?"

"We'll see about that," said Adele, moving her arms as though to conjure a lightning bolt.

The confused look on her face said it all as nothing happened.

Gary raised his gun towards its head, a moment later pulling the trigger. There was a **bang** as the pistol's hammer hit the primer at the back of the bullet. Instead of flying through the air and into the thing's skull however, the bullet weakly slipped out of the barrel and fell into the dirt in front of them.

Teren laughed. "Naught other than a blade will serve you here," came the unnaturally deep voice.

Alistair, who had until now been standing behind the others, stepped forward.

Teren, thus far displaying naught but confidence, suddenly seemed a little less sure of himself, staring intently at Alistair as though he had seen a ghost. Seemingly recovering his composure, the sinister grin spread back across his face.

"So we **meet again**. This time you shall not be so fortunate."

"Errr, what's he on about Aris?" Alistair said looking over his shoulder.

Aris spoke, "Teren certainly is a formidable foe, but the part about him being undefeated is not entirely true. During the last invasion, you became the only person on record to best him in sword combat, claiming the reward he guards. The workings of this place are a mystery to this day, projectiles and magic being rendered ineffective in Teren's domain as you have no doubt just observed. This is the part Jean and Ulric needed you for. You are the only man capable of defeating him. I know it's a tall order, but it is the only way to save the realm. Never fear though, you have beaten him before, I'm sure you can do it again."

"I could be a little rusty after 999 odd years you know. Forgive me if I don't share your confidence."

A shadow danced in the torch light as Hadron stepped forward. "Then it shall be my honour to assist you," he replied, drawing his two swords, throwing one to Alistair.

Teren Antes opened his hand, a wisp of black smoke slowly forming a long black flamberge, the otherworldly blade gleaming in the torchlight as it gave off an ever so slight flow of black smoke.

CHAPTER 57 - HADRON

Hadron and Alistair stepped forward cautiously. Hadron began to circle right as Alistair circled left, trying to position themselves either side of Teren to gain as much of a positional advantage as possible. It was difficult within the narrow hallway however, which was probably part of the reason Teren had been so successful when outnumbered in the past. The thin hallway limited the potential arc that Teren had to defend in front of him.

Standing as far apart as possible, an approximate seventy degree arc existed between Teren and his two opponents. As they closed in, Teren lunged at Hadron with a grunt, his movements not dissimilar to Alistair's, seemingly unnaturally quick. Hadron was just fast enough to parry the flurry of blows that came his way. Instead of attacking at the same time, Alistair used the opportunity to gain a positional advantage behind his opponent. Upon moving, Alistair immediately bent backwards almost 90 degrees just in time to avoid Teren's spinning swipe, the dark blade cutting through the air just above his chin, being parried by Hadron a moment later. Teren was now at a real disadvantage. He had one man either side of him and the angle between the three was now 180 degrees. Irrespective of position, Hadron was struggling. He was good. There was no doubt about it, but he was good through hard work and practice. No amount of hard work or practice could compete with the unnatural skill of the foe he currently faced. Consequently, he was barely fast enough to defend, yet alone have time for counters in spite of the fact that Teren had to defend and avoid

Alistair from behind, which thus far, he was doing exceptionally well.

Teren Ante's successful dance of death on two fronts led Hadron and Alistair to the worrying conclusion that if either of them were to fall, the other was certainly not up to the task alone. Teren lunged at Hadron, forcing him further backwards than he would have liked resulting in Alistair having more ground to make up than normal. The cunning trap had been set. Alistair, almost overcompensating, came to a stop mere inches from the demon swordsman's waiting blade. Teren seemed to have been relying a little too heavily on Alistair over committing however, as Hadron was able to land a kick directly under his chin. Teran reeled backwards as Alistair moved to drive his sword into the oncoming opponents back. Teren, off balance, responded by diving backwards. Flipping past Alistair, he rotated on his vertical axis in mid-air causing Alistair's sword to pass harmlessly by his back instead of through it.

The positions had now been reset, Teren once more only having to defend and attack on one front. Hadron and Alistair were sweating profusely, their breathing heavy as both men began to tire. Conversely, one could be forgiven for thinking Teren had partaken in no more than a morning stroll, not looking nearly as fatigued as his opponents. Their spirits sank with every movement, the enemy seeming to possess a supernaturally plentiful stamina. If they couldn't win with the positional advantage and an even level of fatigue, what hope did they stand now? Hadron looked to Alistair as their opponent backed off for a moment, toying with his prey. The look lasted less than a second, but his eyes said it all. Alistair wanted to stop him, but he knew that if he telegraphed Hadron's next move to his opponent, his sacrifice would be in vain.

Hadron stepped forwards clumsily as Teren plunged his sword through Hadron's belly moments before Hadron could bring his own sword down on the demon's bald head. Alistair couldn't imagine the pain as the tip of Teren's sword pierced Hadron's midsection, moments later emerging from his back. If that weren't painful enough, Hadron then spun on the balls of his feet, using the twisting motion of his impaled torso to pull the sword before Teren could withdraw it. Teren, not expecting any man to be mad enough to attempt such a thing, was pulled towards his impaled foe as Hadron slammed the oncoming swordsman's head into the wall with his palm, giving Alistair the precious seconds needed to slice it from the demon's shoulders. Hadron fell to the ground immediately as Alistair slid on his knees to the brave man's side, Teren's head rolling to a stop next to them. Alistair, a mixture of exhaustion and emotion, barely noticed the others rushing forward.

"Make way! Make way!" shouted Morris as he pushed past Aris and Adele, pulling something from his bag.

Alistair moved aside, looking into Hadron's eyes as he did so, bowing his head in honour of his sacrifice. Hadron wearily raised a hand, muttering something before Morris grabbed it and shushed him.

"Quiet now, old Morris will fix you up," his expression not quite analogous to the words he spoke. The expression was short lived however, changing quickly from concern to confusion.

"There's no blood?" he noted, pulling on Hadrons baggy attire.

It was then that he realised what had happened.

"So that's why you wear clothes that are ten times too big for you," Morris said with a smile as he realised the blade had not in fact stabbed Hadron, but had merely pierced and then got caught in the oversized canvas jacket he'd heard Hadron refer to as a kendogi.

"I was about to tell you," said Hadron between breaths as he pulled the black sword from his clothing.

The look of concern on Adele's face melded almost instantly into one of anger as she pushed him on the shoulder.

"Did you really find it quite necessary to lead us on after you knew he was dead? I hardly think this is the time for such jests."

"Believe me, I wasn't leading you on. I've barely enough energy to move my tongue," he said staring at the ceiling, not really focusing on any of the faces above him.

"Very nice Hadron!" said Moran, admiring the prevalence of cunning over raw skill.

"Oh, aye Laddy! Now that's a battle and a half if ever I saw one!" said Gary excitedly, still in awe of the scene he'd just witnessed. "Bloody good show!"

"Not bad," said Dagath, nodding his head.

"A more fitting coup de grace there could not be," commented George.

Aris congratulated them on their victory after which Alistair spoke.

"What if he had attacked you with the blade horizontally instead of vertically? You would have been gutted the moment you attempted that little spinning trick."

"I know," said Hadron quietly, still so exhausted he wasn't really sure if he was conscious. "It was a risk I had to take. We were outclassed. It was only a matter of time before one of us fell, which would surely have meant the demise of the other. I know for one that I was on my last legs. Even if he had of, it would still be a better outcome than both of us dying, not to mention what will happen if we do not succeed in stopping Ulric. The fate of two worlds rests on us retrieving the substance he was guarding Alistair. Don't forget that."

CHAPTER 58 - ARIS

A panel at the end of the long hallway slid open, the dust cloud that followed speaking volumes of the time that had passed since it had last been accessed. The room inside was almost bare save three noteworthy objects. Some kind of commotion could be heard just beyond the back wall of the room as though something mechanical were in motion. Dripping from a hole in the ceiling, the green glowing liquid that had been the cause of so much chaos was falling ever so infrequently into a bowl-shaped stone artefact below it. Alistair guessed this must have been the substance.

The second object of note, albeit far less attention grabbing than the substance, was a shiny block of metal approximately 2 feet wide by 1 foot high then 1 foot deep again. Sitting atop a platform that jutted out of the back wall in the direction of the mechanical locomotion, the reflectively shiny metal seemed very out of place in the dust filled grimy room.

The third object Gary recognised from his previous journey to the Alman temple, a dragon shaped stone figurine approximately one foot tall, the key to ending this terror and saving the realm.

George removed a large metal flask from his pack, dipping it into the bowl of substance as he did, the liquid radiating an eerie green glow as it was disturbed on contact. George put the flask in his rucksack as Aris directed Dagath and the others to help him drag the chunk of metal down. The chunk of metal fell from the edge of the platform. Instead of a loud clang as one would have expected however, its contact with the floor was accompanied by almost no sound at all. The shiny metal splattered as it hit the ground, expanding horizontally and contracting vertically as though it were some sort of malleable material, not the solid piece of metal it seemed. As if the malleability and lack of sound on its contact with the floor were not surprising enough, it reformed its previous shape a moment later.

Aris wrapped a net around the piece of metal, delegating its responsibility to Dagath, who begrudgingly began dragging it along the ground behind him as they made their way back to the entrance.

"What's that?" asked Alistair as they exited the cave.

"That," replied Aris, "is what your RG32 is made of. A metal unique to this world, stronger than any other known element, its form can be restructured through the application of an electrical charge.

"Electrical charge? Seems our friends are talking gibberish again," said Moran to Adele.

"To put it in terms more familiar to one of your background, this block can essentially shape shift into any conceivable form," Aris said, accidentally bumping into George as he turned to face Moran.

"Ah, I once knew a mage who could do that," said Morris. "Oh wait, I still do. Lo and behold, here he stands beside me."

"Tell me about it," George replied, rolling his eyes as he did.

"Well actually, that was technically possession rather than shape shifting, and she WAS the enemy at the time" Moran protested. "You would have done the same thing in my shoes...well... if you had any talent."

Alistair ignored the banter and idol bickering as they continued back out of the rift in the mountain. Arriving back at the entrance, a sudden wave of shock washed over all but Dagath, he being the only person present who had not yet had the displeasure of meeting the familiar, yet most unwelcome arrival.

CHAPTER 59 - ARIS

"Why, who do we have here?" Ulric said, smiling as the large group of Val Thane wolves behind him bared their teeth. "So good of you to pick up the substance for me Aris. You have indeed saved me quite the bit of trouble."

"How could you?" replied Adele, "All these years... is it true?"

"Is what true my dear?"

"Do me at least one courtesy and refrain from feigning ignorance. Moran has enlightened me. You may inhabit my father's body, but I know the truth of it. His soul was put to rest so many years ago."

"And you would believe that treacherous snake over your own father. Listen not, for he sows discord in all he touches."

Moran stepped forward. "This is most peculiar. Why would you bother to deny it? What do you have to gain? Unless... No... You've become attached to her after all this time haven't you. You've played the role of the father so long that somewhere along the line you started to believe your own deception."

"First you killed my father, our father," Adele said looking back at Hadron, Morris and Moran. "Then you condemn the people of this realm to death so you can live another thousand years and you have the gall to deny it?!!" she shouted, her voice wavering now as her eyes began to blink more frequently, the beginning of tears.

"To hell with you Moran!" Ulric snapped, his tone shifting from patronising to anger in a flash. "So a few peasants have to make a sacrifice for their ruler. That's what the masses do! I may not be your father by blood, but I raised you as my own. Do you know how much pressure I was under to simply dispose of you? One of the last known members of the family that almost crushed myself and my allies. But no, you have the right of it, I couldn't do it. That matters naught now though," he said, his tone changing from anger to sadness as he turned his gaze, no longer able to look at the woman he had called his daughter all these years.

"Aris, hand over the substance before I take it from your cold dead corpse."

"So be it," said Aris, drawing his sword. Ulric stared at Aris, his face forming an annoyed expression. With a sigh, he commanded the Val Thane to attack. The others drew their weapons alongside Aris as the Val Thane began to close, preparing for an impossible battle against the demons in front of them. But then something strange happened. As the nearest wolf came within two yards of Alistair, it howled and whimpered, its body language conveying a new emotion - FEAR. Making one last defiant gesture, it meekly snapped at the air before proceeding to flee. The same reaction played out as the other Val Thane came closer.

"That's right!" said Aris, pacing in front of Ulric. "Last time we defeated Teren Antes we exited this very tunnel only to be ambushed by a group of your new-found friends didn't we," said Aris, pointing at the whimpering huddle of what a moment ago, were menacing monstrosities. "They greatly outnumbered us and we were sure that was the end of our story. Remember the surprise when one by one they retreated. I hypothesised then that killing Teren Antes set off some sort of hierarchical fear system in their brains but forgot all about it till just now, as I'm guessing you did too. It has been so long."

"Ah yes, how fortunate for you," Ulric said sarcastically.

Aris turned to Alistair. "Basically, they won't dare engage whoever killed Teren. Therefore, to put it in simple terms," Aris said, turning back, pointing his sword at Ulric's throat. "You are fucked."

"Wait," cried Adele. "Please don't kill him, I... I... need answers."

Ulric's brow furrowed as Alistair caught a momentary glimpse directed at George.

George let out a sigh. Shaking his head, he reached out and

grabbed Adele about the throat, putting his pistol to her head.

"Bloody Murphy," he said as the others turned towards him in shock. "If something can go wrong it always does, doesn't it. Well, when plan A fails you can always take a hostage I suppose. Aris, be a good fellow, drop the steel and the keystone would you."

George shuffled Adele past them towards Ulric, moving his shoulder as he did to reposition the pack on his back that contained the substance.

"No wait..." Ulric said, suddenly worried about the fate that might befall the woman he still called his daughter.

"Shut up Ulric! If you'd have more thoroughly researched these bloody things we wouldn't be in this mess. Tie her hands for me would you. We don't want anyone randomly combusting now then do we."

Ulric tied her hands behind her back, quietly reassuring her everything would be OK. As George turned her around so she came face to face with Ulric, she spat in his face.

"You are pathetic scum, you are no father to me."

"Feisty one isn't she," George said, raising his eyebrows. "Hurry up Aris, I've no time for games," he said, cocking the pistol next to Adele's ear to prove he was serious.

"I'll give you the steel but you are not getting the keystone. These people don't deserve this fate."

George weighed up his options and agreed reluctantly.

Dagath dropped the ropes attached to the net.

"Alright, back up," said George. "If I see any of you following me, you'll be down a sorceress. Otherwise, you can retrieve her at the gateway in two days time."

Alistair and the party moved away from the steel as George commanded one of the beasts to grab the netting and drag it. They could only look on as George and his minions disappeared down the mountain trail.

CHAPTER 60 - ALISTAIR

"Fucking two faced bastard!" yelled Alistair as he paced to-and-fro. "What's to stop him killing her now and just leaving?"

"Oh, I don't think he'll be killing anyone any time soon, or straying too far for that matter," replied Aris, holding up a large metal flask for all to see.

"How the..." Morris stated, "I saw him retrieve it from that room."

"Initially, I thought Alistair's escape from the Silent Twins was a mistake, but the more I thought about it, the more it made sense. The set up at the Baron's residence and subsequent capture were simply the distraction. The slight-of-hand came in the escape, tricking Alistair into achieving their goal while to everybody else involved, it seems as though the mystery schemer's plan has been foiled by random chance. This wasn't enough to be sure though, maybe I was simply obsessing over recent events, twisting the facts so as to draw erroneous conclusions that supported my hypothesis. Then the next clue came as an all too eager George scooped up the substance. Still, this was probably just due to fact he was carrying the flask at the time. I likely would have been just as excited and hasty if I were seeing the elixir of life for the first time. The third clue though, in concert with his most recent actions, leads me to a more dire conclusion. Not only is George a traitor, but I believe we've had a very old someone in our midst these last few days. The phrase 'coup de grace' does not exist in this realm and it is rarely used on Earth. As such, the instance in which Jean Pierre used it so many years ago, in conjunction with King Mordren's imminent demise, has lingered within my subconscious all these years. The moment I heard George use the words to describe Teran Ante's death, my suspicion transformed into an almost certainty. I believe George is actually Jean Pierre! Ergo, the second member of the duo orchestrating these most dire of events having been right under our noses the entire time. If my suspicions are true, which I am almost certain they are, George needs the substance before the end of the year. The metal won't mean anything to him if he's not alive to use it."

"So Adele is his bargaining chip?" replied Morris.

"What are we waiting for then? Let's get after them," said Moran.

"Once George realises he doesn't have the substance, he'll find us. You can be sure of that.

I know Adele means a lot to all of you bar Dagath, but closing the Val Thane gateway is our first priority. Not only does it doom thousands everyday it is left open, once George realises the position he is in, he may try to prolong the Val Thane's presence, essentially using that as leverage instead."

Alistair paced towards Aris, his face conveying a single-minded determination the likes of which were rarely seen.

"This should be simple then. The Vale Thane fear me now, so what are we waiting for? Let's replace the keystone and get this over with."

"Ah," said Aris. "The part about the Val Thane fearing you. That is somewhat of a half-truth. For obvious reasons, I may have left a detail or two out when speaking in front of those two. Most of the Val Thane fear you. There is still the matter of their leader however, the Chimon. It, unlike the others, will still kill you where you stand given half a chance."

"That lizard thing?" said Morris. "How the hell are the six of us supposed to fell that."

"The six of us don't," replied Aris. "Yourself and I Morris, do. But I will get to that in a second.

Now that the Val Thane will not attack Alistair, he should be able to make his way back to the Alman Temple unharmed. That is of course, if he avoids the Chimon. I know Jean too well. There isn't a snowball's chance in hell he'd have given up the keystone if he thought we would actually make it to the Alman Temple. He may have been remiss in his recollection of the way the Val Thane react upon Teren Antes' defeat, but you can be sure those very same events will have jogged his memory. No doubt as we speak, he will be re-tasking the Chimon to guard the temple.

"Looks like checkmate then..." said Dagath, trailing off as he did.

Aris smirked, "Not quite..."

"And there it is," interrupted Dagath. "Aris the fox conceives a master plan at the last minute, once again. A betting man might be inclined to say the game's rigged. The gambler might just be the one dealing the cards me thinks."

Alistair trusted Dagath even less than he did Aris, but at that very moment he found himself questioning Aris's intentions. Dagath was scum, but he had a point. Aris did seem to continually find his way out of the most dire situations. Not entirely convinced however, Alistair decided to take a cautious wait and see approach. Aris was as intelligent as they came. If he was up to something, Alistair reasoned he'd have a better chance of thwarting whatever it was if the party being scrutinised was unaware of the extra attention.

"We don't have time for this rot Dagath. I've done everything in my power and more to stop those two, losing everything I held dear in the process I'll have you know. Believe me when I say, nothing in this world would make me happier than to run you through where you stand."

"Blah, blah, blah... Wait, let me guess, you still need me for something?"

"It seems you're not quite as stupid as you look," Aris replied mockingly. "I do need you for something Dagath, but I will get to that in due course. Courtesy of yourself, my reputation is mud. No doubt false word of my involvement in King Ervoule's and Prince Cartian's assassination will have spread to the North by now. I and every other living soul in this world needs you to warn, and then rally the Northern Kingdoms before the Val Thane reach Velderwood Neck, it being the ideal location to make a last stand. Know that you are far from my ideal candidate for this task. However, in the absence of anyone else well enough connected, you will have to do."

"Well I guess that means you'll have to release me. And here I was beginning to get used to these ropes. Why, I think I may actually miss them. Say Aris, what makes you think I won't simply ride off into the night?"

"Because you know as well as I that all our fates, not simply my own, depend on your actions in the coming days."

Aris swung his sword true, wishing afterwards he'd stood a foot closer, the blade easily cutting through the ropes that bound Dagath's hands. Finally able to stretch his arms, Dagath turned with a chuckle, shaking his head as he walked forth and mounted his horse.

Aris turned reluctantly as the large man's image faded into the distance.

"So then, where was I... Ah yes, the Chimon. George will no doubt have sent it south to the Temple, as he is yet to realise he does not in fact possess the substance. Oh! what I would give to see the look on his face..." Aris said, trailing off. Focusing once more, Aris continued, "The Chimon's breath is so intense, it melts stone, and the flame that emerges from its hideous mouth is anything but concentrated. Upon George's realisation that we still have the substance in our possession, he will no doubt return the Chimon to the main bulk of the Val Thane, not wishing to risk the precious liquid to such an imprecise deterrent.

The bulk of the Val Thane should have overrun Castle Brin by now and be heading North towards the smaller Kingdoms. If it did not come at the cost of every life in Barathax, I might have even allowed myself to revel in the knowledge that Ludwig's occupation would be so short lived. We cannot let their sacrifice go in vain. Only madmen would venture south now, back towards the Alman temple, the horde likely having reduced Trescot, Eboda, Barathax and Bledith to a pile of corpses. Therein however, lies our opportunity. With the Val Thane marching North, the Chimon should be separated for a time, it initially having moved South to the Alman Temple. If a small group were to circle around the main bulk of the horde, they should therefore be presented with an opportunity to ambush it while it is still isolated from the lesser minions."

"With Alistair, Adele and Dagath otherwise occupied that only leaves four potential candidates," replied Moran. "Correct me if I am wrong, but I believe even 'small group' may be somewhat of an exaggeration. Unless there is yet another mystery twist in your grand scheme, I hardly think four is enough to fell the beast."

"That is where I was hoping you may be of assistance Moran," Aris said with a nervous smile. "I know you abhor the term mercenary, but you have taken gold in exchange for the completion of some rather unsavoury tasks for quite some time now," Aris said weakly as Moran's eyes narrowed, focusing intently on the insolent man before him, his jaw involuntarily clenching. "Surely over such a long period you would have come across others of a similar persuasion," Aris continued.

"Are you asking me to raise an army Aris? You do know, as you so bluntly put it, what motivates a 'mercenary' don't you? Unless you've an invisible pot of gold under that tunic of yours, I think we may be a few pieces of yellow metal short."

"I don't need an army, just say three dozen proficient men. And there's no need for modesty Moran. Your reputation throughout the land being second to none, I'm sure there would not be a shortage of men willing to work for the great Moran Cheldore on a task first, payment later basis."

Moran looked slightly upwards bringing his hand to his chin as he did so.

"I suppose that's true," Moran said as Aris smiled to himself internally, making a mental note of the powerful man's hungry ego.

"I'll get you your three dozen men Aris, but know that when all this comes to its conclusion, I shall be reimbursed in full along with a fee for my services."

Aris agreed reluctantly, shaking his head as he wondered how the man could be thinking of money at a time like this. It was then that he was hit by equal parts pain and relief as he realised there was no way he could keep that promise, any title and fortune he once held having been whisked away the moment Ludwig Steiner accused him of regicide. The relief came upon the realisation that Moran seemingly had not realised this, still viewing Aris as the man he once was and should rightfully still be.

"All this talk of ambushing the Chimon sounds all well and good in theory," interjected Alistair as he turned to Aris. "In practice however, that thing took a shot to the eye from a rail gun and was up and on its way again in no time. How do you expect to succeed where I failed?"

"During the last invasion 1000 years ago, you successfully killed it after closing the Val Thane gateway. Post our recent unsuccessful attempt on its life, I have hypothesised that it draws its supernatural regeneration from the Val Thane home world. Once the gateway is closed, I suspect it loses this ability, essentially rendering it mortal. This would explain why you were able to defeat it after closing the gateway last time."

"Hypothesise and suspect!" Alistair replied, more than a little surprised at the blind faith Aris seemed to possess in his completely unproven theories. "You're telling me that you are going to attempt to ambush something that may not even be killable? Shit, it's a long shot even if you're right."

"If you have a better idea, I am more than open to it, but failing that, our time to act is scarce and potential course of action singular. Just make sure you do not delay in closing the gateway. Morris and I shall take care of the rest."

"I what?..." Morris replied, more than a little daunted by the prospect of fighting a potentially immortal demon.

"Your specific talents would be of great assistance, if you would be so good as to join myself and Moran in felling the Chimon."

A smile made its way across Moran's face as he stifled a laugh.

"'Specific talents'! I suppose there's no need for mercenaries after all! Why, with its superior sense of smell, the thing should fall dead the moment my brother comes within 200 feet."

Morris shook his head as the others burst into laughter, a welcome momentary respite from the gravity of the situation.

Aris handed Alistair the substance as an awkward silence ensued, Alistair's expression conveying he had something else to add, but for some reason wasn't.

"What is it Alistair?" Aris asked.

"You do realise that if I were to destroy this, the realm would never be threatened by the Val Thane again."

"You're not going to do that," said Aris, "Jean would kill her instantly. If that man were to have been born with a moral compass, well, let's just say it would only point south. You give him that substance when, and only when he gives up Adele, not a second before."

"I've held my tongue thus far but I cannay' any longer," interjected Gary. "I'll not let George or Jean or whatever that bastard's name is get away with murdering my men. There'll be blood for that, I'll not settle for less."

"I know you want revenge Gary," replied Aris. "But is losing another life going to bring them back? George has had to make a compromise here and in the process has let us save millions by deactivating the Val Thane portal. Sadly, we have to make one too and let him go."

"Bollocks to that! I'll find him, even if it takes me 1000 years! His time's borrowed," Gary said, snatching the substance from Alistair and taking a swig.

"Gary, what the hell, NO..."

"There's more than enough left for that fucker. You get your lady friend back and me and the lads get justice," he said, handing the no longer quite full flask back to Alistair.

"I dinnay care what ye say, I'm going with ye Alistair. It was me and the lads that released those terrors. The least I can do is help shut it down. This is on condition that we go after the fucker George... Jean... whatever his name is as soon as we're done."

"No arguments here," said Alistair, taking a sip of the substance himself for good measure. "George and Ulric WILL pay for this."

"Well, I guess that isn't quite how I imagined it," replied Aris. "Sounds fair enough though. That just leaves one," said Aris, turning to the reticent as ever Hadron Kado. "Slay the lizard or save the princess?"

"Under differing circumstances I would be remiss to not pursue my kin. I believe, however, that there is one more suited to this task and as such I shall defer. My sword is yours Aris. The Chimon shall feel its wrath."

"Well then, I suppose this is where we part," said Aris. "Seems I've a giant fire breathing lizard to kill."

"Bring her back safe," Moran said to Alistair and Gary.

"Will do," replied Alistair.

"Good luck with your lizard," Moran said, shaking Morris's hand.

Morris clasped his hand, unexpectedly embracing Moran in hug, slapping him on the back as he did. Moran stood with his other hand by his side, not returning the gesture, coming off as extremely awkward, the man far from a master of social conventions. It didn't help that he had to muster all his strength to not instantly recoil from the foul stench that assailed his nostrils, but somehow managed to do so.

Following the most cringe worthy of embraces, the groups went their separate ways. As soon as he was out of earshot, Moran began to cough profusely, dusting off his now dirty and tattered tunic, it having seen many days on the road.

"My god, a million gold pieces to the person that finds a spell to cure that man's odour."

CHAPTER 61 - ALISTAIR

Gary and Alistair arrived back at the small village that housed the temple, or what was left of it. The temple had ceased roaring and the pillar of light that had been shooting out of it when Gary escaped was now gone. From where they were standing they could however, make out a red glow, approximately as far up as Motel Whiskey had ventured, the hellish colour not quite fitting the weather-beaten stone surrounding it. Corpses littered the ground, the smell and state of decay indicating they weren't recently killed.

"Ah shit," said Gary holding his nose. "This is what happens when you dinnay bury em."

They made their way past the now destroyed inn and over the wall where Gary and his squad had fought off the would-be muggers. A sudden wave of melancholy washed over him as his surrounds triggered memories of all he had lost. Up until now, he'd been too preoccupied with revenge and staying alive for the loss of his comrades to really sink in.

Turning to Gary, Alistair spoke, "Looks like Aris was right about the Chimon. I don't see any sign of it."

"Maybe he's hiding over in those trees?" Gary replied, attempting to use humour to lighten his mood.

Stopping a moment, his expression becoming serious once more, he paced off to the left.

"Seems our lizard friend did have a change of heart," Gary said, observing a massive indent in the ground, the shape of a reptilian foot. "These tracks are fresh, not more than an hour ago," he said following them towards the river. "Aye, ye mate Aris, he's a sharp one isn't he. Looks like it's headed back north, just like he said."

Sure enough, as they rounded what was left of a palisade fence on the other side of the river they observed a trail of destruction as though something enormous had crashed through the forest flanking the river.

"I know they're supposed to be scared of ye and all but I haven't seen one yet," Gary said, observing the complete lack of Val Thane encounters thus far.

"Well, you won't hear any complaints from me."

"Think it's a trap?"

"Knowing George... or should I say Jean, and Aris for that matter, I wouldn't discount anything.

Could be that they can sense me from the other side of the portal. They might be too afraid to come through."

"I hope so," Gary replied, still not completely convinced.

To their pleasant surprise, they carried on up the temple without incident until they reached the red glow. There it was, the thin red film of the gateway to the Val Thane home world. Unlike the gently flowing matter that made up the surface of the Earth gateway, the film covering this gateway's opening zigg-zagged and gnashed about violently, leaving little to the imagination as to what lay beyond.

Gary handed the keystone to Alistair and pointed to the dragon artefact he'd naively inserted previously.

"No way I'm getting any closer," Gary said, "it's you they're scared of, not me."

"Thanks," Alistair replied sarcastically, taking the keystone from Gary.

Alistair's heart started racing as the artefact didn't seem to budge. He tugged and pulled with all his might but nothing happened. Turning back to his companion, he saw Gary make a twisting motion with his hand then shrug his shoulders as if it were a wild guess. Alistair twisted the artefact as he pulled, exhaling a sigh of relief as this time it responded, coming out freely. There was a chorus of snarls and growls from within the gateway as a clawed hand briefly protruded from the other world. Upon seeing the claw appear from the other side, Alistair didn't hesitate. He pushed the closing keystone into the newly formed recess, the swirling red film covering the gateway's surface reacting instantly, contracting away from the gateway's circumference symmetrically. There was one last roar of protest as the swirling portal of death finally disappeared into the stone face, the two worlds safely separated once more.

CHAPTER 62 - ALISTAIR

"It worked! It worked!," Alistair said overjoyed, not quite believing it could be over. For a brief moment, he even forgot about George, Ulric and Adele. Gary gave a stoically silent nod of approval and was about to speak when they heard a noise in the distance. Getting louder, it became clear the sound was that of a horse at full gallop. From atop their perch on the temple, they could just make out a man on horseback, followed closely by another, the duo just shy of the small bridge that led into the village of Alman. As the two crossed the bridge towards them, Alistair sprung to action, running out across the plateau then down the stairs two at a time. Gary, having seen it as well, followed suit, sprinting down the stairs after Alistair. As the first of the rider's pursuers crossed the bridge, it glanced past its prey, noticing the two men coming towards it as it did. The oversized wolf tripped in its haste to stop, rolling clumsily in the dirt before turning tail to flee, its foul brethren joining it in retreat. Moran and Hadron's horses began to slow, eventually coming to a stop next to the wall at the end of the cul-de-sac where Motel Whiskey had encountered the muggers.

"Many thanks!" Moran said between laboured breaths as Hadron dismounted his horse and bowed.

"What are you doing here!" Alistair exclaimed. "Aris needs you to rally the mercenaries, not to mention the fact it isn't safe this far south."

"No need to fret. Aris's little militia is raring and ready to go."

"Then why are you both here? I thought you would be helping

Aris with the Chimon."

"Moran has enlisted the services of the Green Suns," replied Hadron. "A more capable band of warriors there is not. As such, my sword is better employed in this task."

Moran spoke. "My sister's life, the family I have been so unjustly separated from for so long, is in jeopardy. I shall not abandon her again, no matter the cost. As such, myself and Hadron shall be accompanying you to the exchange."

"Nothing is quite as it seems with you is it Moran. Well, no arguments here."

"I could not care less if you did present an argument, I will be accompanying you regardless. On another note, were you able to close the gateway?"

"Oh yes," replied Alistair. "The Val Thane's famed infinite numbers just became finite. Now we just have to hope there are enough soldiers left to defend the realm from those that remain."

Moran, who when being described by anyone who knew him would certainly not elicit terms such as "fun-loving" or "happy-go-lucky", surprised his two companions as he punched the air, expressing one very out of character cheer as Hadron seemingly learnt to smile.

CHAPTER 63 - GEORGE

George dismounted his horse and sat on the stone step next to the gateway. Adele had given up struggling, lying tied to her horse, hands behind her back, mouth gagged with an old dirty rag. Ulric moved to console her but her eyes told him she was having none of it. Mouthing the word "sorry" he turned away in shame.

"Shit!!!!!" yelled George, throwing the leather bag on the ground as if that would fix the problem. "Bloody Aris! That slippery fish!"

"What is it?" inquired Ulric in a concerned tone.

"Aris has the bloody substance, I don't know ho... you sly devil," George thought, remembering Aris bumping into him as they left the cave. How long had he known?

"They figured it out," he said turning to face his partner in crime.

"I'm fairly sure that became apparent when you took my daughter hostage," Ulric replied sarcastically.

"No not that. Aris knows my real identity and therefore knows what happens if we don't get that bloody substance back before the year's out."

"Hmm," replied Ulric scratching his chin. "The lesser Val Thane won't go near Alistair, but if I remember correctly, Dejant defeated the Chimon AFTER grabbing the keystone last time. I seem to remember it wasn't very scared of him then. Came close to taking his head off more than once."

"I think I see where you're going with this..."

Ulric continued, "We have control of the Chimon. Why don't we just re-task him from the battle and instead have him wait in close proximity to the temple? Dejant doesn't possess the sword this time around, and he's still not as deadly as his former self if what you tell me about the battle with Teren is anything to go by."

"So we have the Chimon kill them and then we retrieve the substance," replied George. "A plan after my own heart, but I'm not prepared to risk the lizard destroying the substance in the process. You've seen what it can do. That monstrosity's turned more than a few battle hardened men into crispy critters. Not to mention the fact that bloody sanctimonious, holier than thou Aris bastard would use his last dying breath to destroy the stuff just to spite me. No, I think the only way forward is to concede a small defeat and let them end the Val Thane plague for now. We'll get the substance when they come for your daughter."

"What if they don't?"

"I wouldn't worry about that. Alistair has grown quite fond of her and her remaining brothers seem to have developed some sort of instinctive protectionist attitude towards their long-lost sibling. I highly doubt they'll give up on her just to deny us a longer life."

Ulric had to work hard to contain the anger bubbling up inside him. George had assured Ulric on multiple occasions she wouldn't be hurt, but the laissez-faire way in which he was currently describing the life of the woman whom he saw as his daughter was beginning to incite a primal rage.

"Alright George, but I swear, if any harm comes to her..." he said shaking his head from side to side, his eyes wide open.

"I am sorry, please forgive my lack of tact in this matter. It's just our very lives are at stake. You have my word. No harm will come to her. 'Tis merely a bluff. One that for our sake I hope they don't call."

Ulric calmed a little.

"I suppose the best course of action is to pull the Chimon away from the temple then and make sure they plant the keystone successfully?"

"Agreed," said George clasping Ulric's shoulder. "Once we have the substance we've got another thousand years with which to have another go."

Ulric looked at the chunk of metal on the ground.

"I suppose we probably don't need to infect the masses

immediately, there should be more than enough here to infect the leaders of both worlds."

"I guess that will have to do for now," said George retrieving the device from his satchel, entering the remote command for the Chimon to move on from its current position guarding the temple and join the brood.

CHAPTER 64 - GEORGE

George heard the clopping of horse's hooves on solid ground.

"A few folk short aren't we?" he said as Gary, Alistair, Hadron and Moran brought their horses to a stop approximately ten yards from where Ulric was holding the cuffs of a bound, gagged and blindfolded Adele.

George reclined leisurely on the stone steps that led up to the smooth surface of the gateway above him. It seemed they had at least created that memory correctly Alistair thought, recognising the large stone ring atop the platform, a gentle blue film flowing across its surface. The location was even familiar, a random clearing in the dense forest not far north of Castle Brin. Under different circumstances, it would have made for a quite picturesque setting, the cool gentle breeze complemented by the warm afternoon sunshine.

"Hold on Adele," said Alistair, "we'll have you freed in a moment."

Adele nodded her head as best she could in acknowledgement.

"Silly me," said George, getting up off the steps and walking slowly towards them, hands behind his back as he stared at the ground.

Going unnoticed by all present, Hadron's forearm tensed as he gripped the sword tighter, his weight shifting as he bent his knees, lowering himself into a stance more conducive to rapid acceleration.

"It seems I've gone and dropped the substance. I am so very

clumsy. You wouldn't per chance have happened to pick it up for me would you?" he said, looking up menacingly at Alistair.

"First, you release Adele, then you get the substance," he replied, returning the stare.

"Hmm, I'd love to believe you Alistair, but you surely must understand my lack of faith in that proposition ending well for myself."

"Would you have faith in this?" said Gary, drawing a pistol from his belt, pointing it at George's head.

"Ahh, easy now, it would be a terrible shame if Adele were to get in the way of a bullet now then wouldn't it," George replied, moving sideways so that the majority of his body mass was behind Adele, drawing his own pistol and pointing it at her back.

"Wait, wait," cried Ulric, visibly concerned for Adele's safety in light of the quickly escalating situation.

"Settle down Gary," came Alistair's voice from behind.

Moran calmly removed the substance from his satchel, placing the flask on the ground.

"Now that's better," said George. "Ulric, be a good fellow and pick that up would you, I'm rather occupied as you can see."

Ulric moved slowly towards the substance, bending down to pick it up as Gary moved to the right, making sure Ulric didn't get between his weapon and George.

"The girl," said Gary, getting impatient now.

"Thank you gentlemen. That wasn't so hard was it," George said as Ulric handed him the flask.

George received the flask without looking at it for even the slightest of moments, his eyes not leaving Gary and his drawn pistol for a second.

"Well, time to uphold my end of the bargain," he said pushing Adele forward toward the safety of her comrades.

Adele stumbled forward and for what would turn out to be the most fateful fraction of a second in her life, got between George and Gary. The obstruction passed in the blink of an eye, but that was all the time George required as he fired his pistol, hitting her in the back, just missing Gary as it came out the other side. Hadron dashed forward across the grass as another shot rang out, the sound rendering the swishing of Hadron's blade parting the air inaudible, the tip coming in contact with the right side of George's face, slicing a gash from his chin to his forehead. George's hand flew to his face as he retreated through the gateway, blood gushing from the wound that had missed his eye by the breadth of a whisker. At the same time Hadron's blade was making its pass up George's face, Gary moved forward to catch Adele's falling body, putting his right arm that was holding his pistol past her, blind firing in the general direction that George would be as he simultaneously caught her with his other shoulder. Alistair and Moran, completely taken aback by the chaos and not close enough to take action regardless, were stunned just long enough for George to escape through the portal.

Gary laid Adele down gently on the grass, removing the gag from her mouth as the others dashed to her side.

"No no no no!" cried Alistair, his mind a blur.

"Oh God," said Moran as he came sliding down beside her.

Hadron knelt by her side, his expression conveying a concern most wouldn't have thought him capable of.

Gary's head remained clear as he immediately started putting pressure on the wound.

"I need a bandage now," he said in the calm tone of someone who had obviously been in this situation many times before.

Alistair quickly ripped a piece of his shirt and gave it to Gary who proceeded to apply it to the wound. Adele's face was pale, even more so than usual, to the point that they weren't sure if she was alive till she moaned in pain. Alistair gently removed the blind fold as he stroked the hair out of her eyes.

"We're here now. You're going to be OK," he said, his wavering voice giving away the fact that he wasn't really so sure.

She grimaced in pain. "Did you... did you stop the Val Thane?"

"Yes, yes, the gateway is closed now, the realm is safe once more." She managed a painful smile and mouthed what Alistair took as I love you, before closing her eyes, her expression disappearing along with her life force.

"I love..."

Alistair was cut off by Moran, "Move now! I can suspend time around her. When it's done, you'll have to place our bodies in a safe location, myself and Adele being unconscious for its duration.

"A safe location?!" Alistair said in shock as he moved aside, Moran beginning to go through the motions.

"There's bound to be a cellar you can lock us in somewhere in the village we just passed through. Have Hadron guard us till your return. I can buy her time, but you have to get that substance back. It's all that can save her now. I can probably keep it active for a week... much longer and..."

"Much longer and what?" Alistair replied.

"Let's just say there will be two dead Vergen's rather than one. Once initiated I cannot release myself. Time for the two of us will only resume upon my death, contact with the substance or the assistance of another mage who has knowledge of the procedure. Therefore, unless you have some magical friends I don't know of, I'd suggest retrieving the substance.

"Moran, you have my word! Just do it!"

Moran continued through the motions of casting the spell, promptly thereafter falling to the ground unconscious. Alistair checked Adele for a pulse. Nothing. He began to worry that it hadn't worked as his forearm brushed her hair. It took a moment to register, but then he suddenly realised that her hair didn't move. He attempted to part her fringe, but to no avail. Some unknown force was holding it in place. A wave of quiet optimism washed over him as he turned to Gary.

"I think it worked," he said, a half smile replacing his distraught expression.

"Good to hear lad," Gary replied comfortingly, standing up and turning toward the unconscious Moran.

Just as he was about to lift the mage from the ground he spotted a third body, one that had completely slipped their attention in the chaos that had ensued. Alistair noticed it now as well. Lying approximately ten yards away was Ulric Vergen, a large pool of red liquid covering the grass next to his head.

"Two shots..." said Gary, more to himself than to anyone else. "The bastard didn't just shoot Adele, he shot his partner in crime too. Aye, this fucker just keeps moving up my to kill list. I mean, I can't say I'm particularly sad this old scum bag's gone, but killing your mates? I dinnay care how shady ye are, that's just not on."

Alistair gently placed one arm under Adele's back and one under her knees, lifting her rigid body onto Hadron's horse, Gary placing Moran next to her. Alistair turned to Hadron as he grabbed his horse's reins, leading it gently forward.

"You take care of them you hear," unable to hide the emotion in his voice.

Hadron smiled for what Alistair thought was probably only the second time since he'd met him as he wiped the blood from this end of his sword.

"This is not goodbye. Destiny will have us meet again, but not before you finish this," he said, holding the rag that was now stained red with George's blood in front of him. Alistair breathed deeply, a flurry of emotions washing over him.

"Come on lad," said Gary. "We've got a week at most if what Moran said was anything to go by."

CHAPTER 65 - MORRIS

"This is my best anti-fire," said Morris, holding a glass jar of green liquid in the air for all to see.

"And this," he said, holding a sealed glass bottle of clear liquid as far away from his body as possible in an almost paranoid manner, "will eat through a five foot thick steel bar. Or, in this case, the fire breathing lizard known as the Chimon's scales. I've dubbed it 'steel rot.'"

"How's that gonna eat through steel when it can't even make a hole it that there bottle?" replied one of the Green Sun's mercenaries.

"Glad you noticed," replied Morris excitedly. "It's brilliant really, the way it burns through everything except glass. The Chimon should have covered itself in window panes," Morris joked. Unfortunately for Morris, the jest went down like a lead balloon, those present seemingly not sharing his sense of humour. Giving a nervous chuckle he continued, wishing Aris were the one laying out the battle plan. Sadly, his currently marred reputation precluded him from doing so. Instead, Aris had devised the plan, informing Morris and then later joining the meeting under the guise of just another mercenary, a hood doing its best to hide his face on the off chance any of them recognised him.

"Make no mistake, his fire breath covers a wide arc, which means access to its underside is going to be much easier said than done. Hence the anti-fire. This should protect the attacker from its flame long enough for them to get into striking range.

"Hate to rain on your parade, but I don't see how your little bottle of green stuff is gonna stop that thing turning us into toasty pork," said one of the gathered soldiers.

"Ah yes, how silly of me not to explain. Cover yourself in the liquid and the fire will do you no harm."

"I trust my sword and I trust my shield," said the soldier. "What I don't trust, is some green potion from a crazy man that smells worse than I do!"

The other soldiers laughed as Morris's eyes darted nervously towards Aris then back again.

"A demonstration then!" he finally replied, a little louder than initially intended. Morris rubbed the substance over his right hand and up his forearm then proceeded to hold it over one of the torches lighting the tent. To the surprise of the men his arm didn't burn, the man before them seemingly indifferent to the fact that it was hanging in open flame.

"Well I'll be damned," said the same soldier who had just finished dismissing Morris's concoction.

To prove it wasn't a trick Morris handed the soldier the beaker then asked another soldier to try the same experiment on him. There was no pain as the flame wrapped around his arm and he did not catch alight. Seemingly convinced, the captain of the Green Suns clapped his hands together.

"Tomorrow we kill the Chimon, but tonight, we feast!"

An almighty cheer erupted as the mercenaries dispersed, ready for a night of feasting and drinking before the inevitable showdown tomorrow.

CHAPTER 66 - ARIS

The mercenaries of the Green Suns hid in the forest either side of the path, not simply fighting for coin today, but for survival as well. Morris, much to his relief, was not present. His mind was his weapon and today he'd supplied the tools the Green Suns would need to complete the daunting task. Sitting this one out, he'd agreed to meet up with his companion after the battle.

Aris waited patiently as time passed by, not a sound to be heard, the birds eerily quiet if they were present at all. After about an hour of waiting, they felt it. Softly at first, the seismic vibrations became stronger as the great beast approached. The demon lumbered forward, an escort of at least twelve lesser Val Thane not leaving its side for a second. The men stood their ground, the Green Suns enlisting only the most battle hardened souls. As it made its way into the ambush point Aris gave the signal, grabbing the branch of the tree next to him as he almost lost his balance, one of its lifted feet slamming into the ground not more than a couple of yards away. The bolts did their job, the flying wood and steel bringing down the escort. Penetrating the lesser Val Thane with ease, any that made their way to the Chimon met an entirely different fate, merely bouncing off as predicted. To the giant lizard they represented no more than a mild annoyance. The men gave a loud rally cry as they charged from either side, buoyed by the knowledge the thing's fire would be rendered useless by Morris's alchemy. The Chimon's immense size was simultaneously its greatest strength and most pronounced weakness. Its bulky frame afforded it immense strength and near invincibility, but at the same time rendered it incredibly slow. Rotating sluggishly on its four legs, the Chimon turned to face the left flank, opening its mouth as it did, bathing the brave warriors in green flame. To the right flank's utter dismay and horror, it turned out that Morris's potion was not effective against the supernatural heat of Chimon's breath, the entire left flank being instantly burnt to cinders. Blame would come later however, there was no time for that now. The left flank's sacrifice had given the right flank time to close the distance, the forward group hammering the giant metal clasps into the ground around its massive right side feet, locking them into place. Struggling in vain to turn its body, the beast let out an almighty roar of frustration, its front and rear feet on the right side not lifting, both having been riveted into the ground. The right flank moved towards its tail, its head only able to swivel so far without the rest of the body following. **Far from defeated however, it whipped its mighty tail in protest. Catching three soldiers that were too slow to react, the force of the blow killed them instantly as the others ducked safely under the swinging biological pole axe.** The remaining men moved into the region close to its side, a sort of safe zone its tail and head could not reach. Although out of immediate danger, they still needed to penetrate its scales if they were to do any damage.

A barrage of glass bottles ensued, smashing on contact with the Chimon's armoured carapace, coating the thing in Morris's concoction. Thankfully for all present, Morris's rot steel was far more effective than his anti-fire. The Chimon roared in pain as large portions of scale were eaten away wherever the concoction made contact. To any outside observer, the Chimon now appeared as though it was covered in sores, the holes in its armour revealing the pink flesh beneath.

Aris held his breath, silently willing the sores to remain open, praying his hypothesis was correct and that Alistair had indeed successfully closed the gateway. The men, conveniently not privy to their foe's potential immortality, needed little encouragement. A frenzied attack ensued, the Green Suns hacking into any piece of exposed flesh they could find. The thing shook its head from side to side in madness, the pain driving it into a wild rage. **The braces** in the ground started to wobble as pain induced adrenaline began to course through its veins. The men had climbed up its leg onto its side and were hacking away with all their might. Sadly, it was too slow a process, the yards of flesh protecting its vital organs taking an age to cut through.

Grabbing another bottle of Morris's rot steel, Aris decided to take a chance. The thick, great oak like leg was all that stood between him and the underbelly of the beast now. He darted around the clawed foot just as it pulled the rivets that had been containing it out of the ground. Rolling under its belly, he made an educated guess as to the location of its heart, tossing the bottle at its underside. Barely pausing long enough for the rot steel to do its work, he thrust his sword into the open wound above, the blade being eaten away moments later, Aris not having had time to wait for the rot steel to dissipate. Aris's heart sank as he dived to the side, holding a hilt, it being all that remained of his sword. A feeling of dread spread throughout his body, in part due to his impending doom, in part the knowledge he'd failed, condemning the realm to almost certain extinction. Aris was oblivious to his comrades screams as they were flung from the Chimon's back, the thing turning towards him, an almighty rage in its eyes. "This is it then," thought Aris as it turned to face him, opening its mouth, the green flame beginning to materialise inside. And then it happened. The Chimon wavered, seemingly losing its balance. The green fire began to subside, instead being replaced by a puff of smoke as the demon let out one last agonising roar, falling to the ground with an almighty crash.

They'd done it! The Chimon was dead! Aris's thoughts however, quickly turned from relief to concern once more. He knew the deception he and Morris had played was not likely to win them any favours with the remaining mercenaries. Getting to his feet quickly, he ran for the tree line, hoping the survivors hadn't had time enough to compose themselves and come to the conclusion that they had been tricked, half of them involuntarily sacrificed for the greater good.

CHAPTER 67 - DAGATH

The call had been sounded, Dagath releasing the pigeons, the small birds carrying news of the looming threat and Aris's plan to defeat it. No actual mention of Aris was made in the message however. All Dagath could do now was pray that the six bickering Northern Kingdoms would put aside their petty squabbles and unite to stop the one true threat to their survival as a whole. Word of the carnage in the South had spread North a good time prior to his message, a more effective motivator to cooperate than potential extinction Dagath was unable to imagine. The issue now was not a lack of information, but whether or not they believed it, the North being a notoriously stubborn people, or so it was said in the South. Dagath had conveyed Aris's convincing argument for halting the horde's advance at Velderwood Neck.

The Neck, as it was more commonly referred to, was a narrow passage between two towering mountains stretching into the sky. Many a man had attempted to reach their summit, some returning unsuccessfully, the others never to be seen again.

The strong interest the mountains garnered from their would-be conquerors wasn't simply motived by bragging rights or the thrill of the challenge (although it would be a lie to say that didn't factor in somewhere). No, there was a much more valuable prize to be had if one were to successfully navigate their peaks. Proving to others that it could be done, the ability to cross into the North without needing to traverse the Neck. The North didn't have the numbers, the craftsmanship and battle tactics that the South possessed, which under normal circumstances would have led to them being overthrown long ago. The one aspect however, that had abated any potential threat from the south for all these years, were those two mountains. Or more specifically, the narrow passage of land that passed between them known as Velderwood Neck.

Many an ambitious King had discovered to their dismay, that numbers meant nothing in the neck, the ground between the mountains affording no more than four men abreast at its narrowest points. It wasn't simply the sheer height of the mountains that caught the breath of each man upon their initial beholding of the monolithic natural monuments, but the passage between them itself. Unnaturally flat, the sides of the mountains rose vertically into the sky on either side of the neck, seemingly as though the two raised pieces of land had once been one, something slicing a gap through the middle before time immemorial.

Dagath was admiring the sheer cliff faces in front of him when the sound of footsteps released him from his thoughts, the noise originating from the other side of the neck. The sounds of an army marching, slowly becoming louder and louder as a sea of armoured men that carried on as far as he could see approached, clangs reverberating off the sheer walls of the thin gap. As they neared, Dagath recognised one of their commanders as Ross Smith of Bincil. His rusted steel armour was typical of the harsh North lands, these people wearing imperfections and shoddy workmanship like badges of honour.

"Strange times these. Never thought I'd see myself working with the likes of Trescot," came his Bincil drone as he approached the ex Trescot commander.

The Bincil accent was similar to Dagath's, only the words seemed to take longer to annunciate and much more emphasis was put on 'Os'.

"I'm told the Val Thane have been released. Don't really believe it myself, but I guess the fact I'm out here says a great deal of how much that matters. I tell you now though, if you've got me all the way out here for nothing there'll be hell to pay."

"Hell to pay you say... I think you'll find that choice of words very fitting in the coming days," Dagath replied as he was approached by three other commanders.

Roderick Luther of Ghotine's wild black beard was as familiar as his guttural accent, but Dagath was yet to have come in contact with the other two.

"Erwin Trigger of Seng Fa," said a slightly built man mounted upon what Dagath could only describe as something between a pony and a small horse. "This is Trin Mitchell of Tyrandale," he said pointing to another of the riders, "and to my right, Yuri Clavchenko of Bletsova."

Dagath greeted them all. "I know Trescot and the North have not always enjoyed the most amicable of relationships, but what lies in the past matters not now".

Dagath had not yet come in contact with anyone from Bletsova, the slow, drawn out, almost slurred words coming as a surprise, Dagath wondering if Yuri had been drinking. Far from the drunks they sounded like, Bletsova actually sported the highest average intelligence per head of population, the high social value they placed upon the progression of what would on Earth be referred to as the 'hard sciences' likely playing a role. If one had a mind for mathematics or engineering, Bletsova was the place to be. If one enjoyed pursuing the fine arts however, Bletsova should be avoided like the plague.

"We may have been more amicable if you and your southerners were not continually attempting to overthrow our lands! Unsuccessfully I might add!"

Biting his tongue, Dagath resisted the urge to comment on his accent, ignoring the slight before continuing.

"Trescot and Barathax are in ruins, along with what we believe to be the vast majority of Eboda and Bledith. The things that destroyed them lie three days march south of here and are intent on bringing the same fate to your lands as they have ours. We can continue our petty squabbles and lose the South and the North along with our lives, or we can put our differences aside, just for the moment, and halt their death march here together."

Erwin spoke, "If what you say is true, it matters not how many we kill, their numbers infinite, they shall eventually overwhelm us. Tell me, where is the sense in such a plan?"

"As we speak, a band of hero's make haste to disable the Val Thane gateway, stopping their reinforcements in the process. A second group will ambush the demon lizard that leads them. The longer we hold here, the more time we give them and the less carnage the Vale Thane exact on the Northern lands - your lands that is."

"And if your so called 'band of hero's' fail?" said Roderick.

"If they fail... well, let's just say there won't be any more debating who is responsible for our less than 'amicable' relationship."

"So we hold the neck in the hope that your motley bunch manages to close the gateway?" said Trin. "Sounds unlikely. But, I suppose, in the absence of any better ideas... I suppose I haven't a choice."

"It seems that for now we have a mutual interest in your plan's success," replied Yuri. "Bletsova will gladly kill any who try to cross the neck."

The other commanders grumbled and moaned, not wanting to seem too eager, but in the end agreed to help, knowing that there was little else they could do if the Val Thane threat were real.

Once they had all agreed, Dagath took Ross Smith aside.

"I don't see any Veblo banners here. Do they not have any desire to last the year?"

"You know Veblo. They don't believe in magic, always coming up with some poor explanation whenever a mage does something they don't understand."

"That's if the mage in question were to make it through the city gates with his head still attached to his shoulders," Dagath replied.

"Yes, well, that's the point. They aren't convinced the Val Thane exist. If you don't believe in magic, you're hardly likely to believe hellish demons from another world have been released into our own, seemingly intent on genocide. King Rufus thinks it a ploy, something merely concocted by Trescot to curry favour with the North now your army has been crushed."

"And none of you thought the same?"

"No, I don't know how good your history is Dagath but Veblo is a relatively new Kingdom. Most of the lands represented here existed in one form or another last time those things were unleashed. Veblo are too young and naive to take the threat for what it is."

"Fair enough. I suppose five out of six will have to do. How many men do we have altogether?"

"About three hundred thousand."

"Alright, good. The plan's simple. We hold the neck as long as possible to give the others time to shut down the gateway."

"Just out of curiosity, there's a rumour doing the rounds that Aris is a part of this band of heroes you speak of. Is this true?"

"It's true, he is. But before you protest, know that I like Aris no more than the next man. So far as skills required for the task, Aris is second to none. Whether or not he can be trusted is another matter entirely, however. A matter I have, and shall continue to pay great attention to."

"I don't think I'd necessarily even agree where his skills are concerned, but I suppose there's not much that can be done about it now. Very well, what say we begin preparations at dawn."

CHAPTER 68 - DAGATH

The men of the unlikely coalition stood a way back from the northern entrance to the neck. For some of them, this would be their first real battle. Others were hardened veterans, the evolutionary process of war preserving traits that would be needed today while culling those not fit for the task at hand. The fact remained however, that a good deal were merely militia, padding the ranks to give the impression the lords of the smaller kingdoms were contributing their fair share. The political spoils of this war if it were won, were almost as strong a motivator to some as the threat of extinction. None of them however, be they veteran or farmer, had faced an enemy quite like this.

The sky clouded over almost ironically as a fuzzy brown black blob appeared on the horizon, or at least the tiny strip of it they could see between the towering cliffs. From atop the stone wall, the gathered army began to discern with greater accuracy the characteristics of their encroaching enemy. All manner of nightmarish creatures proceeded towards them. It was almost as though someone had combined all the horror stories ever written then materialised the characters into reality, a terrifying horde of demons moving ominously towards them. Fear and dread began to spread through the ranks as some began to question why they were here in the first place. Most of them, if they were to be honest, believed the word of the Val Thane invasion merely a typical exaggeration, the South inflating the reality of the foe that had defeated them, man's pride known to be a most valuable commodity. Their preconceived beliefs had turned out to be quite wrong this day however. The South it seemed, had described the threat as it were.

Yuri helped change their mind, the telling look upon his unforgiving face speaking volumes of what would happen if anyone so much as thought about deserting. What was initially a brown black blob, was now a wave of Val Thane. The beasts could smell their prey's scent in the air, seemingly driving them into a frenzy as they closed the distance. Lurching forward, what could be best described as a four-legged vanguard set off at a charge.

"Archers ready!!!" came the call from Ross Smith, soon to be echoed by the other commanders.

A line of arrow heads promptly raised towards the sky, not quite parallel as would be the norm, the geography rendering depth and hence power more important in this instance than breadth, the goal being to fill the neck with as many shafts of death as possible. A tense few seconds that must have seemed like a lifetime to the archers finally culminated with the command.

"Release!"

A flurry of wood and metal pierced the sky before falling onto the horde, taking with them a considerable number of Val Thane. The speed with which they covered ground however, had taken the commanders by surprise. The line of archers had barely strung another arrow as the first of the Val Thane crashed through the valley like water bursting through a dam. All manner of things began to funnel through the gap. Larger Val Thane had to go through single file, others not fitting at all, screaming wildly in frustration as they were denied their prey. The men on the other side, although horrified, fought valiantly and after an exhausting couple of hours that seemed more like a couple of days, they appeared to have defeated the last of the horde. Their victory however, was not without loss, be it psychological or physical. The Val Thane took with them at least a tenth of the coalitions forces and the vast majority who remained would never to be quite the same after what they had witnessed this day. Regardless, the mood lifted as the last remaining demons were slain. All that was left was the incessant screaming and roars of those stuck on the other side.

"It seems this legendary evil is not quite the genocidal hell swarm you southerners make out," said Yuri to Dagath, stepping between the corpses, bow still in hand.

"I always thought you southerners were weak, but I never in my wildest dreams thought you that feeble. They're certainly not pretty, but world destroying? I hardly think so," said Roderick.

"My regards for the bit of sport, but really Dagath, I think your friend Aris may have a bit of a dramatic tongue," said Erwin.

Dagath stood in an embarrassed daze. "Was that really it? Had this been another of Aris's schemes? Make me look like a fool in front of the smaller kingdoms?" His question was soon answered as one of the soldiers searching the corpses on the ground yelled something as he pointed towards the horizon. There was another brown black blob forming, only this one was larger than the last and it was coming right for them.

"Seems it's going to be a bit more than a warm up," said Dagath, ironically somewhat relieved that he hadn't been had as a total fool.

"Back to your positions men!" came the cry from Trin as the second wave approached.

As the second wave of Val Thane reached the south side of the neck the men observed a far greater concentration of large demons, providing comfort in the knowledge that they couldn't fit through the gap. Little did they know, that comfort would later turn to horror, the sounds of the large burrowing rat like creatures becoming audible in the mountain walls as they tunnelled through, eventually digging tunnels large enough for their hulking kin to traverse. That eventuality was a ways off yet however. The direct concern now was the addition of the skeletal looking flyers as Dagath turned to the skies.

"Man the ballistas!" yelled Erwin. "We're going to need them."

CHAPTER 69 - GARY

Gary spoke, "Listen, you're not going to be able to stop him on your own, ye might be a fancy pants swordsman here but that means shite all back on Earth. I've got some friends back home that can help us out."

"Thanks, but what are you going to tell them? They'd think you've lost the plot if you say we're chasing a thousand-year-old man that just tried to destroy an entire civilisation."

"All they need to know is that this fucker played a part in Renfield, Winters and Burnley's death and they'd follow us into the gates of hell."

"Fair enough," said Alistair, putting a hand on Gary's shoulder. "Thanks."

"It's me that should be thanking ye lad, if ye and your friends hadn't shown up, at best I'd be stuck here and at worst I'd be some oversized mutt's dinner. Not to mention, I get a shot at this bastard."

Alistair nodded then put one finger into the thin semi translucent veil that stretched the surface of the gateway. The stone frame always looked so out of place. If not for the blue liquid veil covering the opening, the frame would just appear to be a set of concrete blocks that had been mortared together, no intricate designs or clues present to hint at who had built it or its true purpose. Alistair guessed they must have valued function over aesthetics as he turned to Gary.

"Think he's waiting for us on the other side?"

"No clue, but we've no other options now do we. Let's just get on with it," he said as he stepped forth into the veil.

The time it took to travel through a gateway was negligible, almost as if the traveller were walking through a door. Once the eyes were past the thin film, the world appeared as it should on the other side. There were no spiralling wormholes or fancy blue tunnels with bolts of electricity snaking across the perimeter, just a simple transition from one world to the next.

"How long's it been lad?" came the voice next to him as Alistair emerged from the other side.

"Too long," said Alistair as he surveyed the scene around him. "But then I guess I've never really been here before, my memory being naught but a lie... It still feels like home."

Squinting as he stepped into the bright sunlight, the sound of birds chirping in the trees, Alistair could just make out a thin road in the distance. Turning about, he was shocked when he realised that he and Gary were both standing in open countryside, no gateway or like structure to be seen.

"Noooo!" Alistair yelled, throwing his hands skywards.

"What?" Gary replied, not understanding the sudden outburst.

"Don't you see? The exit and entry points, they're not one and the same. We can't get back. She's dead!"

"Aye, seems you're right about the entry-exit, but dinnay worry, ye will be going back right soon. Just means we need to take three things from George now 'stead of two."

"What?!" Alistair snapped, frustrated by his companion's seeming lack of comprehension.

"Well, before we were just gonna take the substance and his life, now we're gonna take the location of the entry gate on Earth too."

As Gary's simple yet instant plan sunk in, Alistair's spirits soared. Alistair attempted his best Scottish accent as he shook Gary excitedly by the shoulders.

"Ye a genious lad!" he shouted, completely butchering the impersonation, Gary laughing all the same.

"Well the good news - George wasn't waiting to shoot us. The bad news - unless you know something I don't, I think we might be lost."

"So it would seem," Alistair sighed.

"Let's go to the road and see if we can't find a sign."

Wherever they had appeared, it seemed the area wasn't short on rain, the lush green grass matching the occasional tree as they followed the road till they reached a large sign.

"Inverness 15 miles!" Gary yelled excitedly the moment he saw the road sign. "Ye can thank your lucky stars, this couldn't have worked out better if I'd planned it!"

"Do tell."

"We need to find someone. James is a bit strange but if ye need someone lost to become unlost in a hurry, there's no one better. The man lives not more than a few miles from here. Come on, we'll be there in no time," Gary said as he set off at a jog down the quiet country road.

CHAPTER 70 - GARY

Alistair followed Gary until they came to a small country house. Not bothering to knock on the front door, Gary proceeded to the rear garden where two large wooden doors had been built into the ground. As he pulled the doors open, a concrete staircase leading down into a dimly lit room was revealed. Inside it seemed like something from a doomsday scenario. The plain grey concrete gave the small room an almost cold war era Soviet feel. There were all sorts of provisions and equipment stacked neatly on the shelves bordering its perimeter, two flickering fluorescent lights only serving to reinforce Alistair's initial perception. Computer parts were scattered everywhere, surrounding a bald, middle aged man with the thickest pair of reading glasses Alistair had ever seen. The malachite glow of the screen he was seated in front of danced across his glasses, the green text on black background command line interface only adding further credence to the geekish stereotype.

"Police, don't move!" shouted Gary.

James flinched, dropping the motherboard he was holding, so absorbed in his soldering that he hadn't noticed someone had entered the room.

"Gary Anders, is that you!" he said in a nasal voice, pushing the glasses back up on the bridge of his nose. "To what do I owe the visit? I don't seem to remember receiving an email?" James looked to Alistair. "Oh you've brought a friend too."

"Apologies for the lack of notice James, but we're in a bind and

255

could really use some of your whiz bang computer wizardry. Oh, and this is Alistair by the way."

James, or 1337UB3RHX0R as he was known online, was every bit as bright now as he was the day his parents bought him his first computer, a Commodore 64. If the obsession he developed was in a more socially accepted field, it would probably have been described as a passion. The long nights he spent programming, researching networking and later security, eventually lead him to the wrong side of the law. Curiosity rather than malice drove him to engage in the activities his target corporations and government bodies were less than pleased with. Their IT security teams were especially frustrated, being made to seem the fool on more than one occasion. James never stole anything or caused any harm. He'd merely break into the system, leaving behind some form of tell-tale before vanishing into the crowd of IP addresses once more. This sort of behaviour however, eventually catches up with even the most paranoid of its practitioners. 1337UB3RHX0R was eventually identified as James Greensill by an international crime investigation agency, his arrest occurring not long after his 25th birthday. The list of companies and governments on which he'd committed what essentially amounted to digital trespass, was enormous. It was to this end that he was given the choice of spending the next 25 years in 'a room without a view', or be hired by an international crime investigation agency under very strict conditions, where he would engage in the same activities, only against different targets, his actions now being sanctioned by a legitimate organisation.

As fate would have it, it was during an operation against an Eastern European Organised Crime syndicate that he met Captain Gary Anders of Motel Whiskey. Providing information to the boots on the ground, James, working in tandem with Gary and his team, was successful in shutting down a major branch of the syndicate. Unbeknownst to James, the syndicate had a proficient networking and security expert of their own. This man was able to ascertain and pass on James' full identity prior to Gary and his team raiding the branch.

A few months later, upon his security detail's scheduled shift change, the relief team never arrived.

Being the paranoid hacker he was, James was distraught, concocting all sorts of conspiracy theories as to why his employer had left him without a security detail. Reaching out to the only person he knew could help, he contacted the man he had just assisted - Gary Anders. James offered an exorbitant sum for Gary to bring a crew immediately, the man now fearing for his life. Most of the time James' paranoid delusions were just that, but in this case, being obsessively cautious paid off. The syndicate made an attempt on his life which Gary and his squad successfully thwarted, killing a dozen men in the process. If one is going to attempt to assassinate a man of James' talents, they'd best be successful the first time. The difficulty in keeping secrets from someone such as him poses a major problem to future plausible deniability, as the international crime investigation agency were to find out. Not long after the attempt on his life, James traced a large donation to one of his superior's political campaign aspirations and a 'clerical error' with the scheduling of his security detail. The relief team had not been rostered on for another week. Gary Anders was a man who oft treated principal, morality and justice above and beyond what was probably the most intelligent course of action, or, much to his superior's frustration, orders. Not one to stray from his convictions, Gary helped James disappear, secretly relocating him to a small property in the Scottish countryside.

It was now time for James to return the favour, 1337UB3RHX0R providing food, water and some couches for them to get some much needed rest, as Gary provided him all the information he had on the man they so desperately needed to find. Gary was somewhat liberal with certain facts of course, the Scot not quite sure a manhunt for a thousand-year-old man from another world sounded quite plausible, even to a man who knew more of the world's secrets than most heads of state combined.

CHAPTER 71 - GARY

After some food and a few hours sleep, Alistair and Gary followed James back to what he aptly referred to as 'The Bunker'.

"That fellow you're looking for, I did some digging, but I initially couldn't find a thing. Then I remembered Gary said the man came from very old money. So I started looking at companies that incorporated at least 500 years ago. There were a few that seemed to fit the profile and are still in existence today, but one in particular caught my eye. You said to look for a Jean Pierre, George Preston, Dannick Veltross or Ulric Vergan with possible connections to James Errol and Co.

Well, lo and behold I found one company of interest. It's changed names and owners throughout the years, but it seems Thane Industries was chaired by one Jean Pierre for a time about 400 years ago. More searching revealed that although it's a common name today, one George Preston is at the current time the majority owner, followed closely by a Dannick Veltross. There isn't anything nearby held directly in their name. However, I later discovered Joram Holdings, a wholly owned subsidiary, has a property in its name approximately ten kilometres from here with hey presto, a private airstrip! If, as you say, he was getting picked up in the same location you were, then I think the next logical destination is this property. Just to be sure, I've pulled footage from the complex's surveillance cameras. Would you believe they're still using RSA without padding... Seriously, you must have been living under a rock to have not heard of Chinese remainder theorem," James said laughing to himself as he leaned back in his chair, shaking his head dismissively.

Gary and Alistair nodded in unison as though they had the slightest clue as to what the man in front of them was on about, the pair not quite sure if James had started speaking another language.

Typing something into the command line and pressing enter, the footage began to play. Alistair and Gary huddled around the glowing monitor, eager to see what the grainy footage would reveal.

A three-vehicle convoy of black SUV's pulled up outside the facility as four large fellows in suits exited the front and rear vehicles. After they'd done some preliminary checks, three more exited the middle vehicle followed by someone clothed in attire that didn't quite match the suited bodyguards. Alistair pointed at the man in ragged clothing on the screen and clicked his fingers excitedly.

"That's him!"

"Right," said Gary, "can you get us some schematics? We need to get going ASAP. He's not gonna want to hang about."

"Done," said James excitedly as he handed them each a radio. "I've uploaded all the relevant information I have on the property and the target to these devices."

Gary slapped him on the back "Nice one. What's the security look like?"

"It would seem their digital security is only rivalled in incompetence by their physical security. Whoever is in charge seems to favour a policy of security by obscurity. Either that, or he just hasn't had time to get organised. I've done a complete fly by with the drone and there's no permanent guard postings. Aside from the guys we just saw then, I've seen no one go in or out since I located the property."

"Alright lads, the boys'll be here any minute now. Let's get a move on Alistair," Gary said as he and Alistair made their way outside, the sound of a vehicle becoming audible as they opened 'The Bunker' doors.

CHAPTER 72 - GARY

"That'll be our ride," said Gary as an old Range Rover came into view, the red vehicle making its way towards them down the dirt track that led to James's house.

Pulling up approximately a metre away, the Rover's three occupants disembarked the vehicle. Alistair could tell from the moment he saw them that they certainly weren't accountants or computer scientists. The tattoos, bald heads and beards giving a quite different impression of their occupation even before the backslapping and handshakes. One could be strong and muscular, but still have the personality and physical presence of a pen pusher, either pasty or orange from fake tan, the sort whose sole goal in life is to take their shirt off at the beach. Gary's friends were certainly strong, but there was no aesthetic vanity here. The strength was functional, their imposing presence best summed up by the phrase, "Not someone you'd like to meet in a dark alley."

The tall one on the left turned to Alistair, "Glad to meet you mate," came a Yorkshire drone. "Terrible thing what happened to the lads. Don't worry, if he's still breathin it's nought gonna be for long."

Alistair nodded then looked at Gary as if to say, "What did you tell them?"

"If it wasn't for this lad here, we'd still be in Basra right now, only six feet underground," Gary said, looking at Alistair as if to say, "Just play along."

"Well if he's alright with you, he's alright with me," came the reply from the shorter man to the right, his voice placing him somewhere around Liverpool.

"This giant of a fellow is Wayne, that's Danny to the right and I'm Connor," said the short one, an unmistakably East London tone.

"Got the kit in the back. We're all pucka! Let's get on with it then," said Connor as he got in the Rover, the others following suit.

"James hey," said Wayne, having to bend forward awkwardly to fit his large frame into the vehicle. "I haven't seen him in years. Still playing with his gadgets is he?"

CHAPTER 73 - GARY

Connor pulled the vehicle to a stop just before the edge of the wood. Approximately one kilometre of open ground stood between them and the solid six-foot-high concrete wall that comprised the complex's perimeter.

Gary spoke into the radio, "Alright James, give us a sit rep and possible points of entry."

"No personnel outside the complex. I assume you'll be ok with the perimeter wall. The building he's most likely in has two possible entry points, a skylight on the roof or through the front door. I'd probably advise against the latter however."

"Just a second lads, I'll find us a way in," said Alistair as he retrieved the RG32 and peered through the scope.

"Find George Preston," he said out loud.

The opaque concrete walls transformed before his eyes into a wire frame as the search process began, just as it had when searching for Aris in castle Brin. After about ten seconds, the portrait of George in the top left corner found a match and the viewpoint zoomed in on his location. He was sitting in a room that was housed in what seemed to be the main building, not far from the middle of the compound. There were two other men in the room with him, presumably some of the body guards they had seen earlier. Alistair passed the scope about the team.

"Piss off!" scoffed Gary in disbelief as he looked through the scope, observing in disbelief the footage of George Preston, no longer simply a wire frame, the image in scope as though someone had placed a high definition camera in the room with him. "Where the hell'd ye get this piece of kit?" Gary said as he handed it to Wayne.

"Well I'll be, give me some lycra and call me Clark Kent, where's the challenge if you can see through the bloody walls! This is gonna be a cake walk."

After taking turns with the scope to confirm George's location, Connor handed it back to Alistair.

"Looks like it wants you to do something."

Alistair peered through the scope. A message was flashing in the bottom right corner, "SUBSTANCE located.....DISPLAY?" Then on the next line "PROGRAMMABLE STEEL located... DISPLAY?"

"Yes," said Alistair quietly.

The scope moved slightly to the right and down, momentarily displaying a wire frame image before morphing into high definition footage of the flask he'd witnessed George use to scoop up the substance. It seemed to be located in a briefcase attached to George's arm. The substance message disappeared but the programmable steel message was still visible.

"Programmable steel?" Alistair said curiously, more to himself than anyone else.

A text document appeared in the scope with a picture of what looked like a blob of steel that was morphing into different shapes.

Programmable Steel:

Metal with unique properties discovered in world designate MX-64. Is similar in composition to Earth native element Ti but shape can be manipulated through the passing of electrical current within element. Closer inspection has revealed trillions of self-organising nanites. Laboratory replication attempts thus far unsuccessful. Potential value: Extreme.

A voice cracked over the radio. "I've looked over the schematics more thoroughly and have derived a third, more optimal path to George. When you're over the perimeter wall and in the compound, make your way to the east section where there should be a small building with a catwalk adjoining its roof. You'll probably need to boost onto it but once you're atop the building, cross the catwalk then go up the set of stairs at the end. From the top, you should be able to jump the small gap to the roof of the adjacent building, which, according to the scope's intel, should be the one he's in. From there you need to rappel down through the skylight and then proceed one floor lower once you're in. This will put you on the same level as the target. He'll be in the second room to your left as you move down the corridor."

"Copy that," replied Gary.

"Here," Alistair said, handing the RG32 to Wayne. "We'll need you to provide sniper support and relay any situational information you can."

"Roger that," replied Wayne, setting up position on a log at the edge of the wood as Alistair gave him a crash course in its operation.

"All of you, DO NOT, I repeat, DO NOT bring down the target unless Alistair or I give you the word," said Gary. "As much as it pains me to say it, we need the contents of that briefcase first and foremost. George is the second priority."

"Understood," came the reply.

"Weapons and comms check everyone."

Once they were satisfied their gear worked, Gary, Connor, Alistair and Danny set off quickly in a crouched position towards the perimeter wall, emerging from the tree line as they did.

Climbing over the wall and landing on the other side, Alistair surveyed the compound. Shipping containers and small demountable buildings were interleaved by a dusty dirt path, weeds and long grass sprouting at random intervals from underneath the raised buildings. As he peeked around the corner of the nearest shipping container he saw the top halves of the two larger buildings in the centre of the compound, one of which was currently occupied by George. There didn't seem to be anyone about and considering they had both an eye in the sky and the RG32 scope, it was probably fairly safe to proceed. Regardless, they moved cautiously, staying low until they had made their way to the demountable wooden building James had mentioned to the east of the compound.

Alistair moved so that he had his back against the wall, cupping his hands, ready to boost the shorter man Connor. Climbing up Alistair, Connor threw his MP5 sub machine gun onto the roof as he did so, needing both hands free to clamber over the edge. Then it happened. A frantic voice came over the radio.

"Hostile across the rooftops! Over!"

As Connor scrambled for his weapon he became aware of one of George's bodyguards staring directly at him, approximately thirty metres away on top of an adjoining building. The bodyguard's gun rose. Connor didn't stand a chance. Scrambling in hopeless desperation for his weapon, the muffled report of a silenced weapon was followed by a thud as the body hit the ground. His fingers clutching the black metal, Connor rolled over and saw the sun. The less fortunate bodyguard however, wasn't going to be seeing much any time soon, the hole in his head making sure of that. The moment he heard the call, Gary had instantly backed away from the wall just far enough that he could make out the bump where the top of the guard's head protruded ever so slightly above the artificial horizon created by the top of the wall. Thankfully for Connor, his aim was true, the silenced round slamming through the edge of the wall between two brackets where its horizontal and vertical faces met, the bullet connecting with the guard's forehead milliseconds before George's man could squeeze the trigger. Not only would Connor be dead, the guards unsuppressed weapon would without a doubt have alerted George and his men to their presence.

Gary spoke anxiously into the radio, "What's the situation with the others? Are we blown?"

"Doesn't seem so," came the reply. "The rest of the guards and George haven't shown any obvious signs of concern."

"What the fuck was that!" Connor whispered frustratedly over the radio. "A little more warning next time?"

"Sorry," came the reply. "I swear he just appeared out of nowhere, and when I squeezed the trigger I just got a red 'X' in the scope."

Alistair spoke into his radio, hiding his frustration as he gave Wayne instructions on reducing the power.

"Ta lad," Connor said smiling at Gary as the others climbed up.

"Up these stairs?" Alistair queried as he observed the makeshift set of metal stairs that bridged the gap between the demountable building's roof and the catwalk James had mentioned.

"Roger that," came the confirmation.

As they came to the top of the stairs and looked out across the catwalk, Gary signaled for them to halt.

"We all clear to cross?" he asked Wayne.

"Affirmative, no hostiles in sight."

"Are ye sure now?"

"Ha ha, that's an affirmative, you're clear to move."

They made their way across the open air catwalk as quickly as possible, it leaving them extremely exposed if any of the guards strayed outside. Crossing without issue, they climbed the stairs on the other side, ending up on the roof of one of the larger buildings when the luck they had experienced thus far abruptly ran out.

"James, isn't there supposed to be a 'small gap' to the next roof? I don't know what you're looking at but I can't see it here."

"Just a moment. Ah I see the problem..." James replied. "Silly me, whoever did the scale on this blue print made a bit of a boo boo. Looks like it's actually a bigger gap than I thought. Idiots right."

"Fucks sake James... we're going to need another route in."

"Well unless you're packing some breaching charges that I don't know about, you're going to have to learn to fly, 'cause there's no other way in except through the walls. That is unless they were kind enough to leave the front door unlocked."

"Shit, shit, shit," Gary cursed.

"Wait! Look down there," said Alistair, pointing just below the roof of the building across the gap.

Gary and the other's gaze followed his finger down and spotted a balcony jutting out of the building they were supposed to jump to.

"You've got to be kidding matey, ye not seriously thinking of trying to jump to that! If ye miss, there's no coming back. That's a massive drop."

Alistair, ignoring Gary's voice of reason, raised his radio, depressing the button on the side.

"James, one floor down there's a balcony with what looks like a set of glass doors. If I can get inside, can I still reach George?" Silence ensued...

"Ok, there's a stairwell from that level that leads down to the floor George is on, so yes, but that's a crazy jump."

"Easy now, easy... I want that bastard dead just as much as ye..." Gary began when Alistair cut him off.

"Good, then I'll see you on the other side," he said, backing up in preparation.

Gary and the others watched in horror as Alistair flung himself through the air then began to drop down towards the waiting balcony. His feet scraping the balcony rail, moments later crashing down on the metal with a smack, Alistair successfully landed. Rolling on impact, he banged into the glass doors with just enough force to crack them but not break through.

Clambering to his feet quickly, he observed the room behind. Satisfied it was clear, he opened the now worse for wear doors, signalling to the others to follow. Gary shook his head, mumbling something incomprehensible as he took the steps backwards and then ran forward and launched himself into the air. Landing successfully moments later, he rolled through the open doors as he hit the ground to reduce the impact of the fall. Next to come flying through the open doors was Danny, clearing the gap with little trouble. It was just the shorter man, Connor now. Stepping backwards then rushing forth, it was obvious from the moment he jumped he wasn't going to make it. Gary, Danny and Alistair's heart's skipped a beat as Connor's head came level with the balcony rail, the only problem being, he was on the wrong side of it. There was a clang of steel as his hands smacked down on the balcony floor just below the railings, clutching the cold metal for dear life as his body swung out into the air below. Alistair and Gary quickly moved over to help but what Connor lacked in height, he certainly made up for in upper body strength, pulling himself up the balcony rails with his arms alone. Alistair later hypothesised a larger man probably wouldn't have been able to take the initial impact, slipping to his doom due to the exponential mass gain any increase in velocity and initial weight would produce. Connor pointed at Alistair as he clambered over the rail.

"You, my friend, owe me a pint."

"I think he owes us all one," replied Danny.

Wayne gave them the all clear over the radio as the trio moved down the stairs and approached the boardroom.

"He's alone in there. The guards seem to have moved on," came Wayne's voice over the radio.

Alistair smiled as he realised the only thing standing between them and George now was a gold coloured handle on a thin wooden door.

"As you enter he'll be slightly to the right. He's sitting at the table facing away from the door looking at what seems to be a television," came Wayne's voice.

"Roger that."

As they stacked up on the door, Gary took place close left, asserting his position as the breacher. Alistair felt for a moment like arguing that he should be the first man in, the high probability that Gary would now be the one to strike the final blow. The feeling was brief however, as he quickly reconciled that in all fairness, Gary had borne the lion's share of the losses thus far. Gary took a deep breath as he stood with his back to the left of the door, Alistair beside him, Connor and Danny on the other side. Raising the MP5 to his eye, he ever so slightly pressured the trigger, Gary of the opinion that every extra millisecond the man in the next room drew breath was an injustice most heinous.

"This is it," Alistair thought as Connor nodded to Gary from the other side of the door, the wild Scotsman slamming his boot into the final barrier with all his might.

CHAPTER 74 - GARY

Gary felt the initial resistance followed by the wood on the other side of the lock giving way as the door swung open, a handful of splinters exploding out of the adjoining wall. Holding the trigger down, the stock of the sub machine gun firmly tucked into his shoulder to control the recoil from the automatic fire, a barrage of metal connected with the chair. Foam spewed from the leather as he moved quickly into the room and to the left so as to not obstruct the others. The chair was riddled with bullets as rounds punched through its back and into its occupant, finally coming to a stop in the wall beyond it. What moments ago would have passed for a board room at any large company was now riddled with holes and foam lining.

A wave of relief washed over Gary and Alistair. It was over. All they had to do now was retrieve the substance. But... there was something wrong with this picture. The chair was facing away from the door but neither arm nor leg was visible, the limbs of any man who'd been on the receiving end of that much fire would have gone limp by now. And to that end, the briefcase he was supposed to be holding, where was it?... As the air cleared it became apparent that George was not in fact sitting in the chair they had just mangled beyond recognition. To their horror, it was empty!

"What the hell! Where is he Wayne? You said he's supposed to be in here!" Gary yelled into the radio.

"You got him, didn't you?" came the reply. "I can see his wire frame in the chair you just destroyed!" ... BANG!

Wayne's transmission was interrupted by a gunshot, the static that followed all but confirming the worst.

"Fuck, get down!" yelled Alistair moments before Connor was ripped in half by a projectile as it tore a hole through the room and out the other side.

Gary and Alistair instinctively ducked for cover, Gary scanning the room for hostiles as he did, still not realising where the shot had originated from.

Danny dropped to the ground, but not quite soon enough, the piece of fashioned stone that smashed through the building like a rock through paper taking his head with it.

Gary looked on in shock as Alistair dropped his weapon, stood up, put his hands in the air and faced the wall.

"What the fuck are ye doing!" he yelled. "Looking to get ye bloody head shot off!"

"You can't hide from that," Alistair said slowly, the tone of a man resigned to his fate.

It was then that Gary remembered the scope on the weapon outside. There was no hiding from a man for whom walls didn't exist. As the ramifications of their failure began to play out in his head, an all too familiar voice came over the intercom.

"We meet again my friends."

CHAPTER 75 - ALISTAIR

"There's a good lad," came George's voice over the intercom as Gary followed Alistair's lead, his weapon hitting the floor. "I know we trust each other, but you see, the fellow holding that gun of yours hasn't been introduced. Therefore, we're going to have to make sure you don't have any other nasty surprises in store. Terrible business, I know."

Two of George's guards stepped into the room and frisked them.

"Now if you'll be so kind as to follow my associates."

One of the guards pushed Alistair and motioned for Gary to follow, the other walking behind them. They were led to a laboratory, George sitting in the middle of the room in a black suit trying unsuccessfully to light a cigar, a bandage covering the right side of his face and eye where Hadron had almost stopped the man.

"Ah greetings," he said as the two walked through the door.

Gary spat in his face as he passed by, which was abruptly followed by the but of a rifle hitting him in the back.

"That's no way to treat your host now then, is it?" said George wiping his face with his sleeve.

Alistair felt the rage surge inside, wanting nothing more than to reach out and strangle the man where he stood as he was marched into the lab. Alistair's jaw clenched so tightly his teeth were in peril, yet somehow he still managed to bring his primal instincts under control. He knew full well the action his emotions were encouraging would be a futile gesture, one that if acted upon would not end well. Surveying the sterile white room, Alistair felt a sudden relief as he spotted what could only be the second part of the gateway to and from Earth. Scanning further right, his eyes came to rest on a disturbing sight.

"What the hell are you doing with that?" he demanded more than asked as he caught a glimpse of the Chimon's head suspended in a large tube, flanked by two werewolf heads.

"Ah yes," said George. "It's going to seem rather cliche, you know, letting the hero's in on the master plan right at the end. I'm surprised myself by the urge to complete the blanks instead of just killing you both now, however, you have both proved extremely capable and it would be such a waste to deny you the opportunity to serve me in the new world order."

"You're kidding yourself if ye think I'd do anything for ye other than separate ye head from ye spine," came Gary's reply.

"Not if you don't have a choice in the matter. Do you believe in free will or fate gentlemen? Do your actions simply represent the sum of your genetics and experiences? I'm personally inclined towards the latter, but it doesn't really matter anymore."

"Get rid of ye guards and I'll show you how I'm 'personally inclined'," retorted Gary.

"I don't doubt you would," replied George. "Sadly for you however, your inclinations will bow to my will, as I'll now elucidate," George said as he snapped his fingers, two burly bodyguards gagging Alistair and Gary.

"Let me introduce you to the creator of your future leash, a good friend of mine and all round genius, Dr Roberto Enzo."

Another guard escorted what seemed to Alistair the living embodiment of the reclusive scientist stereotype into the room. Far from the smooth talking, olive skinned Italian his name implied, this Roberto Enzo was as pasty as they came, his beady little eyes made to seem much larger than they actually were, the black and white balls magnified by the thickest pair of glasses Alistair had ever seen. To say his eyes were magnified, Alistair and Gary hardly saw them as the Doctor avoided eye contact with anyone present as much as was humanly possible, his head occasionally having to dart awkwardly as his gaze came dangerously close to one of those present. Alistair thought it a great shame that like so many great minds, the gift of intelligence came hand in hand with the burden of poor ability to recognise social customs, the man in front of him most likely not aware of how awkward he appeared, walking without moving his arms, both limbs stuck fast by his side.

"Dr. Roberto is the one responsible for my being able to control those unpleasant things back in Aris land. Oh, and on a side note, he designed the RG32... Seems he must have 'accidentally' introduced a bug into its programming making you think I was watching television in the boardroom. Silly Dr. Roberto. I must say though, it's quite the feat of engineering that scope. I really don't know what I'd do without my good doctor. Oh yes, that's right, silly me. I know what I'd do, I'd slaughter his family. Anyhow, long story short, Dr. Enzo developed some very tiny devices that when inserted into the right parts of the subject's brain allow us to manipulate it. Lucky for us, the brother of this charming fellow," George said, pointing to the Chimon's head in the tube, "seemed to control all the lesser minions. So, what was the problem? Glad you didn't ask," George replied, answering his own question, Gary and Alistair not sure if the blabbering man in front of them was at all sane. "The problem was, the location these devices attach to in the brain has to be very specific which therefore requires some intense operations and a large dose of anaesthetic. I don't know about you, but I wasn't too keen on trying to sedate big brother," he said with a feigned look of fear. "So we had this wonderful technology, but it seemed we were at an impasse. How do you implant the device without getting up close and personal? As you know, the machine in Aris land doesn't only create the substance. It also creates this," said George holding up a seemingly normal piece of metal. "This my friends, is programmable steel. What's that I hear you say? Looks like any old chunk of metal? Well, I thought so too at first but upon closer inspection, one finds that it is made up of trillions of self-assembling nanites which react to different signals. Essentially, one can stimulate the material to almost instantly change shape or even move. That brings me to the question you asked during our brief stay at Raven's Contact. How does the RG32 cope with the stress of repeated firing? Well, now you have your answer – the steel repairs itself through reassembly."

George looked to the Dr, "I am getting this correct, aren't I?"

Roberto sighed, "Close enough I suppose," came a

disappointed nasal reply.

George continued. "So, and this is the brilliant part. We got an unsuspecting mule," *cough* "I mean Alistair, to shoot some of this into the prime demon... I mean, what did you call it... ah yes, the Chimon. I know what you're going to say, why not just shoot it yourself, blah blah blah. I admit, I didn't know it would work for sure. It would however, seem that my lack of total confidence in the good Doctor's abilities was unwarranted. I apologise wholeheartedly."

Roberto shook his head in disapproval, wondering to himself how such a clown could wield so much power.

"You can't really blame me though, I mean, who wants to be on the receiving end of this fellow after he's taken a sting from a supersonic slug. Better you than me, I'll tell you now.

Anyway, once the material is in the beast's body, some fantastic code splits the pieces into tiny, tiny particles that can travel through the blood stream. Not only that, but each particle forms a small rudder like attachment at its rear, the nanites oscillating to create what is basically a mini boat motor to propel them through to the correct parts of the target's brain. Once they arrive, they then reform into the necessary shape to facilitate control of the host. Ta da! Impressed? Of course you are.

Now, all I have to do is distribute it throughout the water system, or maybe even the air, and voila! I rule this world explicitly rather than implicitly. You two lucky fellows will be the first of my subjects. I'm sure you feel honoured," George said as he spun on his heels to leave the room.

CHAPTER 76 - ALISTAIR

Dr. Enzo had heard all he could stand. His pride no longer capable of suffering this fool, he finally broke. Pressing the button on the wall next to him before anyone could react, two panels parted to reveal a cage containing a deer and a tiger. As the people in front of him turned towards the noise, he pressed another button to which the cage responded by opening, unleashing the test subjects into the lab. The tiger roared, launching itself at the nearest guard.

"Fuck it, kill them all!" yelled George as he made a dash for the exit, the laboratory plunging into chaos as a gun raised towards Alistair's head.

Deflecting the arm attached to it moments before it fired, a bullet smashed into the wall to his left. Alistair began to act on instinct now, his brain outputting actions without first passing information to his conscious mind, an audible crunch of breaking bone as his fist connected with the guard's nose. He then proceeded to wrap his forearm around the stunned guard's neck, using him as a human shield. Gary simultaneously dispatched the guard closest to him with a brutal strike to the man's throat, crushing his windpipe as the tiger ripped into the other. Alistair spun himself and his human shield about, firing a shot at George in desperation. Unfortunately for Alistair however, the reinforced steel door was not on his side, the bullet bouncing off moments after George slammed it shut behind him.

Having cleared the room of George's men, Gary was more

concerned with the tiger that seemed to have lost interest in mauling its prey. He raised his gun to shoot but was interrupted by Roberto.

"No, he won't harm you. He'll only attack what I tell him to. You've got to..."

Roberto was interrupted as an RG32 slug ripped through the near wall and then out the one opposite, the bottom half of the guard in Alistair's grapple being separated from the top, leaving Alistair holding a torso. The friction from the blast burnt Alistair's midsection, forcing him to keel forward as he dropped the body. His hand feeling the amalgamation of cloth and burnt skin, the pain was intense as he began running laterally across the room in an attempt to make the next shot from outside a more difficult one.

"Run!" he yelled as another blast ripped through the wall just behind him.

The third shot was way off, smashing through the building at least two metres away.

Roberto jumped down from his console.

"I've disabled the scope on the RG32, he's effectively blind out there."

The fourth blast brought down a large section of the ceiling, splitting the room in two, separating Alistair and Roberto from Gary with an almighty crash.

"Ye OK lad?" Came a yell from the other side of the wreckage.

"Still in one piece, you?"

"Seen better days but I'll be alright. Not getting to that door any time soon though."

As the dust settled Roberto spoke to Alistair.

"George should have ordered him to cease fire now as there's a good chance he could be hit unintentionally if that goon keeps firing blindly. Outside there's a helipad. I'm not supposed to know of it, but I have heard them landing and taking off from behind that door. It's quite thick, which no doubt means the helipad can't be far. George has likely arranged a pick up and therefore should be waiting outside. If he leaves here today... well, you know what happens. The risk I've taken is enormous. You've got to stop him, but you must also promise me you'll protect my family! I've jammed his outgoing communications in a seven-kilometre radius.

If he gets clear, he'll contact his men in Belfast. I think it goes without saying what happens to my family if that were to play out."

"Trust me, I want him dead as much, if not more than you. The sooner the better," Alistair said, looking at the large section of roof that had cut him off from the others and the door George had escaped through.

"If we make it out of this mess, you have my word, Gary and I will do everything in our power to ensure your family's safety."

"Looks like he's laying off the shooting!" came a yell from Gary's side of the rubble.

"Roberto disabled the scope, he can't keep blind firing in case he hits George!" Alistair yelled back.

"Well at least that's one good thing!"

"George is going to board a chopper that we need to take down, any ideas?"

"Well, if we could get a hold of that rifle of yours he'd fall out of the air like a skydiver who forgot his parachute. Good luck getting to the gun though. Going out there now is a death sentence. Scope or no scope, the run to the forest line is as open country as it gets. There's no way you could get in range before he slots you." A brief pause ensued... "I suppose with the scope disabled you could lay down smoke, but you're gonna need an arm like an Olympian to throw it far enough to reduce the distance to anything close enough to get in range. Actually... " said Gary, "I have an idea. This is going to sound crazy, but it's probably the best chance we've got."

CHAPTER 77 - ALISTAIR

Alistair stood on the inside of the compound's perimeter wall.

"Have you ever done this before?" he asked, the whirring sound of the dinner plate sized quadcopter becoming audible as it floated down towards him.

A resounding "Nope," came back through the radio. "Let's hope James's toy has enough juice to make it happen."

Alistair tied the smoke grenade to the underside of the copter with a scrap of cloth from his shirt and let go. Rocking back and forth, it initially threatened to fail under the added weight, but eventually stabilised.

"Alright, ready when you are," came James' reply over the radio. "All set Roberto?"

"Yes, the hack was successful. I've overridden the gate control. Those fools!"

"I'm releasing the pin now," said Alistair, removing it from the smoke grenade.

After a couple of seconds, smoke slowly began to flow from the canister.

"Oh no! I can't see! Crap!" said James as he barely managed to navigate over the wall before the slow flow of smoke became a billowing cloud engulfing the drone.

"Now Roberto, now!" yelled Alistair into the radio.

The gates in front of him swung open as he began the mad dash behind the grey cloud heading towards the tree line in the distance. There was a whooshing sound as a projectile flew past him, ploughing through the smoke, creating an intricate swirling effect that Alistair might have admired under different circumstances.

"Looks like he's given up on the cease fire," Alistair thought as he continued behind the levitating visual obstruction.

Without warning, the cloud abruptly veered to the right, momentarily exposing Alistair before he darted back behind it.

"James, what are you doing?! Left mate, left!" he yelled into the radio between breaths.

"Sorry Alistair, I can't see a damned thing!"

Another shot flew through the air but this one was further off than the last. A sudden surge of adrenaline coursed through his body as the tree line got ever closer either side of the cloud. Alistair was just thinking it odd that the gap between shots seemed to have increased when a small metal ball like object appeared under the cloud. "You've got to be kidding," he thought as he jumped to the left just in time to avoid the explosion from the hand grenade. On the bright side, the explosion kicked up enough dust to cover his position. On the not so bright side however, it knocked the quadcopter off course, James having no way to right it now in the smoke.

"Alistair, Alistair, are you still with us?!" came a nervous voice over the radio.

"Yeah I'm still here," said Alistair, lying in the dirt, his ears ringing. "But I think you're about to crash our little smoke screen".

"Oh dear," came James' reply as the quadcopter crashed into a tree, right next to George's man, covering him in smoke.

As the smoke slowly dissipated, Alistair spotted the sniper. He'd dropped the RG32 and was moving towards the quadcopter's crash site with his pistol up, seemingly not having noticed Alistair lying in the dirt a small distance from where the grenade exploded. The next bit was easy. Without hesitation, Alistair drew his pistol and fired two shots into the man's head.

"You still in one piece?" came Gary's voice over the headset. "Cause if you are you might want to hurry up, I think the chopper is about to take off."

Alistair quickly made his way to the RG32, informing Gary to relay the message to Roberto to reactivate the scope. Alistair lay down in the short grass at the edge of the tree line, using a moss-covered log to steady the rifle.

The scope came to life, a magnified view of the complex filling the screen as he turned the power dial up to the highest level that it was safe to fire without being mounted. He didn't have to wait long, a set of whirring blades appearing over the top of the complex followed by the cockpit of the helicopter carrying the man who had caused so much grief. Alistair aimed at the column just below the rotating blades and was about to squeeze the trigger when a revelation most dire stabbed at his mind as much as it did his heart.

"Gary, if I shoot him down, the substance goes down with him along with any chance of reviving Adele."

"Look mate, we've all had to make sacrifices to get this far. Lord knows, if there was a better way to do this I'd be all for it, but if that man gets away today, the result will be far more tragic than the loss of Adele's life. The others will understand with time, ye cannay always save everyone. You'll probably regret the sacrifice the rest of ye life and there's not gonna be word of thanks from the billions you'll save from slavery, but you'll make the sacrifice and save them all the same. I know ye lad. You'll do what's right, not what's easy."

Alistair didn't reply. With a heavy heart, knowing it would condemn her to death, he squeezed the trigger.

CHAPTER 78 - ALISTAIR

A flurry of sparks ensued, as through the magnified view, Alistair saw the rotating blades separate from the body of the helicopter. With nothing to supply lift, it dropped like a lead balloon. The separated rotary blades flew off at an angle, cutting through the top of the laboratory wall like a knife through butter, finally coming to a stop about a metre from Gary's head.

"Might just be my lucky day," Gary thought as he kicked the edges of the wall where the blades had come through, creating a gap just big enough for him to squeeze out onto the tarmac. As he made his way through the gash in the wall, he noticed something most peculiar. There were no flames outside. The helicopter hadn't exploded as he expected. Instead, it seemed the shot had completely sheered the rotary column from the rest of the aircraft, the cockpit falling to the ground. The impact had crumpled the compartment somewhat, but it was otherwise in good shape. Also surprising was the fact that George and the pilot were nowhere to be found, the crumpled cockpit absent of corpses.

"Alistair!" he yelled over the radio. "Get here quick, the chopper's down but it's still intact and there's no sign of George or the pilot."

Alistair's spirits soared upon the realisation he might be able to save Adele after all. Drawing a second wind he wouldn't have thought possible a moment ago, he sprinted as fast as he could back to the compound.

Gary had made his way to the top of a building that he supposed was the control tower and was surveying the surrounds for the missing pilot and his passenger. It wasn't long before he spotted them. For some unknown reason, they were moving back into the compound through the door George had initially used to escape.

"Alistair, they're back in the lab, be careful," Gary relayed as he moved, crouching along the wall, attempting to get behind them.

Alistair stopped outside the lab. The rest of the world faded out as all his mental faculty concentrated on the door his pistol was pointing at in front of him. Gary was saying something into the radio but it didn't matter now. He knew everything he needed to.

After what seemed like an eternity, Alistair was rewarded for his patience, the hydraulic hissing sound music to his ears as the door slid to the right, the pilot on the other side instantly receiving a round between the eyes.

George spun 180 degrees as he was splattered in blood, running back into the lab only to collide with Gary's fist. Dazed on the cold metallic floor, George saw through hazy eyes, the figure of the man he had sent to do the unthinkable followed by the flash of the Glock in his right hand.

Alistair made his way into the lab from the front entrance. He observed Gary standing over a barely conscious George, his gun aimed at his head, the briefcase containing the substance still attached to his right arm.

"What the hell are you doing?!" he yelled as he observed Gary purposefully miss George's head by a millimetre.

"Waking this fucker up. He's gonna feel every second of it, just like the lads did," said Gary through gritted teeth as George was rocked back into reality by the bullet smashing into the ground next to his ear.

Roberto, emerging from his hiding place now that they'd subdued George, nodded in agreement with Gary's request. Turning back to the figure on the ground, Gary whispered in his ear before backing away. "Winters, Burnley, Renfield."

The confused expression on George's face lasted but a moment, instantly morphing into that of genuine fear and horror as the previously docile tiger's form emerged slowly from the shadows, its eyes focused menacingly on George to the exclusion of all else.

The giant cat's large padded paws gracefully transported the apex predator towards its prey.

Alistair retrieved the briefcase before returning to Gary and Roberto's side, the trio observing a moment of silence as the sickening sound of blood curdling justice ensued, its terrifying melody never sounding so sweet.

EPILOGUE

Roberto sat staring at his multiple monitors. It felt so good to be able to straighten his back and remove the ridiculous glasses, his current solitude not requiring the facade at which he'd become so accomplished. Gary had made his way to Belfast now to protect the doctor's family. Roberto's family had never really been in danger as he didn't actually have any, the Scot being sent on a wild goose chase.

Turning to the screen on his left, he focused on the window entitled Alistair, the video stream capturing an emotional event as the substance was administered to an unconscious woman, the large exit wound in her midsection noticeably healing in real time. Roberto averted his eyes, the affection her face conveyed towards the man standing over her jarring his psyche, the feeling akin to a metaphysical knife being thrust into his chest. The wound was just too raw, the display acting as a painful reminder of all he'd lost.

Pushing the thought of them aside, he turned back towards his monitors as something caught his eye, something so disturbing he barely noticed the two progress bars on the next screen finally complete their journey to the right, signalling the synthesis was complete.

"Synthesis successful," appeared in their place as Roberto took the liquid from the laboratory machine, pondering the other revelation a brief moment before downing it.

Wiping his lips, he clicked the button labelled 'contact' on yet another of his monitors. Waiting till he could hear the breathing of

the man on the other end of the communication channel he spoke.
"We have a problem... Aris."

www.ingramcontent.com/pod-product-compliance
Lightning Source LLC
Chambersburg PA
CBHW031257170626
46807CB00001B/188